McDonald lives on a large farm east of Esper-
n Western Australia, where she and her husband
ony produce prime lambs and cattle, run an
cattle and White Suffolk stud and produce
ll amount of crops. They have two children,
lle and Hayden. Fleur snatches time for her
ng in between helping on the farm. *Red Dust* is
rst novel. www.fleurmcdonald.com

Red Dust

FLEUR McDONALD

ARENA
ALLEN&UNWIN

This is a work of fiction. Geographical locations are not necessarily described
exactly as they are in real life.

This edition published in 2010
First published in 2009

Arena Books, an imprint of
Allen & Unwin
83 Alexander Street
Crows Nest NSW 2065
Australia
Phone: (61 2) 8425 0100
Fax: (61 2) 9906 2218
Email: info@allenandunwin.com
Web: www.allenandunwin.com

Cataloguing-in-Publication details are available
from the National Library of Australia
www.trove.nla.gov.au

ISBN 978 1 74237 005 7

Set in Granjon by Midland Typesetters, Australia
Printed in Australia by McPherson's Printing Group

20 19 18

MIX
Paper from
responsible sources
FSC® C001695
www.fsc.org

The paper in this book is FSC® certified.
FSC® promotes environmentally responsible,
socially beneficial and economically viable
management of the world's forests.

To Anthony, Rochelle and Hayden, you are my world.
To Carolyn and Jeff with heartfelt thanks
and to Louise Thurtell for the opportunity.

Prologue

Tears rolled down her cheeks as Gemma stood looking into the grave, a lonely figure in the hot January sun. All the other mourners had since left for the coolness of the church hall, seeking welcome cups of tea or cold drinks.

With her arms wrapped around herself she couldn't decide what hurt most: the fact that he was gone, or what he'd said before he died.

In her mind's eye, twenty-nine-year-old Gemma saw herself driving over the hill in the ute. There was dust everywhere; more than was usual for shifting a mob that size. The red dust was swirling, the wind was blowing so hard she could only hear the roar in her ears, not the bellows of the cows nor the noise coming from the plane. All she saw was the plane coming into land as usual ... but then something was wrong. He wasn't supposed to land there – there wasn't room – *and* he was coming in too fast. *What the hell?* had flashed through her mind as the plane carrying her husband hit the ground.

Beside the grave Gemma shook herself. *Don't dwell*, she told herself. *You've got to be strong*. She turned towards the hall.

If she'd turned only moments earlier she would have seen a man she didn't know leaning against the doorframe of the church hall, staring at her with such intensity it would have startled her.

Heads turned as Gemma walked through the door and a hush came over the room. Everyone started to talk again, trying to fill the silence. Someone rushed forward with a cup of tea and someone else whispered how sorry they were. It was all a blur.

'Gem?' A voice at her shoulder made her spin around. Seeing her best friend brought tears to her eyes again.

'Jess,' was all she could manage.

Jess put her arms around Gemma. 'Come on, let's blow this joint. You don't need to stand here like some sort of freak show.'

Gemma allowed herself to be led away, as family, friends and neighbours watched in silence.

Chapter 1

Gemma woke in a sweat. Another nightmare. The plane coming down, her rushing over to it, to Adam. His face bloody and his body twisted. Her screaming in frustration at not being able to open the door. Then Adam had opened his eyes.

'Not going to make it, Gem,' he'd gasped. 'Be careful, I'm in trouble and they might come after you when I'm gone. I'm sorry. Sell the station.' They were his last words.

Although it was only 2 am Gemma threw off the covers and got up. Padding out to the kitchen she made herself a Milo, knowing from experience there was no hope of sleeping again tonight. Picking up her jumper and ugg boots, she headed towards the office, which she'd searched high and low for a clue as to what sort of trouble Adam might have been in. She'd found nothing. Tonight, however, she put that to the back of her mind and fired up the computer. It was time to start working on the accounts and trying to decide what she was going to do with the one hundred and ninety-five square kilometres she'd been left by her husband.

Her inheritance had made her one of the most asset-rich young women in the district. No one had thought she would be able to manage the property on her own, but she had. So far. She employed two stockmen to do a lot of the grunt work – and she wasn't afraid of getting her own hands dirty when push came to shove – but it was Gemma who made the decisions and ensured things ran smoothly.

Despite what Adam had said, she had never had any intention of selling Billbinya after his death. Her land was good productive land. It was just on the northern side of Goyders Line but close enough to get a bit more rain than those areas further to the north of South Australia. The phone calls from the real estate agents had come thick and fast with offers, good offers, but the answer was always no. She would keep on farming. It was all she knew and all she wanted to know.

Her decision had caused surprise and resentment among the other landowners.

While Adam had been by her side, Gemma's hands-on involvement with farming had been accepted. Now, she was a single woman in a man's world and this caused a wariness amongst the women of the district who had always been involved in the CWA, trading tables or tennis, rather than agriculture.

The men looked at her with a mixture of respect and contempt. She knew that the men thought she couldn't manage the land on her own. As she was leaving the Hawkins & Jones Stock Agents & Farm Merchandise store one day she heard one of them say, 'She must have balls to take that on but you watch – she'll get sick of playing farming when the money runs out. It'll end up on the market before long.'

If asked, Gemma would admit that running a large station was hard, but no one had bothered to ask. It would have been completely impossible without her dependable stockmen, Bulla and Garry. They had worked overtime in the six months since Adam's death. They hadn't complained, but she was going to need more manpower so they could have some time off. Besides, there were places on Billbinya she hadn't been to in weeks and goodness only knew what was going on with the sheep and cows in those areas. The station could use another bloke, she decided, and went about wording a situation vacant ad to run in magazines.

Once the email had been sent she turned to the batch of bills and letters that had arrived in the last mail. Opening them, she felt her heart start to sink. Billbinya was running mainly wethers, with a few ewes to breed replacement stock and some cows thrown in, and wool prices hadn't been good for a long time. Gemma was beginning to think that there would have to be changes to the enterprises she ran on the station. Obviously wool wasn't going to make her the money she needed on its own. But she needed to work out what would, and how she could do it.

By the time she'd updated May's debits and credits, reconciled the last month, and calculated the GST, the sun was just beginning to creep over the horizon. She stretched and got up.

Walking to the doors that led from the office onto the verandah of the rambling homestead, she threw them open and breathed in the icy morning air. She'd stood at this same spot most mornings in the eight years she'd been living on Billbinya.

Billbinya was, for the most part, gently undulating country. Running through the middle of the station was a creekline with big old gum trees and moss-covered rocks.

The homestead was snuggled into the bottom of a granite hill surrounded by large gardens full of rambling ivy, geraniums and lawn. Pepper and almond trees were dotted all around the edge of the garden fence. Once there had been a vegetable garden with an orchard that had produced most of the food, but Gemma had let the garden go now that she was so busy on the station.

The house itself was a stone construction with a tin roof, built by Adam's great-grandfather. The windows were small but the house was of generous proportions, with five bedrooms, a dining room, formal lounge and an expansive sunroom that looked out over the native bush that led to the summit of the mount.

The side of the house where the office was situated opened out to the wide plains of the farming land.

Gemma could see the dog kennels under the trees and this early in the morning, all except her faithful work companion were still snoozing. Scoota sat outside his hollowed log which passed for a shelter, with his ears cocked, listening to the movements of his mistress inside the house.

To the right stood an old shed full of machinery needed for cropping and feeding stock. Behind that, the shearing shed and sheep yards stood silently in the morning light. The cattle yards were on the other side of the station, near where Bulla and Garry lived.

As she watched, the golden rays of the sun picked up the edges of the gum leaves and made them glow. She loved this time of the morning, but it was one of the worst times for missing Adam. They had always risen early and had their first cup of coffee watching the sun come up and talking quietly. They would work out who was doing what for the day, make decisions and just enjoy being together.

With a burst of determination, Gemma pushed away her feelings of loss. Replacing her uggies with her Rossi work boots, she jumped over the railing of the verandah and raced to the ute which was parked under the lean-to, off the house.

Let's get an early start to the day, she thought. She revved the ute, fishtailed down the drive and laughed out loud. Shaking her honey-coloured hair, feeling the wind in her face, she felt the day was going to be a good one.

In another house, in another part of South Australia, a man looked at his files and tapped his fingers against his mouth, thinking. He had no idea what Gemma knew – or if in fact she knew anything. Had Adam managed to convey a message to her after the plane crash? The man had heard that Adam had been conscious briefly, but what had happened in those final minutes? He *had* to find out ...

Chapter 2

Gemma decided that there was nothing better than checking around your own land, seeing green grass, fat stock and their progeny running, bucking, and chasing each other. There had been many years in the north when there hadn't been any green grass to see. Drought had turned the grass to dry and dusty soil, so to look at the wonderful spread of green now was good for the spirit. The fact that she was listening to Sara Storer sing about drovers and people who worked the land also helped Gemma feel inspired to keep doing the things she was doing. Tapping her fingers in time to the music, she sang loudly, ignoring the fact she was tone deaf.

By twelve thirty, not having found anything amiss, Gemma turned the ute towards home. Walking into the homestead she put the kettle on and went straight to the office. The message light was blinking on.

'Hi Gem, Jess here. What's going on? No word from you for yonks. Hope you're okay. Give us a call when you've got time. Seeya!' Gemma smiled at Jess's happy but concerned voice – she must ring her.

'Ah, hello. It's Mike Martin from Australian Transport Safety Bureau calling. I just wanted to let you know that the report on the fatal accident involving the aircraft Foxtrot Juliet Papa is being released today. The findings will show that a catastrophic engine failure caused the aircraft to make an emergency landing, impacting with a large tree and resulting in the fatality. If you have any questions, please give me a call. I will be in the office for the rest of the day.'

'The fatality?' Gemma mouthed as she wrote down the number which followed. She steadied herself against the office desk as a picture of the plane entered her mind. She could see the wings wobbling madly, the wheels buckling beneath the body, the metal crumpling like a tin can as the plane hit the ground.

'Gem, it's me again.' Gemma looked blankly at the answering machine. 'I reckon I'll come and visit this weekend. I'll be there Friday night about seven thirty. I'll ring as I'm leaving town. Catchya, mate!'

'Brilliant!' said Gemma out loud as her friend's voice banished the vivid images of a few moments ago.

'You on the channel, Gemma?' The two-way crackled to life with the voice of Bulla, one of her stockmen. Turning to where the radio sat on shelves that held the past three generations of records, she picked up the handset.

'Yeah?' she answered.

'Yeah, Gem, I'm getting these sheep in and I think there might be about another four hundred-odd more than we thought, so we'll need more gear for lamb marking.'

'Oh,' said Gemma in surprise. Adam had always kept such up-to-date records of stock numbers, yet it was the third time since Adam had died that they had found mobs with increased numbers. 'That's weird. Well, no worries, I'll get it organised. Everything else going okay?'

'Yeah, we'll be at the yards in about half an hour.'

Gemma signed off and went to the kitchen to fix herself some lunch. While she was eating she started making a list of things she'd need in town. She knew she would have to return Mike Martin's call at some stage, but she couldn't deal with it now. Instead, she'd focus on the lamb marking – and looking forward to Jess's visit.

Gemma was excited. Jess had rung – she was on her way – and Gemma couldn't wait to have some female company. Although she had loved Adam to distraction, there was no denying that marriage had affected her female friendships as she'd devoted herself to working and spending time with her husband. Not that she was complaining – that was the way she wanted it – but she'd missed partying till the small hours with her brilliant, energetic friend. She and

Jess had a history! Growing up as farmers' daughters, they had travelled on the same school bus, until Jess's parents sold up and moved to Port Pirie. The girls had been ecstatic when they realised that they would be attending the same boarding school, along with other friends from the local school. They had been inseparable ever since.

Of course, Jess's partying had calmed down slightly since she shifted back to town, so she could practise her profession – banking. Gemma shook her head every time she thought about the profession Jess had chosen. Gemma had thought her wild, outgoing friend would do something that would turn the world upside down – instead, Jess had become a boring old loans manager. It was almost as bad as being an accountant!

Chuckling, Gemma put on some music, mixed herself a rum and Coke, and sang along while she made the gravy for the roast lamb she'd bred, butchered and cooked herself. The breeding and butchering were her forte, she noted ruefully, not the cooking.

Hearing the dogs bark, Gemma raced outside and saw Jess's red Holden ute pull up. It looked every part of the souped-up ute that a young bloke would drive, complete with huge spotlights and aerials, autographs from famous country singers on the tail gate, and the bar runner she'd pinched from Oodnadatta pub when they had been up for the races running across the dash. It was always sparkling clean and hardly ever saw dirt roads these days. Flying towards her friend, with her arms outstretched, Gemma pulled her into a huge bear hug.

'Jess, you made it!'

'Gem, wonderful to see you, gorgeous.' Jess returned the hug with vigour. 'Man, I forgot it was such a long way out here. I didn't even think to get some roadies as I came through town, I'm so used to not drinking and driving. But the cops wouldn't even know this road existed!'

'You poor bugger, it must be hard to drive a whole hundred and fifty k without a drink!'

'Well, you know a girl can get kinda thirsty.'

'Obviously,' Gemma said dryly.

'So how are you?' asked Jess as they headed back to the house, their arms slung around each other.

'I've had my moments. But mostly I'm okay.'

'I knew you would be. Any word from the out-laws?'

'Hey, let's just have fun tonight,' said Gemma. 'We'll talk *that* stuff tomorrow.'

Walking inside with her friend's arm warm around her shoulders, Gemma felt a peace she hadn't known since Adam died. It was nice to feel almost whole again, to know that whatever happened, she'd be all right.

The smell of burning met them at the door. 'Oh bugger! That's what's left of the gravy,' said Gemma, running to the stove. Jess – a fabulous cook – laughed so hard she almost had tears running down her cheeks.

'You haven't improved on the cooking front then! So what *is* for tea? I'm starving,' asked Jess, opening the fridge and pulling out the Coke to mix with her scotch. Popping the top, she leaned against the kitchen counter. 'Is it eggs on toast? Grilled cheese sandwiches?'

'Get away! I'm not that bad a cook! I just don't do a lot of it now that there's only myself to cook for. Anyway, we're having roast lamb - without the gravy!'

'Roast lamb? Yum, I haven't had that for ages!' She nudged Gemma out of the way. 'Allow the master!' She started trying to salvage what she could of the gravy. 'I think we might have to make some more. Where's the flour?'

'In the pantry.' Gemma looked at Jess. Her red hair hung below her shoulders and her freckles and green eyes stood out against her pale skin. 'You've been indoors too much,' she observed.

'Ah yes,' sighed Jess dramatically. 'Well I do have to spend some time in the office and that tends to play havoc with the complexion. However -' she held up her finger to make a point, 'that's why they invented makeup!'

'You're awfully cheery,' said Gemma. 'Is there anything wrong?'

'Like you said, we'll talk *that* stuff tomorrow,' replied Jess with her head deep in the pantry. 'I cannot find *any* flour in here of any sort. I can't believe you have a pantry without - oh, here's some. Gemma Sinclair, it's about a year out of date! You'll poison yourself one day. Oh well, beggars can't be choosers.'

'Flour is not exactly big on my agenda at the moment,' Gemma said defensively.

'C'mon, let's eat and I'll fill you in on all the gossip from town. You would not *believe* who I saw yesterday at the hairdresser.'

'Tell me,' said Gemma.

'Gabby Clarke. Do you remember her from school? Blonde, with legs up to her ears and really skinny. I couldn't believe it was her – she's got three kids hanging off her.'

'You're joking!' interjected Gemma. 'I didn't even know she'd got married.'

'Yeah, she married some guy from the city about five years ago.' She threw her hand up against her forehead for dramatic effect. 'Oh, and guess who I had a wine with last week at the pub?'

'I couldn't guess. Do you actually do any work?'

'Of course, but only if it doesn't interfere with my social calendar,' Jess stated solemnly, and then burst out laughing. 'But you'll never guess who I heard was back in town,' she continued.

'Who?'

'Paige Nicholls.' There was silence as both girls remembered the accident that had killed one of their friends, another committing suicide, and the part that she had played in that.

'Well, that's interesting. I wonder what she's doing back here.'

Jess shrugged. 'No idea. And I don't really care.'

They laughed and talked into the night, soaking up one another's company. At midnight Gemma stretched and said, 'Well, this is the latest I've been up in ages. I need to go to bed. I've got to check the heifers in the morning – I've given Bulla and Garry the weekend off.'

'Yeah, I should go to bed too. Where am I sleeping?'

'Where you did last time. Second on the right. Do you remember where the bathroom is?'

'Yep, dishes?' asked Jess, yawning.

'In the morning, I think. Do you want to come with me tomorrow?'

'What time?'

'About five thirty.'

'No way! Sorry, Gem, you're on your own.'

'Night, Jess,' said Gemma with a smile. 'It's good to have you here.'

Jess moved forward to hug her friend. 'I'm glad I came. It's taken me too long. Night.'

It felt good to have someone else in the house, Gemma thought as she settled into bed. For the first time in months she slipped easily into a heavy, dreamless sleep.

Chapter 3

By 5 am Gemma was up making coffee and looking out at the cold, clear day. Pale sunlight was just visible on the horizon. As welcome as the sun was, when she switched on the radio for the weather report, Gemma found herself hoping that the week would hold some rain. They had had good rains this year, but she would never knock back more.

By five thirty it was nearly light enough to see, so she wrote a note telling Jess not to expect her back before eight, though she knew it was likely she'd be back before Jess got up anyway.

Untying her dog Scoota, who ran madly around her legs in a morning greeting, she jumped in the ute and made her way towards the heifer paddock, her thoughts drifting to Jess. Something wasn't right with her, but Gemma knew her friend wouldn't talk to her about it until she was ready. They had had angry words more than once when Gemma had offered help before Jess was ready for it.

After opening and shutting several gates and driving over a couple of cattle grids, Gemma finally arrived at the heifers. She methodically counted the hundred cattle in the paddock; there weren't any problems this morning. She would come back this afternoon and check again.

Jess had woken when she heard Gemma leave. Tossing and turning, she finally decided that coffee was a better option than lying in bed alone with her thoughts, so she rose and dressed. Coffee in hand, she walked over to the fire and stoked it up, then went and stood in front of the wedding photo hanging on the wall in the big sunken lounge room. Looking pensively at Adam, she asked aloud, 'Were you the weak, untrustworthy bugger I think you were?'

She stood there for a long while, sipping coffee and looking at the photo, recalling her conversations with Adam, searching for any clue that might substantiate the rumours she'd heard in town, but nothing came to her. Sighing, she put down her cup and wandered outside. Instinctively, she headed towards the shearing shed, passing the kennels on the way. Gemma loved dogs, and whether they were good or useless, she always had at least five of them. Jess untied the house dog Scoota; he'd give her some companionship on her walk. A Lab look-alike with about a dozen different breeds in him, Scoota had belonged to an old grader driver who was going to have him put down because he couldn't take him on the road anymore. These days many people on farms objected to contract workers bringing dogs with them.

Jess hadn't spent a lot of time on Billbinya. Between her social life and work, there hadn't been the opportunity. She had quickly risen through the bank to loans manager, and though Jess told no one, she loved her numbers and her job with a passion. She specialised in agribusiness accounts that put her in contact with farmers, her past, which she also treasured. Because of her farming knowledge, she often received phone calls asking for her guidance on the industry and its opportunities, but even though she subscribed to many of the leading agribusiness and farming magazines, the answer wasn't always immediately clear. Jess would research the issue and return with good, professional advice.

With Scoota bouncing at her feet, she resumed her path to the shearing shed. She'd always loved the old lanolin smell of shearing sheds, the way everything was oily to the touch. Wood of the railings smooth from years of sheep rubbing against it. She breathed deeply, finding peace in the silence, then went outside to survey the scene she could see from the shed.

Walking on towards the creek, she bent down to pat Scoota and picked up a stick for him to chase. 'Do I tell her?' she asked the dog.

* * *

As Gemma approached the house she could smell the bacon and eggs already sizzling. Entering the kitchen, she arched an eyebrow and said, 'Well I didn't think I'd see you this early.'

'Oh, I'm still *able* to get up early most days – I just choose not to. Do you want a coffee?'

'Is the Pope Catholic?'

'So what's the go for today? Do you have anything you have to do?' Jess asked as she moved about the kitchen getting coffee and turning the bacon.

'Nope, I'm all yours. Is there anything special you want to do?'

'Well, I was thinking that it would be fun to go camping. We could camp down by the creek where we used to go when you were first seeing Adam. Take the swags, have a fire – you know, all that sort of stuff we used to do before we got old and sensible.'

Gemma nodded slowly, the idea growing on her. 'Yeah, camping in winter. A fire, crisp air and some port to keep us warm. That sounds great. We can leave this afternoon after I've checked the heifers.'

'You've got a new ute,' Jess commented after they piled their swags and provisions into the tray late that afternoon and set off.

'Yeah.' Gemma rubbed the dash of the new white

Toyota LandCruiser affectionately as they bumped across the paddocks. 'I got it after Adam died. All the other vehicles on the station are old and pretty clapped out. I thought that if I was going to be out on the station, doing long distances by myself then I needed something reliable.'

'Good idea. Be horrible to get stuck out in the middle of nowhere and have to be rescued,' Jess agreed as they pulled up at their old camping site. It was exactly as Jess remembered – a sheltered spot on the side of the creek where native pine trees grew. There was a granite outcrop covered in old moss and the creek gravel was soft.

Setting the fire, Gemma laughed. 'I can't believe we're doing this. How old are we? We're supposed to be mature and responsible. This feels like we're teenagers again camping on Mum and Dad's place just so we could play our music up loud and smoke without getting caught!'

'Hey, want a rum and Coke? Let's party like we used to. We don't get many nights like this anymore.'

'That sounds like a plan.' As Jess got the drinks from the esky and Gemma set up the camp site she threw some more branches on the fire then rummaged through a box in the tray of the ute for a barbecue plate, chops and flour.

'Are you making damper? Fantastic! Well, I think fantastic – how old is that flour again?'

Gemma laughed and threw some of the flour at her. 'Here, make yourself useful. Grab some of those spuds and the foil and chuck them in the fire. I thought we could go the whole hog.'

'Ah, I've needed a night like this for a long time,' said Jess, leaning back against her swag and staring deep into the heart of the flames. 'So tell me, Gem, how are you really? You haven't said much at all about you or the farm or what's happening.'

Gemma took her drink and sat on her swag looking at Jess.

'I'm going okay. I thought it would be harder – well, no, that came out wrong; it's been bloody hard and I miss him so much, and would give anything to have him back again . . . but I'm doing all this stuff I never imagined I could do. And I *can* do it.'

'Well of course you bloody can,' said Jess indignantly.

'Yeah, but there are so many things I've wanted to ask and I can't and that always makes me feel frustrated. And going to bed without him . . . no one to cuddle or talk to . . .' Gemma's voice was getting softer and softer. She looked down at the ground and fiddled with the can in her hand. 'It gets a bit lonely, especially when I don't see anyone except for Garry and Bulla for days on end. I must admit that when the stock agents come, I quite enjoy it. There's a bit of news from around the district and someone different to talk to. Someone to throw ideas around with about stock and markets, that sort of stuff.'

Getting up she went back over to the card table to finish the damper.

'But I think that has helped me out emotionally, you know, being so busy on the farm and not having a lot of time to think during the day. Making sure that Billbinya runs smoothly and that there's enough money in the bank to pay all the bills isn't easy. I mean, I know I used to do some of the office work, but Adam did most of it and he was the one who knew when the big payments were due, like tractor payments or the payments to his mum and dad. To tell the truth, I'm not even sure how he managed to make some of the large payments. Sometimes there isn't enough money in the bank to pay the wages with, let alone make a loan repayment. I don't know how I'm going to come up with the money for the next repayment to his mum and dad, but I'll work something out. I've got a while yet, and shearing is coming up.'

There was a silence broken only by the crackling of the fire, and Jess noticed the card table wobbling as Gemma kneaded the damper harder than necessary – the only sign that Gemma was upset. She couldn't help but think that her friend wasn't really dealing with the emotions of losing her husband at all. Gemma had always been good at sweeping her feelings under the carpet.

Without looking up from what she was doing, Gemma said, 'I feel like I'm achieving something, but then I'll overhear some bloke in town talking about me "playing farming" and that really hurts. I know that people are gossiping, but it's awful to actually hear it.' Looking up she smiled sadly. 'I'm not playing, Jess; I really want to make this work.'

'Oh, Gem, I never thought for a minute that you were playing. I've always known that you can do this. It's all you've ever wanted to do – even when we were stuck in that stupid, pompous boarding school you only ever wanted to get back out to the farm. It has to be wide open spaces for our Gemma!'

'I miss Adam every day, but life goes on and I plan to have the best life I can for the rest of it,' Gemma said quietly.

She turned her attention to the damper again, muttering something under her breath that Jess couldn't quite hear.

'What was that?' asked Jess.

'I said I wish I could ask Adam about the discrepancy in the stock numbers,' Gemma repeated.

'What stock numbers?' asked Jess with a feeling of dread in the pit of her stomach.

'Most of our ewe numbers are up for lamb marking, which means the lamb count is up too. It's strange because he was always so good at keeping accurate figures. Bulla reckons that Adam always knew how many were in a mob, and some of these mobs have been up by five hundred. That isn't an insignificant amount. I've got the stock agent coming next week and we are going to get all the mobs of both cattle and sheep in and do a proper count. I need to be sure before 30 June so I've got the numbers right for the taxes.'

Jess was quiet. This was her opening. 'You know, Gem ...'

But Gemma was still talking. 'I remember him being on the computer, using the stock management program saying he had shifted stock from one paddock to another, when I knew they hadn't been shifted at all, but I just figured he planned to shift them the next day or something like that.' She shrugged and gave Jess a big smile. 'Come on, the damper's ready to go in the fire and I need another drink.'

Jess opened her mouth to speak then closed it again. The moment had passed.

After dinner Jess undid her swag and pulled it up to the fire, then took off her boots and climbed in. Gemma put another big log onto the fire and did the same.

'Are you still having trouble with Ian and Joan?' asked Jess.

'Ah, the dreaded out-laws . . . No, not really. They were so upset about losing Adam that they really couldn't see past that and I was the obvious one to take it out on. They couldn't understand why he left the station to me rather than passing it back to them, but I think we've sorted that out. As long as they get the money they're owed, we get on pretty well. I go and see them when I'm in town and they ring occasionally to see what's going on, but we don't have that much to do with each other really. Ian thinks that a woman has no business running a station, but I just let him think that Dad is helping me make decisions.'

'And how is the money situation? Is it as bad as you just said?' asked Jess tentatively.

'Oh, I don't suppose. Farming is tight. Cash flow is the main problem, but I'll get it sorted in time. Anyhow, what's bothering you? I know there's something wrong. Is it a bloke?'

Jess's stomach constricted. 'Me?' she said brightly. 'Nothing's wrong with me. Working hard at the bank, and not enough time to do all the things I want to do, but other than that everything is fine.'

'Uh huh,' said Gemma, clearly not convinced but deciding not to pursue it. 'What about that bloke you've been seeing . . . what was his name? Brad, Chad, Gonad?'

'Brad!' cried Jess huffily, leaning over to thump Gemma through the swag. 'He's wonderful,' she said dreamily.

'Aren't they all?' Gemma teased.

'This one is different,' Jess said.

'You always say that.'

'Well he is. Tall, dark hair . . .'

'Tall, dark and handsome,' interrupted Gemma. 'What are you going to do if they break the mould, Jess?'

'He's great,' continued Jess, ignoring Gemma. 'He's an agronomist and he only moved to Pirie a year and a half or so ago. He's just started his own business after being with one of the main stock firms, but he reckons he can do better out by himself.'

'So, why is he different? What's the best bit about him?'

'Well,' Jess said coyly, 'I can't really tell you that – but I'm sure you can use your imagination!'

'I should have known better than to ask!' said Gemma with a laugh.

'Nah, really, he's just different. He listens to me, talks to me, and we enjoy just hanging out together. Life can be pretty lonely. I've got lots of friends but they don't know me like you do – and I think Brad is beginning to know me better than anyone. But he's a real man's man, if you know what I mean. Plus he likes to have a good time.'

'Well, Jess, I hope he's *the one* then. I can't see you tied down though!'

'Yeah, I know! I can't see it either – but I haven't got cold feet yet, and he's spending a lot of time with me.'

They lay back without speaking, looking at the stars and watching sparks from the fire crackle up into the air.

Jess left Billbinya on Sunday afternoon to head back to Port Pirie, work and Brad. Leaning on the airhorn and watching Gemma wave in her rear-vision mirror, she berated herself for not coming clean about her suspicions. But Gemma's plate was full enough without adding something from left field.

Chapter 4

The next few weeks were busy ones for Gemma. No time for trips to town or anything but work. Her ad had garnered some responses, and she had interviewed a couple of blokes, but neither of them had really stood out. She had to get someone, so against her better judgement she'd hired Jack Marshall, a man in his mid-thirties who had spent most of his life on stations in the north of Australia. A tall man with a thick bushy beard and a cracked front tooth that showed when he smiled. He had arrived in a white Holden ute with a bad-taste picture of a naked blonde woman on the rear window. He seemed quite surly but his references from previous employers had been impeccable. So far he'd worked hard and there hadn't been any trouble, which was just as well – while Bulla and Garry lived away from the main house, on another part of the station, Jack had moved into the shearers' quarters near the shearing shed, within a few hundred metres of the house.

The shearers' quarters had seemed the obvious place for him to move into since there weren't any spare rooms at Bulla and Garry's house. The shearers' quarters had eight rooms that were used only during shearing time. Gemma was also short of a work ute for him so she had asked Garry to fix up an old Yamaha bike that had been forgotten in the depths of the shed.

On the last day in June, Gemma received a phone call from Ned Jones, a partner in Hawkins and Jones Stock Agents and Farm Merchandise. Whenever he was in the area he'd called to let them know and they had got a few mobs in to count. It had taken some weeks and a lot of Ned's time, but he was happy to help out. A middle-aged man with a big beer belly, big hat and a red face from being outside all day, he was quick with a joke and a laugh. Gemma thought him the epitome of the old-style stock agent.

When Ned pulled up at the cattle yards, he had someone with him in the car. Gemma went over to greet them.

'Hi, Ned, how are you going today?'

'Hi, Gemma, how are ya? I'm good.' Heaving himself out of the car, he motioned with a calloused hand to the passenger side. 'Gemma, this young bloke is Ben Daylee. He's come on board with us as a new stocky. Ben Daylee, Gemma Sinclair.'

Gemma looked over as the 'young bloke' got out of the car. Expecting to see a nineteen- or twenty-year-old, she was surprised to see he was about her age. Looking at him she drew in a breath, and then blushed, hoping no one had noticed. He was gorgeous.

She held out her hand. 'Pleased to meet you. Do you know what you're letting yourself in for, hanging around with this one?' She gestured to Ned.

Ben smiled. Perfect teeth. Was there anything not perfect? wondered Gemma.

'Sure, but does Ned know what *he's* in for? I could probably teach him a thing or two!'

'I bet you could,' said Gemma. 'Now about these cattle . . .' She turned and headed toward the yards, Ned and Ben close behind.

'These are beautiful beasts,' said Ben appreciatively as they gazed at the mob.

'Thank you. Adam and I bought these from my dad, who breeds Angus cattle. Have you had a lot to do with cattle?'

'I'm from a cattle background. My parents have about four thousand acres right down south. They breed Angus as well, actually.'

'Oh, what bloodlines are they on?' Gemma asked, more to test his knowledge than out of genuine interest. So many new blokes thought they understood the stock industry when really they were very green.

'Well, there are three different families essentially. We mainly do artificial insemination and embryo transfer work with sires from the US.' Ben talked knowledgeably about genetics and Gemma listened intently; he really did know his cattle.

'I do a bit of AI for Dad,' she told him. 'I did a course a few years ago so that we could do it ourselves, but we – I – don't use it here since I don't breed my own bulls. I like to buy them in from registered studs. Dad usually, but others as well to keep the bloodlines fairly separate.'

'Right,' Ned broke in, 'these cattle need counting.'

They ran all the cattle through the gates, with both Ben and Ned counting. Bulla and Jack kept the cattle coming through, while Garry brought more mobs in from different paddocks. After they had finished, Ned, Ben and Gemma went back to the homestead for a coffee, while Garry, Bulla and Jack returned the cattle to their paddocks.

Ned busily added up numbers from counts done in the weeks before and laid them all out on the table for Gemma to go through when she sat down.

'Now, Gemma, these figures don't square up with what Adam had recorded. Most of the sheep numbers are up; some mobs by five hundred, but most only a hundred and fifty or so. The cattle numbers are pretty much on track. Except the steers. There are five hundred and seventy-three steers when usually you would sell around one thousand in a year. You've got the three hundred contracted to the feedlotters and then you usually put up about seven hundred in the January sales. You're down by four hundred-odd steers.'

Gemma let the teaspoon she was holding fall to the table with a clatter. 'Down four hundred? What contract? Adam didn't tell me about a contract!'

'The contract he's signed for the last three years. You know, with the feedlotters on the other side of town.'

'Oh,' said Gemma in confusion, racking her brains. Contract? Last three years? 'I must have forgotten,' she stammered. 'Um, look, I'm not sure, Ned – how many did you say were contracted?'

'Three hundred.'

Gemma shook her head, puzzled.

'Did you definitely get all the mobs in?' asked Ned.

'I'm pretty sure we did. I've been to every paddock on Billbinya in the last two weeks, and unless the guys made a mistake bringing in the cattle I don't see how we could have missed them.' She thought for a minute. 'Maybe he had something in mind with Dad.' Even as she said it she felt herself relax. That must be it. 'I'll give him a call and see what he says. When was the contract for?'

'End of October.'

'Right, no worries.' Gemma was suddenly professional again. 'I'll talk to Dad tonight and give you a call.'

'Okay. Well …' Ned pushed back his chair. 'We have to head off – we're due over at the Carters in about a half-hour. Got to finish introducing Ben around to all his new clients.'

They rose from the kitchen table. Ben collected the cups and carried them over to the sink.

Walking them to the car, Gemma asked: 'So, Ben, are you my new stock agent?'

'I'm not sure; that's up to Ned. But I certainly hope so.'

Ned laughed and clapped Ben on the shoulder. 'He thinks he can take on the world. Doesn't realise that if he takes on all my clients he'll be as burnt out as I am! That's the reason me and Bert hired him – so we could finally manage to have some time off! Oh yeah, that reminds me, Gemma – I'm taking some holidays in about three weeks. Taking the missus up to the Alice for a fortnight. Ben will be filling in for me while I'm gone.'

'That sounds wonderful, Ned! I can't remember you ever taking a holiday and I've known you just about my whole life.' Gemma was genuinely pleased.

'Yeah, well Rose's wanted to go up there for a while and now that young Ben's here we think that it's the perfect opportunity.'

Opening the car door, he leaned over and squeezed Gemma's shoulder. 'Look after yourself, girl.'

'You too.'

Ben handed Gemma his card. 'You can reach me any time,' he said, and shook her hand. 'Seeya later.'

As soon as they left, Gemma hopped in the Toyota to have a drive around Billbinya. News of the contract had come as a nasty surprise, but by hell she was going to get to the bottom of it. And find these three hundred cattle she would need if she were to fulfil the agreement.

Ned and Ben turned out of the driveway and onto the single-lane bitumen road.

'Phew,' said Ben, leaning back in his seat. 'She's amazing.'

Ned glanced across at him. 'Now don't you go getting any ideas, boy,' he said sternly. 'She's been through enough in the last year or so. You leave her well alone.'

'Mate, I haven't got any *ideas*, but she's still amazing.' He shook his head. 'She had no idea about that contract,' he said after a pause.

Ned rubbed his face tiredly. 'I know.'

'What do we do about that?' asked Ben. 'Is it something we should warn the feedlotters about?'

'Well, let's just see what she comes back with tonight. Sinny was a shifty bugger at times and might not have told her. He might've forgotten or just thought she didn't need to know.'

'Sinny? Is that what they used to call Adam?'

'Yep.'

'Is it really possible that he'd spoken to her father about the contract?'

'I sincerely doubt it, but you never know.'

'Have you heard the rumours about stock stealing?'

Ned looked over at Ben with an annoyed expression on his face. 'Yes I have, Ben,' he replied in a clipped tone. 'But no one has reported anything to the cops and I can tell you that no one from Billbinya would be involved. No one around this area has reported missing stock – it's all been over the west side of town – so just leave it, will you?'

Ben stared silently out the window at the passing country, but his vision was full of Gemma's pretty face.

Chapter 5

After driving around the whole of Billbinya and consulting Ned's counts, Gemma was sure that all the stock on the property had been counted. Heading home, she called Bulla on the two-way and organised to meet him and Garry at the homestead for a beer after work. She wanted to pick their brains.

She was in the office when they pulled up in one of the station's old utes. 'How goes it, guys?' she asked, walking out to greet them.

'Goes well,' Bulla replied. 'We got that mob of a thousand ewes and shifted them closer to the yards for Millsy and his crew to lamb mark next Monday.'

'Great. Want a beer?'

'Thanks,' they said in unison.

She led them to the kitchen and got them a beer each from the fridge, pouring a rum and Coke for herself. They sat down at the table and Gemma looked at the two men seriously.

'So what do you reckon the deal is with these stock numbers? They've got me buggered,' she said.

Garry and Bulla had worked for Adam's family for many years before he'd taken over the farm from his parents. When Adam and Gemma had married, she'd earned their respect and loyalty by working as hard as they did and taking pride in her work. Neither had had any hesitation in staying on with Gemma as boss after Adam had died; they knew she'd be as good a boss as Adam had been, if not better.

'Well, Gem,' said Bulla, 'I'm blowed if I know what's going on. Sinny used to know what was going on with every mob, sheep or cattle, but I reckon for the last eight or nine months before the accident he spent so much time going off in that plane of his, that maybe he lost track of what was going on.'

'Did either of you know about a contract for three hundred steers to go to the feedlotters at the end of October?'

Bulla and Garry looked at each other, puzzled, and each took another swig of beer without realising they were mirroring each other's actions. Gemma laughed to herself. They were so similar, but she guessed they had lived and worked together for so long that it was bound to happen.

'I dunno nothing about any contract for the feedlotters,' said Garry. 'Don't remember him ever signing a forward supply contract. Do you, Bull?'

'Nah, don't reckon I do.'

'Really?' said Gemma, surprised. 'Ned said today that he'd done it for the last three years.'

'No way,' said Bulla strongly. 'Not while we've been here, and definitely not in the last three years. We'd remember 'cos we would've had to get them in, and Sinny would've taken us out to look at them in the feedlot. Ya know how he liked to follow the stock all the way through to the abattoirs. Ned must have it wrong.'

Gemma looked thoughtful. 'Yeah, that's a good point. He always took you guys or me with him to look at the stock. Don't know why I didn't think of that.' She took a sip of her rum and Coke. 'Do you think he was doing something with Dad?'

'Nah, mate,' Bulla replied without hesitation. 'Don't reckon that would be a goer. No offence to ya old man, but it's not like Sinny and Jake were good mates.'

Gemma nodded. Adam hadn't always seen eye to eye with her dad, but that was okay; she didn't see eye to eye with his folks at times either. Mostly they got along well, although Gemma sometimes felt that his parents hadn't really understood Adam and the pressures that they placed on him.

Gemma finally smiled and said, 'Well, I reckon we're organised for a while. The stock and little bit of crop that we have are looking good and we're all organised for lamb marking next week. What are you two up to for the weekend?'

'Reckon we'll probably go to the pub, what do ya think, Gazza?'

'Yeah, think that's where we'll end up. Gotta go to town on Sat'dy mornin' to get some supplies, so I reckon we'll probably pass through the pub.'

'Sounds like a good plan. Well, I guess I'll see you both in the morning.'

The pair got up from their chairs, downing the last of their beers as they went. Bulla stopped abruptly before he got to the door.

'Gem, I'm not really keen on that Jack. Make sure you watch out for yourself. Make sure you lock ya doors at night, okay?'

'Why's that, Bulla? Are you being overprotective?' She smiled at him affectionately.

'Nah, I've got me reasons. Just you be careful, hear me?' he reiterated gruffly.

'I'm always careful, Bull,' Gemma said gently. 'See you tomorrow.'

'Seeya,' they echoed.

After a dinner of eggs on toast – not that she would ever confess to Jess how close to the mark she had been! – Gemma took a deep breath and picked up the phone.

'Hello, Sarah speaking,' her mother's voice carolled.

'Hi, Mum, it's me.'

'Hello, darling. How are you?'

'Pretty good. What's happening over there?'

'Oh you know, the usual. Your father's pretty busy with calving. He's gone to bed early tonight actually – he's feeling a bit poorly. And I had a phone call from Leisha today. She and the children are fine – and guess what?'

'What?' It had been a couple of weeks since Gemma had spoken to her sister.

'Zac has been offered a job in Canberra. Higher-paying than where he is now. They'll be shifting sometime in the next month or so. It'll be such a great move for them. Much colder than Melbourne, of course, but a wonderful opportunity and plenty of good schools for Zoë and Kate. And here's the best bit – oh, that's right, I can't tell you that yet. Leisha wants to tell you herself. Anyway, how are things going over there? Are you eating properly? You've lost so much weight. I wish you would come over here more often for meals.'

Gemma raised her eyes heavenwards. 'I'm fine, Mum. It's great – about Leisha, being pregnant again, I mean.' Gemma waited for the reaction.

'Oh, has she rung you already? Isn't it exciting?'

'No, Mum, she hasn't rung – I was just guessing.'

'Oh, Gemma, you do get me every time. Now don't you go telling your sister I told you. I didn't really tell you, anyway. Now I must go, your father is calling me. The poor darling, he was feeling so awful that I had to send him to bed. Have a lovely night. Bye!'

'Bye, Mum,' Gemma put down the phone and shook her head, smiling. She sent an email to Ned explaining that she hadn't spoken to her father yet, then she had a shower, jumped into bed and picked up the book she was reading . . .

Jack took another swig from his bottle of rum and gazed through the window of the shearers' quarters. A short time later he threw on some clothes and grabbed his torch. Opening his door quietly he listened. Not a sound – maybe tonight was a good bet to check out the widow's house. He made his way softly across the yard, talking quietly to the dogs who growled in return. Looking around he paused and listened again. Nothing. His hand rested on the doorknob, then Jack turned it slowly. The dogs started to bark excitedly. He abruptly stopped and let go of the knob, cursing, and made his way quietly back to the shearers' quarters. Lighting another cigarette he lay back thinking about how he could get into the house and have a look around. His mobile phone beeped with a text message.

Chapter 6

Gemma sat up with a start. What had woken her? The clock showed 12.20 am. Then she heard the phone. Who on earth could be ringing at this time of night?

'Hello?'

'Gem, it's Mum here, darling.'

'Mum, what's wrong?'

'Well, nothing to be too alarmed about, dear, but Dad has had a bit of a heart attack and we're in at the hospital. We thought you might like to come in.'

'What?' Gemma gasped. 'Is he all right? Was it a bad one? I'm leaving now. Where are you?'

'Now calm down, darling. It was only very mild and he's going to be fine. We're still in Pirie but we'll probably be off to Adelaide tomorrow or the next day.'

'See you in an hour or so.'

Gemma threw on some clothes, her mind in a whirl, and ran to the ute.

Driving through the dark her mind kept wandering back to when she was a little girl and her dad was teaching her about stock and farming. She remembered his big hands, rough and cracked. The cracks were embedded with grease and dirt that no amount of scrubbing would get rid of, but those big hands were always gentle. She remembered him helping a lamb to get its first drink, speaking soothingly to the ewe while his hands carefully guided the lamb towards the ewe's udder. She remembered him picking up the fleeces off the sheep they were shearing, his hands all shiny with the lanolin from the wool. Shearing time was the only time her dad's hands were really soft. She remembered him gently rubbing her dry after swimming in the sea on a holiday they had when she was little.

She pressed her foot down on the accelerator.

Unexpectedly lights blinded her as she neared the crest of a hill. Swearing, she flashed her lights until the driver of the oncoming vehicle dipped his. Glancing in the rear-view mirror, Gemma saw a truck with a stock crate loaded behind it.

As she reached the outskirts of town, Gemma took some deep breaths and tried to calm herself. She wished Adam was with her. She felt panicky, as if events were hurtling out of her control, just as she had the night he'd rushed her to the hospital, when she was bleeding while pregnant with their child. She could still hear the doctor telling them both he was sorry, but they had lost the baby. But as devastating as that had been, at least she had still had Adam. He had taken her in his arms and they had cried together. Now she was alone.

I will not lose my dad, she thought. *Not after everything that has happened. He'll be okay – he's got to be.*

She pulled into the car park of the hospital and, closing her eyes and leaning her head against the steering wheel, said a little prayer. Then she grabbed her purse and mobile phone, shoved them in the pocket of her jeans, locked the car and headed inside.

The sterile smell made her feel ill. The fluorescent lights played havoc with her eyes that were used to darkness and the white lines of the road. Thankfully the casualty department was quiet. The nurse looked up and smiled as she entered.

'Hello, Gemma, I've been expecting you. Don't worry – he's going to be fine.'

Gemma looked at the nurse and blinked. The nurse laughed. 'Do I look that different from school? I guess I do with my hair pulled back like this.'

'Paige? Paige Nicholls?' The night was beginning to feel surreal. 'I heard you were back. What are you doing here? Is he really okay?'

Paige laughed. 'I work here, and yes, he really is okay.' Her voice sobered. 'I heard about Adam. I'm really sorry, Gem. You must have been through hell.'

'I'm doing okay,' Gemma told her, 'and I'd love to talk, but I need to see my dad. Let's catch up later though, once all this has blown over.'

'He's on the second floor in 32B. I'll wander up and give you my phone number before I get off work.'

Gemma headed off in the direction that Paige had indicated and took the lift up to the second floor. When the doors opened, she saw her mother leaning tiredly against the wall of the corridor.

'Mum,' said Gemma, almost running towards her. 'Where is he? Is he okay? What's going on?'

'He's fine, Gem, don't panic.' Sarah took her arm and led her to a grey plastic couch near the lift. 'Before you rang he'd been having some angina pains and had decided to go to bed after taking some of his tablets. While we were on the phone the pain increased and he was having a little trouble breathing so he asked me to take him to the hospital. When we got here the doctor ran some tests and told us your father had had a mild heart attack. We're probably going to have to go to Adelaide for some more tests, but at the moment he's resting and he's feeling all right.'

'Oh, Mum, I was so scared. So the doctor really thinks he's going to be fine?'

'He should be as fit and strong as you can be once you've had a heart attack. He may have to have bypass surgery, but we won't know that till the tests have been done.'

Gemma started to get up, then sat back down again and hugged her mother. 'What about you? Are you going all right?'

Sarah nodded, but Gemma saw the glimmer of tears in her eyes before she swiftly rose from the couch. 'Coming?'

Gemma stood and followed her down the corridor. When Sarah opened the door Gemma paused at the threshold, swallowing hard to control her emotions.

When she entered the room her eyes flew straight to the bed where her father lay, his eyes closed and hands resting on his stomach. Gemma felt her throat contract when she looked at his hands, so familiar but in such alien surrounds. He had monitors on his chest and fingers, and they beeped quietly as she glanced at the green lines that measured his breathing and any movements made by his heart.

'Hi, Dad,' Gemma said softly.

His eyes opened and she was relieved to see that, although he looked tired and pale, his eyes still held their usual sparkle.

'Hi, Gem. Didn't hit any roos on the way in?'

Gemma smiled and moved across to sit on the bed. She picked up one of his hands. 'Not this time. They didn't have time to see me!'

'Good. Now don't you go worrying yourself about me. Everything will be fine.'

'I'm supposed to be the one telling you that,' Gemma said in jest. 'I guess you'll be up and about in no time. I won't even have time to get over to the farm and check the stock for you.'

'Well, you might get to check them once or twice while I'm in Adelaide, but other than that you ain't getting your mitts on my land yet, missy!' Her father smiled to show he was teasing.

'Well, don't worry about anything on the farm. Bulla, Garry and I can deal with it. Just you get better.'

'Mmm,' said Jake as his eyes began to close again. Gemma settled into a chair on one side of his bed and her mother sat on the other side, each holding a hand.

'Gemma, I need to talk to you about something.' Her father's tone was quiet but serious.

Gemma looked across at him.

'Is it really important, Dad? You really should be resting now.'

There was a look of indecision on his face, battling with fatigue.

'You and I need to have a long talk when I get back from the city, okay? Promise me you will make time.' The intensity of his words alarmed Gemma.

'Of course, Dad, whatever you want,' she said, looking at her mother with her eyebrows raised in query. But if Sarah knew what it was Jake wanted to talk to Gemma about, she gave no indication.

As her dad drifted off to sleep, Gemma let the soft beeps of the monitors lull her into a doze.

Gemma woke with a start as she heard rustling in the room. As her sleep-filled eyes focused, she remembered where she was and why. Her eyes flew to the bed but she relaxed as she heard the rhythmic breathing of her father. He was still asleep, as was her mum, who dozed with her head against Jake's shoulder. They had been married for thirty-five years and were as much in love now as the day they married. This must be hard for them both.

A nurse was checking Jake's monitors and feeling his pulse. She smiled when she saw that Gemma was awake.

'Hi,' she whispered.

Gemma returned the smile sleepily. 'Hi, what's the time?'

'About four thirty.'

'If they wake up, could you let them know that I've just had to make a phone call and I'll be right back?'

'Sure.'

Gemma slipped from the room, pulling out her mobile phone as she went. Walking outside she smelled rain on the bitumen and heard the engine of the occasional passing car. She wrapped her arms around herself to keep warm, but relished the brisk air. It made her feel alive. Breathing deeply, she began to dial Bulla and Garry's number, then stopped. She would go to Jess's, get a coffee, have a shower and borrow some clothes. Then she'd be in a better condition to deal with things.

The town glistened with overnight rain, the road wet beneath the wheels of her ute. Driving down the quiet tree-lined streets her eyes took in the small gardens. She'd often wondered how people could bear to live with their neighbours so close.

As she entered the street where Jess lived, a white Toyota ute pulled out onto the main road. A farmhand heading out to work, Gemma assumed, her quick glance taking in the muddy bullbar and line of four large spotlights perched on the roof.

She turned into Jess's driveway, surprised to see the light on. It was unlike Jess to be up this early. She got out of the ute and went to the door. She had just raised her hand to knock when the door flew open and there stood Jess in a flimsy green negligee. Her happy voice cut through the morning air: 'I knew you wouldn't be able to resist . . .' Jess's voice trailed off when she saw Gemma. 'Gem, what are you doing here? Are you okay? What's going on?'

'Dad's had a heart attack,' Gemma choked out.

Jess's hand flew to her mouth then she rushed forward to hug her friend. 'Oh Gem, is he all right?'

'I think so, but – Jess, what is happening to my life? I'm so scared.'

Jess didn't answer but hugged her again, then she looked at Gemma and laughed. 'Look at us, me in my lingerie and you – looking rather crumpled, I must say – in jeans and a jumper. I've *got* to get dressed or I'll freeze. I'll be two secs. You make the coffee.'

A little while later the two of them were sitting at Jess's kitchen table with steaming cups of coffee.

Gemma shook her head. 'Jess, I'm just not sure what's going to happen now. I can't think straight or even work out what step comes next. I feel so helpless.'

'Give yourself a break, Gem,' Jess advised. 'It only happened, like, twelve hours ago. It'll take some time to get used to the idea. It's only threatening to overwhelm you now because you've had so much happen to you in the last little while. Just go with the flow and give yourself some time to adjust. Stop trying to control everything.' Gemma opened her mouth to speak but Jess held up her hand. 'I know, I know. This is how you handle things – but this is a situation you can't control. So breathe deep, and relax.'

Gemma smiled. 'I'm glad I came to see you.'

'Well of course you are. How often does someone meet you at the door looking the way I did? Now go have a shower and then get back to the hospital. I'll give you a key to the house and you can stop here tonight, get a decent sleep. Your mum can stay here too if she wants but I reckon they'll find a bed for her at the hospital if she wants to stay there.'

Heading out into the wet streets again Gemma felt much better – stronger, which she needed to be for her mum and dad. Looking at the clock she saw it was nearly 6 am and if she didn't get in contact with Bulla and Garry soon they would be at work. Pulling over to the kerb, she dialled their number on her mobile phone.

'What?' answered a grumpy voice.

Gemma laughed out loud and said, 'Why are you

so grumpy? It's a beautiful morning. There's been rain!'

'Damn it, Gemma, you know what time it is, girl? Don't you ever sleep?' Bulla grumbled.

'Yeah I do, but it's still a great morning.'

'I'll tell ya after I've had me first cuppa. Whaddya want?'

Gemma knew he was putting on an act. He'd probably been awake since before light. 'Got some bad news. I'm down in Pirie. Dad had a heart attack last night.'

Bulla let fly with a curse.

'He's okay – was only mild – but I'm going to need you or Gazza to go and check the stock over at Hayelle. I'll probably be home later today, maybe tomorrow. I'm going to stay here until they don't need me anymore. There's talk they'll be sending him down to the city today or tomorrow to have some more tests.'

'Yeah, no worries, you just stay there for as long as you need to. Gaz and I'll handle everything out here. You just tell the old man to get better.'

'Thanks, Bulla,' Gemma said quietly.

Gemma bought a cup of coffee for herself and one for her mother from a sleepy-looking girl at a cafe outside the hospital.

As she entered the ward one of the nurses said to her, 'You had a visitor while you were gone.' She held out a piece of paper.

'Thanks,' said Gemma. Unfolding it, she saw it was from Paige.

Dear Gemma,
Sorry I missed you. I was hoping to have a chat.
I've moved back to town for good now, so maybe
when you have some time we could catch up
over a meal or something. I've missed you since
we left school. Hope we can get together soon.
    Love Paige

Beneath her name Paige had written her phone number.

Gemma thought back to the boarding school she, Jess and Paige had attended in Adelaide, and how their group of friends had promised never to lose touch. They had been friends since primary school – Paige, Jess, Kathy, Claire and her. She thought hard, trying to place where everyone was these days. The occasional Christmas card was about all the contact that Gemma had had with Paige and Kathy for years. The last she'd heard of Kathy she was travelling overseas. Kathy had always had the travel bug. As for Claire, Gemma would never forget the parting words of rage she had flung at her boyfriend before flying out the door of the restaurant.

'You're nothing but a two-timing prick, Tim Milton. I can't believe I thought I loved you!' Claire had flung the photos of him and another woman at

Tim as Gemma and Adam watched open-mouthed. She jumped into her small car and sped off down the road. Ten minutes later she was dead after colliding with a road train. Tim had committed suicide a year later, out of guilt.

Gemma shook her head. Bugger the memories. Too many of them, and bad times always brought the worst ones back. She took the coffee in to Sarah.

Both her parents were awake, and as she handed the coffee to her mum, Sarah asked Gemma if she'd call her brother and sister to let them know what had happened.

'Sure, I'll go outside and give them a call now. What time will the doctor be here?'

'Sometime after eight, I think, so we have a bit of time to wait.'

'Okay, I'll make the calls. Then I need you to tell me what's happening on the farm, Dad, and if there's anything coming up that we need to know about.'

Jake nodded his assent. Gemma thought he looked tired and grey today, but that was probably normal after a heart attack, she reasoned.

Stepping outside she dialled her sister's number.

'Hello?' Leisha sounded harassed and Gemma could hear the two girls, Zoë and Kate, arguing in the background. She smiled, imagining Leisha with her brown hair pulled back into a ponytail, phone tucked between her ear and shoulder, frantically trying to complete the million and one jobs she would have on the go at once.

'Hi, it's me, is it a really bad time?'

'No. But I've had enough of your two nieces. They've done nothing but argue all morning. Anyway, what's up with you?'

Half an hour later, all the arrangements had been made. Leisha and the two girls would arrive by the beginning of next week, and their brother, Patrick, would be coming as soon as he could get to Brisbane and a flight. He would meet up with Jake and Sarah in Adelaide, then come out to give her a hand with Jake's farm, Hayelle, and Billbinya. He would be welcome company for a couple of weeks.

When Gemma rang Ned to say she wouldn't be at Billbinya for a day or so, Ned told her that he and Ben were following the police out to Kettles' farm. With her mind too full of other things, she didn't question him, but felt a twinge of apprehension without knowing why.

Chapter 7

On Wednesday morning, Ben walked into the Jones and Hawkins Stock Agents and Merchandise office ready for a full day with clients. Ned was sitting at his desk talking into the phone in an animated sort of way, Bert was leaning against the wall talking on his mobile, and the merchandise blokes were firing up the computers in readiness for the day. The office always hummed madly in the early morning. Ben made his way to the kitchen to make a coffee.

'Ben!' Ned's voice vibrated through the office. 'Get in here!'

Ben turned and hurried back. 'What's wrong?'

'Jake Birch has had a heart attack and the Carters, Smiths and Kettles think they have all had stock stolen overnight – out of their own yards, if you don't mind – and are going to the police. The cops are going out to interview all of the surrounding neighbours today.

All of those farmers are within about a thirty k radius of Billbinya, Gemma's in here at the hospital and there isn't going to be anyone on Jake's place. Reckon we should take a trip out there and see what's going on.'

Ben abandoned all thoughts of coffee and headed towards the car. He had some thoughts on this stock-stealing business.

Ben came from a long line of farmers, but he'd recently leased his farm out for three years in order to embark on a new venture. He'd always loved farming, but his enthusiasm had waned – finding it could be incredibly lonely and time-consuming. He hadn't managed to see his friends, or go to a B & S ball or concert, for at least a year. The weekly trips to the pub and the unwanted attention from single girls in the small town he frequented hadn't lessened his thirst for company, so he'd decided he needed some time away. Ben had come to Ned through his own stock agent down south. Knowing the rural industry as he did, and understanding how farmers thought, had made him an invaluable addition to Ned's team.

'Is Jake all right?' asked Ben as Ned sped towards the main road that led to Billbinya.

'Yeah, sounds like he's going to be fine. It'll put some pressure on Gemma though with no one on Hayelle. But she said her brother is coming down from Queensland to give her a hand so that'll be some help.'

'What does he do?'

'Oh, something with horses – breaking in stock horses, maybe? Dunno. He's a nice enough bloke, but I haven't had a lot to do with him since he was a kid.'

'Ned, why are we racing out to Billbinya just because the cops might be going out? Why are you so protective of Gemma?'

'Did you think that Billbinya could have stock stolen too? No, I didn't think so,' Ned said as Ben shook his head. 'She's a good girl and a hard worker. If Jake and Sinny aren't around to protect her, then someone needs to and that someone will be me. I don't like the way those sheep numbers are up and there is something wrong with the contract for the steers. Gemma just doesn't own that number of cattle. Where are they going to come from? I want to talk to Bulla and Gaz before the cops get there too. I noticed some foreign earmarks and I just wanted to check if some sheep had got through the fence and they hadn't noticed. Maybe the neighbour had bought some sheep in from outta town. I know that Sinny never dealt with another stock agent but Bert and me, and I know that I didn't sell him those sheep otherwise I'd know the earmarks. I don't think they're from around here. But where are they from and how did they get here? See? Best to have a chat to the guys, see what they know and if Gemma needs me then I'm right there.'

Ben listened in silence. It was the longest speech he'd ever heard Ned make and he was surprised by the note of hysteria in the older man's voice. Why was he so concerned? Earmarks were important – it was how farmers could tell their stock apart from their neighbours' – but it didn't seem out of the question that Gemma would have other earmarks on Billbinya; it was a big place and he was sure that they couldn't breed all their own ewes. They would have to buy some in, so it stood to reason there would be different earmarks. Besides, sheep had been known to jump fences or walk through gates that had been left open accidentally – they could have just wandered through from the next station. Well, he'd just listen to what everyone had to say and see if he could make some sense of what was going on.

The shed on Billbinya was a hive of activity on Wednesday morning. Garry's feet could be seen sticking out from under a ute as he serviced it and Bulla was loading materials and tools into the tray of his ute in preparation for the day. Jack received his allocated jobs and climbed onto the farm motorbike. He was putting on his helmet when he asked: 'Where's Gemma? I heard the ute take off in the middle of the night.'

'She's with her father who isn't well.' Bulla said shortly, reluctant to reveal that she might be away for a few days, then clattered down the drive in his old yellow ute, with Jack heading in the opposite direction to start a stock run.

Later, Garry was headed towards Hayelle when he passed Jim Carter. His two-way crackled to life.

'Gotta minute to have a yarn, Gaz?' Jim asked.

'Sure, mate.' Garry slowed and did a U-turn. Parked by the side of the road, the two men leaned against the side of the Billbinya ute.

'How's it going?' asked Jim.

'Not too bad, mate. What's happening with you fellas?'

'Well, we've got a bit of a problem. There's some sheep gone missing off our place.'

'What?' Garry said in surprise. 'How many you missing?'

'About three hundred wether lambs. I know that isn't much by your standards, but I need every one of them with the wool prices being so low at the moment.' Jim scratched his head in a worried fashion and rubbed his hands over his face. 'Trouble is, I don't think this is the first time. Reckon I've lost lambs before but not realised it until it's too late, but definitely not like this – this time whoever took them is being really brazen. These lambs were in the yards for crutching and the buggers just came and loaded them out of the bloody yards. Can't believe it. Got over to the shed this morning to make sure everything was all ready and there's no sheep!' Jim shook his head. 'There are truck tracks in and no sheep tracks anywhere, so it's not like they've got out of the shed and walked out of the front gate onto the road. It's blatant theft. Never come across anything like this in my life!'

'Bloody hell,' said Garry, shocked. 'Have you called the cops?'

'Yeah, they're on the way out. But that's not the worst of it, mate. Sam Smith and John Kettle have had some stolen too – the same as me, straight out of the yards. They had theirs in for crutching too.'

'You're kidding me? Who would know that all you fellas are crutching on the same day? It's not like that would happen often.'

'I just don't know, Gaz. Look, if you hear anything let me know, all right? I'd better keep going and pick up Sam and John. The cops are going to meet us at our farm and then we're all going to drive around together and see what we can find.'

'I s'pose you tried to follow the truck tracks?'

'Yeah, we did,' said Jim. 'But it's all single lane bitumen roads from here back to the main drag, and you can see the tracks heading out the drive until they hit the bitumen but you lose them after that.'

'Well, if we can do anything, you let us know,' said Garry. 'You know Gem was out late last night, she had to go to town unexpectedly – she may have seen something. I'll ask when I catch up with her next.'

'Yeah, that'd be good. Thanks, mate.' Jim thumped Garry on the back and walked back to his ute.

Garry drove on to Hayelle to check the stock. But really what he wanted to do was go back to Billbinya and talk to Bulla.

* * *

Bulla was checking the boundary fence when he saw from a distance a mob of sheep walking around a paddock. They looked like they had just been put there and they were checking out where the water was, and looking for the best tucker.

Strange, he thought. *There shouldn't be anything in that paddock.* He turned the ute around and headed back to the gate that was just off the one-lane bitumen road. As he pulled off the road he could see there were truck tracks leading to the gate and that the gate's padlock had been opened and left unlocked. Any gates that weren't used regularly or that were a long way from houses or the coming and going of people were padlocked for security. Billbinya was such large acreage and had a lot of road frontage; when Adam's parents had owned the land they were forever finding people camping on it or stomping through the bush looking for dams to throw their yabby nets into.

As he drove into the paddock he could see that the sheep were young wethers and they were not Billbinya's.

Bulla was waiting at the shed when Garry returned. The latter jumped out of the ute and asked immediately, 'Have you heard about the missing sheep?'

'What missing sheep?' asked Bulla.

'Jim Carter, Sam Smith and John Kettle have all had wether lambs stolen out of their yards. They had them in for crutching and someone has brought in a truck and just taken them *out of their yards*! Can you believe it?'

Bulla raised his eyebrows and rubbed his chin. 'Well, that's a bit interesting,' he said slowly. 'Reckon someone has dumped about a thousand wether lambs in our paddock – Reimer's paddock to be precise.'

Garry looked shocked. 'What the hell is this?' he asked in horror.

'Who knows?' Bulla said as he handed Garry Ned's card to indicate that he had called in early in the day but had not caught either man. 'Maybe Ned knows something.'

They heard the revving of a motorbike and knew Jack was close by. 'Don't say anything, I'll fix this,' said Bulla.

'All okay?' asked Bulla as Jack got off the bike.

'Actually it's not,' said Jack, pulling off his helmet and running his fingers through his hair. 'I was over on the north side and the cattle have busted a couple of fences so I'll need to get back and fix that this afternoon. I'll need to borrow a ute to carry the fencing gear though. Plus there are two mobs of calving cows that have got boxed in together. Not sure what you want to do about that – it might be a bit hard to get all the calves back with their right mums.' He took out the little green notebook that fitted snugly into his pocket to read out the rest of his notes from the stock run.

'The cement tank in Middleton's paddock has cracked and is leaking pretty bad and the windmill on that dam needs fixing. Compensator buckets look shot. There's a cow stuck in the middle of Mackay's dam – probably going to need the tractor to pull her out. And just for a bit more fun, the rams have got out into the Woolfords' place. Looks like a dog or roo or something has pushed them through the fence.'

'Blast it all,' said Bulla. 'Yeah, all right, Jack, get some lunch and head back out. Take Garry's ute and all the gear you need for the fence. See if you can bring those rams back too. Gaz, you might need to take the tractor and deal with the cow, and I have some things in my ute that I can use to pull the windmill. I bet the tank's going to need relining so it won't leak. Have to organise for someone to come and do it.'

As Jack headed towards the house for lunch, he overheard Bulla say, 'I was hoping to get those wether lambs into the yards and then call Jim Carter, but guess we'd better fix these problems first. I'll give the police a call when we get home tonight, and see what they want us to do.'

Jack smirked. His boss's plan had worked.

The work that Jack had created would keep the men on Billbinya so busy for the rest of the day they'd have no time to work out what to do with those wether lambs – and by tomorrow morning, there wouldn't be a wether lamb in sight.

Chapter 8

The workshop and sheds were quiet when Gemma pulled up at the homestead around 2 pm and there didn't seem to be anyone around. She really hadn't been gone all that long but she felt grimy and tired and longed for a shower and to curl up in her own bed. The doctor had said that Jake wouldn't be able to work for some time and he'd be in the city for at least a month. She definitely needed sleep before facing the ramifications of that ...

BANG, BANG, BANG! Gemma looked at her bedside clock. It was nearly four. She climbed out of bed and went to the door, squinting with bleary eyes at the police officers standing there.

'Hello?' said Gemma, puzzled. Then as her brain started to work, she said in a panic, 'It's not Dad, is it?'

'Mrs Sinclair?' asked one of the men.

'Yes, what is it, what's wrong?'

'I'm Geoff Hay and this is Ian Paver. We're from the police station in Port Pirie. Could we come in? We need to ask you some questions regarding some stolen sheep.'

'Oh, okay.' Gemma opened the door wider. 'Please, come in. My dad had a heart attack yesterday and I've only just got home from the hospital. I thought something must have happened to him,' she explained as she led the way through to the kitchen. 'Take a seat. I'll be back in a sec to put the kettle on.'

Taking refuge in the bathroom, Gemma splashed her face with icy water and tried to get her head together. Being woken up from a deep sleep, by two policemen wanting to talk about stolen sheep, was a bit overwhelming. Tears welled in her eyes but she impatiently blinked them away and returned to the kitchen.

'What can I get you both to drink?' she asked, filling the kettle.

'Coffee, thanks – white, no sugar,' said the officer who seemed to be in charge. Tall and slim, in his late forties, he had a stern look on his face, but his brown eyes seemed friendly.

'Tea, black, thanks,' said the other one, who looked remarkably similar to the first but about five years younger. It must be the uniform, Gemma decided.

Gemma busied herself getting the drinks and then sat at the table. 'How can I help?'

Geoff Hay spoke again. 'The police department had a phone call this morning from one of your neighbours, Jim Carter. It seems he's had about three hundred wether lambs stolen. He had them yarded ready for crutching and someone allegedly brought in a truck in the middle of the night and took them straight out of his yards. Same thing happened to Sam Smith and John Kettle.'

'You're joking? Who did it? Have you found the stock?' Gemma was horrified.

'Hello? Anyone home?' called a voice at the front door.

'Ned,' called Gemma with relief. 'In the kitchen.'

Ned and Ben walked through into the kitchen. 'G'day again,' said Ned to the two policemen. Ben nodded and leaned against the doorframe.

'G'day,' said Geoff. 'I'm afraid we've caught Mrs Sinclair on the hop a bit. Woke her up and now we're just explaining what has happened.'

'Ned, you knew about this?' asked Gemma incredulously. 'How come you didn't ring?'

'Come on, Gemma. As if I'd worry you about something like this while you were at the hospital with Jake. We only heard about it early this morning. Ben and I got out here as quick as we could to see if we could help. We've sort of been following them around from farm to farm. We went to Hayelle after not finding anyone here first thing, but no one was around either. Thought we might have caught Garry or Bulla doing a stock check and feeding the dogs.'

Gemma was back at the bench making more coffee. She sat the cups in front of Ned and Ben and motioned for them both to sit down.

'Okay,' Gemma said to the police officers when she resumed her seat. 'What did you need to ask me?'

'What time did you leave to go into Pirie?' asked Geoff.

'I think it was about twelve thirty or so. I remember looking at the clock when Mum rang and that was twenty past twelve, I think. I basically just ran out the door.'

'Did you see a truck or anything suspicious when you were driving to Pirie?'

'I was lucky to see the road! I was just hellbent on getting to the hospital to see Dad.'

'Have you ever heard anyone talking about having stock – sheep or cattle – stolen?'

'I haven't heard any rumours, but I haven't really gone anywhere since Adam died. I avoid town if I can and I usually just ask Ned to bring what I need from town or get things sent out on the mail run.'

'Why don't you go to town much?' the young officer asked curiously.

Gemma looked at Ian, who had stopped writing notes. 'People stare and talk about me,' she said frankly. 'They don't think I should be running this property. They think I should've sold when Adam was killed.' Out of the corner of her eye, she saw Ned wince. She knew he'd tried to protect her from all these things, as had her family, but she wasn't blind or deaf.

'Do you think you've ever had any animals stolen from your property?'

'Well, I don't think so. Adam used to keep all the records and I never really had anything to do with the office until he died. But I know he'd have said something to me if he thought that we'd had stock stolen.'

'Yeah,' Ned agreed. 'He wasn't the type to take something like that lying down.'

'Do you think you have ever had stolen animals on your farm?'

'What? No way! What are you implying?' Gemma looked at Geoff angrily.

'I'm not implying anything. I'm sorry if I offended you,' Geoff assured her. 'We need to ask these questions to form a clear picture of what has happened.'

'I'm sure we haven't.'

'Okay, what do you do when your neighbours' sheep or cattle stray onto your property? Are your fences pretty good?'

'We put them in the yards, ring the neighbour and ask them to come and pick their stock up. The same way we have done it since time began. Our neighbours do the same if our stock goes through the fence onto their place. Mostly our fences are in pretty good nick, though.'

Geoff sighed. 'We're going to have to call in the stock squad from Western Australia since South Australia doesn't have one.'

'Well, I'm happy to help in any way I can.' Gemma was exhausted and it showed.

Ned spoke up. 'Do you reckon we could do this another time? Gemma looks a bit whacked and she's been through a fair bit in the last twenty-four hours.'

'Yeah, look, that's as much info as we need at the moment anyway. We have to get back and make some arrangements with the stock squad now, but if you think of anything further you can give us a call, Mrs Sinclair.' Geoff dug out his card and placed it on the table, Ian following suit. 'Thanks for your time; we'll probably be in touch.'

Ned stayed with Gemma, getting all the details of Jake and his illness, while the policemen prepared to leave, and Ben walked them to their car.

Ben pushed open the door into the corner pub. He'd been told this was where the best meals were, and he was looking forward to a big steak and a cold beer. After ordering a drink, he sat at the bar near a few other young guys standing around talking. Amongst the general chatter and warmth of the pub Ben was starting to relax when he heard Gemma's name mentioned. Tuning in to the conversation, Ben looked to see who was talking.

A tall, thick-set, good-looking man was saying: 'After all, it's been known that stock stealing has been going on around here for two or three years, but I guess a lot of us thought it would stop when Sinny died.

Gemma must be pretty good at it to keep it going by herself.'

'On ya, mate,' snorted another one. 'She wouldn't know how. She has enough trouble running Billbinya. She couldn't manage that as well.'

'But what about if Bulla and Gaz were helping her?' asked another.

'Nah, no way,' said the tall man. 'One thing I do know about those two, they're as straight as the day is long. Nup, must be Gemma.'

'Well you'd know – aren't you making it with her best mate? What's her name, that red-headed piece?'

Ben casually shifted closer to the men to hear their conversation as the man holding court said, 'You guys know me, mate – I just take what's on offer. Jess is fun to hang out with but we're not joined at the hip or anything.' His mobile phone beeped suddenly. Ben watched as he grabbed the phone from his belt and looked at the text message. 'Better take this one, guys,' he said, and threw down a fifty-dollar note. 'Get yourselves another – I'll be back soon.' He disappeared towards the men's room.

Ben thought it was a shame that the conversation had been interrupted as he would have liked to have heard more of their thoughts.

He raised his hand to order another beer, then moved down the bar towards the other men. 'G'day, I'm Ben Daylee. I'm the new stock agent with Ned Jones and Bert Hawkins. How's it going?'

'Good, mate. I'm Scott Forrester – call me Frost, and these guys are Shadow, Pusher, Jonesy and Floro.'

'Good to meet you all,' said Ben, shaking hands all round. 'Can I get anyone a drink?'

'Nah, we're right at the moment, mate,' Frost said. 'Hey, if you're working with Ned then you should know all about what happened today with the stolen stock. I hear there were about two thousand ewes stolen from five different farms.'

Ben smiled and shook his head. It was amazing how information could get so distorted. 'I don't think it was that many, but yeah, there have been some go missing. You fellas farmers?'

'Nah, but we've got mates on the footy team that are and they're all talking about it. It's got round town real quick,' said Jonesy.

The tall man was making his way towards them, putting his phone back on his belt. 'G'day.' He nodded at Ben.

'Bradley, mate, this is Ben Daylee – I think we should call him Hills.' Pusher paused. 'You know, like Dales, Hills . . .' His voice trailed off as all the men looked at him blankly. 'Anyway, he's working for Ned and Bert, the stock agents down the road.'

The two men shook hands.

'Is that right?' said Brad. 'I'm the local agronomist, so I guess we'll be running into each other a bit on farms.'

'I guess so.' Ben took a swig of his beer. 'Well, I'm off to get a feed, anyone want to join me?'

The other men made their excuses, but Brad stayed. 'Yeah, I'll have a bite with you; I might be able to fill you in on the good farmers and the not so good, if you're interested.'

'Sounds great.'

They talked generally while they waited for their steaks, chips and salads to arrive, then suddenly Brad said, 'So you would've met Gemma Sinclair in your travels with Ned?'

Ben was cautious, while he formulated his response. 'Yeah, I've met her a couple of times.'

'I knock about with one of her mates a bit. Jess Rawlings. I haven't met Gemma yet, but she seems to be a bit of a legend around here.'

'Why's that?'

'Oh, well, you know with her husband dying in the plane crash like that and her taking on running the farm. She's obviously got some get-up-and-go about her.'

'Mmm,' responded Ben noncommittally. 'Had heard something.'

'Rumour has it that the Sinclairs are involved, but no one can prove it. Don't really know how much truth there is to it, but where there's smoke there's fire, hey?'

Ben sat back, pushing his empty plate away, and nodded for Brad to continue.

'Well, look.' Brad leaned across the table. 'I'm not one to speak ill of the dead, but it seemed that every time the Sinclairs had people over for dinner, stock would disappear from their guests' farm. It could be just coincidence but I think there might have been something in it. Sinny was a bit of a rogue.'

'Did you know him well?'

'I used to catch him in the pub occasionally and we had some common interests but that was about it.'

'All pretty interesting anyway,' said Ben. 'Well, I guess I'd better get going – another big day tomorrow. Good to meet you, I guess I'll catch you round.'

'Yeah, no worries, mate. Good to meet you too. Oh, by the way, don't suppose you play footy? We're looking for a full forward.'

'Well, I have kicked the footy a bit, but I'm a bit rusty. I haven't played this season.'

'If you want to have a kick, we're playing a home game on Saturday. Come down, put the boots on and I'll introduce you to the rest of the blokes. Training's on Tuesday and Thursday.'

'Okay,' said Ben. 'I'd be into that.'

Ben sauntered home reflecting on all that had happened throughout the day. The stock-stealing business was on everyone's lips and had fuelled the local gossip. He wondered about the guys he had met at the pub – most of them seemed like decent blokes. Brad, though, made him uneasy. There was something malicious about how he spoke of Adam and laid the blame with no real evidence. He made a mental note to watch what he said in front of Brad in the future.

Chapter 9

Gemma looked at Bulla and Garry aghast. 'What do you mean you think the stolen sheep were here and now they're not?' They stood at the entrance to the shed, where they met every morning to talk about the day's work before heading off in different directions. But it wasn't often Gemma was dealt such bizarre news.

Bulla scratched his head. 'Well, I spotted a mob of about a thousand wether lambs yesterday just before lunch out in Reimer's paddock. We had things that were urgent to do yesterday out in other paddocks and when I went back this morning, the sheep were nowhere in sight.'

Gemma started to shake. She took a couple of deep breaths and tried to pull herself together. 'Right, I'll need to ring the police and let them know. We didn't have anything to do with it, so we have nothing to fear, right?'

'Yeah, right you are,' said Bulla doubtfully.

Neither of the policemen were available, so Gemma left a message and hung up. She was just about to head back outside when the phone rang.

'Hello?'

'Hello, lovely, what's happening?' asked Jess's happy voice.

'Jess, you wouldn't believe what's going on here. You always ring at the right time.' Gemma's voice cracked.

'What's wrong? It's not your dad, is it?'

'Not this time.' Gemma proceeded to fill her in on all that had happened in the last twenty-four hours.

Jess was silent for a while and then said, 'Right, this weekend you're coming to town. That festival Taste of the Outback is on and there's a jazz concert over at one of the wineries. We'll have a meal out under the stars, drink some wine and listen to some music. And on Saturday we can watch Brad play footy. It'll do you good to watch some guys running around in footy shorts.'

'I don't know, Jess ...' Gemma's voice petered out. 'I can't leave unless Bulla and Garry are around to look after everything. You know that.' As an afterthought she added, 'Maybe Jack can.'

'That's sorted then. See you Friday . . . No arguments. See you at my house at five thirty. Don't be late!'

Gemma put the phone down and it rang again immediately, startling her.

'Gemma Sinclair?' she answered, expecting it to be the police returning her call.

'G'day, sis, you're sounding very professional there. What's up?' It was her brother's familiar voice.

'Patrick, oh it's so great to hear from you. Are you in Adelaide yet?'

'Not yet, but I'll be there late tonight. I've talked to Mum and everything seems okay. The hospital is just running more tests and Dad is comfy so all's good.'

'How're you getting up here?'

'I was thinking I'd hire a car, but now I reckon I'll catch the bus up to Pirie. I'll use a farm ute when I get there anyway. Can you meet me?'

'Yeah, no worries. Actually that'll fit in well. Jess has just talked me into going to a concert over at a winery, so I'll be in town already. When?'

'Probably Sund'y. I want to spend a bit of time with the folks, ya know?'

Gemma smiled as she hung up the phone. Despite the worry that shadowed her, the thought of having Patrick and his happy-go-lucky nature around was cheering.

Jack's mobile phone rang just as he was emptying the last of the rum into his glass. 'Bugger,' he swore as he spilt the amber liquid onto his jeans.

''Lo?'

'How's it going, Jack?'

'Great. I was gonna ring ya tonight. The widow's away for the weekend. I'm looking after everything on Billbinya and the other two are doing 'er old man's place so they'll be out of the way. Good time to get into the house, I reckon.'

'Good. Talk to you after you've done it. You know what you're looking for, don't ya?'

'I ain't stupid.' He skolled the rest of his drink and pulled another bottle from the cupboard.

Jack's bender lasted for the weekend. He had visited Gemma's house on Friday after the girls had left but hadn't gone in. Scoota had growled and then barked furiously as Jack had turned the handle. With a quarter of a bottle of rum already inside him, his urge to see the young jillaroo who could match him drink for drink grew. Jack and responsibility didn't go together and without thinking, he left the home-stead and Billbinya and made the hour drive north to see her. He didn't return until Monday morning.

Chapter 10

Gemma and Jess were having a lovely night. The winery, set on the bank of a creek, was beautiful. Camp fires had been lit along the creek's edge, and next to the fires were old wine barrels that had been cut in half and filled with poinsettias and other flowering plants. Further out into the creek, spotlights had been placed beneath two old gum trees, and their ghostly limbs gave the scene an enchanted air.

The stage where the jazz band was setting up was covered in fairy lights.

'Wow,' Gemma breathed when she saw it.

'C'mon,' called Jess. 'Let's get set up.'

There were heaps of people milling around, setting up their picnic blankets or chairs; some carrying hampers, others going back and forth from the food and beer tents. The atmosphere buzzed with the anticipation of a special evening.

They had just set up their deckchairs next to a huge boulder and were taking the first sip of wine when they heard a voice behind them.

'Gem, Jess, hi!'

They turned to see Paige Nicholls clutching the arm of a tall blond man.

Gemma smiled warmly. 'Hello, Paige, enjoying a night off?'

'Yep, Daniel and I are looking forward to the concert. We used to see a lot of jazz bands when we lived in Melbourne, so this is a real treat. This is Daniel McDavis, by the way.' She snuggled in closer to the man, who nodded without smiling. 'How are you, Jess?' asked Paige.

'Fine thanks,' Jess said coldly.

Paige's smile faltered. 'Well, good to see you both. I guess we'll go find a spot.' She gave a small wave, and they were gone.

'I don't know how she has the guts to show her face around here,' said Jess furiously. 'After Claire's accident and Tim's suicide. I still can't believe she had an affair with Tim, right beneath our noses while pretending to be Claire's friend. I cannot stand that woman.'

'Jess, it was a long time ago,' Gemma said gently, 'and I'm sure if Paige had known what the outcome would be, she wouldn't have started the affair. And don't forget, she said she loved Tim too. I miss Claire and I hate what happened – but imagine what Paige must have suffered.'

Jess smiled. 'You always were a lot more forgiving than me.'

'I wasn't at the time, remember? I called her a harlot and all sorts of names. But I guess when you lose someone you love, it puts things in a different perspective.'

'Do you know what she's doing now?'

'Didn't I tell you? Sorry. She's a nurse. She was on duty at the hospital when I went in to see Dad.'

'Well, I don't know if leopards really can change their spots,' Jess said, standing. 'I'm off to find a loo. Can you get more drinks?'

Struck by a thought she turned back to Gemma and asked, 'Hey, did the cops call you back?'

Gemma shook her head. 'I don't know what's going on there. Not a sound from them. Maybe they've found the sheep and everything is okay. Who knows?'

Gemma weaved through the crowd to the bar, not stopping to talk to anyone, but nodding and smiling at people she knew. On the way back to their seats, she stopped off at the food tent and loaded up plates full of pork from the spit with vegies.

'Need a hand to carry that?'

Gemma turned to see Ned and his wife Rose. 'What are you doing here, Ned? Looking for some culture?' Gemma leaned forward to kiss Rose on the cheek. 'How are you, Rose?'

'Culture yourself. You're the one who never goes

anywhere. Who dragged you along?' Ned asked gruffly.

Rose smacked his arm gently. 'Ned, mind your manners. How are you, Gemma? It's lovely to see you out and about.'

'It's looking like a great night. I'm here with Jess Rawlings, my friend from school. She thought I should get out more, so she dragged me along. Not really like the B & S's we used to go to, but I guess you have to grow out of them sometime!'

Bidding them farewell, Gemma hurried back to Jess. She handed Jess her plate, then moaned with delight through a mouthful of pork. 'I haven't eaten like this in so long.'

'That's 'cos you don't eat,' Jess retorted as the spotlights flashed on and off to signal the start of the show.

The chatter of the audience died away as the jazz band started to play. Gemma felt all the worries of the last few months begin to disappear as the musicians' fingers flew over keyboards and guitar strings.

At the interval, Gemma volunteered to refresh their drinks. While she waited for the queue at the bar to lessen, she stood looking into the embers of a dying fire, lost in the memory of the music. She didn't realise Ben was behind her until he spoke.

'Didn't recognise you without your work clobber on,' he said quietly. She spun around, and found herself staring straight at his chest. Looking up, she found his brown eyes regarding her curiously.

'G'day,' she managed. 'What are you doing here? Do you like jazz?'

'Not really, but I thought it would be a good place to meet people.'

'Definitely is. Most of the town is here, plus a heap from Adelaide and other towns by the looks. I guess these concerts are pretty big these days. People from the city seem to enjoy a country fix.'

'That they do.' Ben's eyes moved to look over her shoulder and Gemma felt a nudge.

'Hi,' Jess said around Gemma's shoulder. 'Who are you?'

Ben looked quizzically at Gemma, who just smiled blandly.

'Uh, I'm Ben.' He looked a little taken aback. 'Who are you?'

'I'm Jess Rawlings, Gemma's best friend, party partner and confidante. Nice to meet you.'

'Ah, I've heard about you. I met Brad at the pub a few nights ago. He managed to rope me into playing footy tomorrow.'

'That's wonderful, they need some people with talent – I hope you have some. They're the most dismal team I've ever seen. I don't think they've won a game this season. Can you kick goals?'

Gemma watched Jess with amusement. It was no wonder that she drew people to her; she had such an open and friendly manner.

Jess grabbed Gemma's arm. 'I've just had the best idea. Since we three know each other and

Gem hasn't met Brad yet, let's all go out to dinner tomorrow night. We could check out the new bistro down on the seafront. Someone told me they serve the best pasta, and I haven't had a chance to try it yet. Apparently it's really hip.'

'Something is really "hip" in Pirie? I'd like to see that!' said Ben, laughing at Jess's enthusiasm.

Gemma smiled and said, 'Me too!'

'Right! That's settled. Tomorrow night it is. What?' asked Jess when she saw Ben shaking his head.

'I have plans tomorrow night. How about next weekend?'

'Sounds brilliant. Now I really have to drag Gem to the bar or I'll die of thirst and I won't make it to the footy tomorrow, let alone next weekend. Enjoy the rest of the evening, Ben.'

'I'll talk to you during the week, Gemma, if I don't see you at the game tomorrow,' Ben said as he waved and moved into the crowd.

With light footsteps Gemma and Jess headed for the bar, Jess bombarding Gemma with questions. 'Who is he? Where's he from? How come I haven't heard about him? Man, he's a dream boat!'

Gemma let her friend rattle on, her gaze raking over the crowds of people, hoping to catch another glimpse of Ben – who had looked rather gorgeous in his moleskins, R.M. Williams boots, blue shirt and dark leather jacket – but he seemed to have disappeared into the smoke of the camp fires. Her gaze rested on two people and, before glancing away, she recognised them as Ned and Paige. Ned stood in the shadow cast by a tree. She couldn't see the look on his face, but Paige looked angry. Gemma watched them for a minute longer, wondering how Ned and Paige knew each other. Then she shrugged. It was a small town. Turning to Jess she told her that if she wanted to know about Ben then it was time to shut up and listen!

The rest of the weekend passed in a blur of fun and laughter. Eating out felt like a new experience to Gemma, it had been so long since she last had. The footy on Saturday brought back memories too. The cars were all parked around the oval, and Gemma found herself remembering things she'd long forgotten, like how everyone beeped their horns whenever someone kicked a goal, or how the teenage girls got so dressed up and hung over the rails of the oval waiting for the guys to notice them. The friendliness of the people who were there also startled Gemma. There were farmers and a lot of townspeople who remembered her and asked how she was, but no one pried or asked if she was going to sell her land.

She met the famous Brad, who was everything Jess had said he was. 'Brad, this is my very best friend, Gemma Sinclair. Gem, this is Brad – the best man in my life at the moment!'

'I've heard a lot about you, Brad – it's great to finally meet you.'

'The same goes, Gemma.' Brad shook her hand,

smiling. 'I hear you're doing an amazing job out on Billbinya. I've been meaning to call in and say g'day, but there isn't a lot of call for an agro out your way. So we're off out to tea next Saturday? It'll be great to get to know you a bit better.'

On Sunday afternoon, Gemma went to the bus station to pick up Patrick. He alighted looking rather cramped up. 'Small seats for a big fella like me, sis,' he groaned in greeting, and gave her a hug.

Gemma looked up at his six-and-a-half-foot frame and the floppy blond hair he was always brushing out of his blue eyes. 'I always said you were too tall.'

'I always said you were too short.' He grinned in anticipation of the next line of their childhood game.

'I'm not short,' Gemma said huffily. 'I'm medium!' They laughed and hugged again.

Driving through the green-tinged hills of the Flinders Ranges, Gemma and Patrick talked about Pat's work breaking in horses in Queensland. They fell silent as Gemma turned down Rochden Road and they approached Hayelle, where Patrick would stay for the next few nights. Patrick smiled as he glimpsed the front gate. 'Home sweet home,' he murmured. As Gemma turned into the driveway, the old homestead came into view with the front dam and hills behind it. The gentle sloping hills were often brown and dry but, with this season's good rains, now glowed a bright green, with purple Salvation Jane flowers blooming and the occasional red of the hops weed.

They pulled up next to the small stone building that held the garage and laundry. The winding path to the house went past the laundry and across a rambling lawn to the sunroom built off the kitchen.

Patrick threw his bag on the floor of the kitchen and opened the fridge. Gemma smiled. That had been Pat's routine from the minute he'd been old enough to walk. The fridge was always full of Sarah's homemade goodies and Patrick had an appetite to match. He quickly moved from the fridge to the cupboard to the cake tin on top of the bench.

'So what's the go?' asked Patrick after establishing there wasn't much to eat. 'What can I do to help?'

'Well, I guess if you could just keep a bit of an eye on everything here it means I can concentrate on what's going on at home.'

'No worries. Hows about we go for a drive now and you can tell me what's going on with everything?'

'Yep, righto. How long can you stay for, Pat?'

'Well, I'm my own boss, so I can basically have as much time as I need. But I won't be getting any money in either. Guess we'll just see how it goes, okay? We'll see what happens with Dad, make some more decisions then. I'm not staying forever, though, sis.' He gave her a long look.

Gemma nodded her understanding.

'Great. Okay, let's have a look around.'

* * *

It had been a while since she'd gone on a farm tour with her dad, and Gemma could see that things had gone downhill in the last few months. Fences weren't as tidy as usual, calves not marked when they should be, and it seemed that there was some work to do on the catchments of the dams. It was important to keep catchments up to scratch so any little rain that fell ran into dams to keep the precious water supplies up. Cattle drank a lot more than sheep. Gemma was lucky not to have water problems on Billbinya as she had underground water. Her main problem in dry times was feed for the animals.

It was quite strange to see Hayelle a bit rundown. Jake was a perfectionist, especially when it came to his stud bulls, and Gemma knew there was definitely something wrong when she came to the young bull paddock and saw there weren't any tags in their ears. There wasn't anything to say who the sire or dams of the young bulls were, and no identification numbers.

'This is a bit weird, Pat,' remarked Gemma. 'Dad is usually a bit more on top of things than this.'

'Yeah,' agreed Pat. 'I wasn't expecting this. There's a fair bit of work to do here.'

'Well, let's go back to the house and have a cuppa, and make a plan.'

Gemma drove back to Billbinya wondering what fresh horrors she might find waiting for her. But there weren't any messages on the answering machine, no new emails and no notes from Bulla or Garry to say that anything had gone wrong. Gemma sighed with relief, made herself some toast for tea and went to bed.

What a wonderful weekend, she reflected. No pressure, no back-breaking work. She wondered, not for the first time, what it would be like to be able to farm a smaller place without any debt and pressure.

She also wondered why Hayelle was as far behind in the stock work. Couldn't her dad manage anymore? Was he sicker than she had been told? It was all a bit strange. The other strange thing was that the police had never returned her call. It looked like the whole problem was going to go away.

Chapter 11

At the Port Pirie police station, Ian Paver and Geoff Hay had just returned from Adelaide, where they had picked up Dave Burrows and Craig Buchanan from the Western Australia stock squad. They talked all the three hours back to Pirie and continued the conversation when they arrived at the police station, discussing what had happened with the wethers, the rumours that had come to the attention of Ian and Geoff when they had undertaken their initial investigation, and the anonymous phone call that had been made to Pav shortly after the investigation had started.

'I think we have an organised stock-stealing ring happening here, fellas,' said Geoff. 'We have unconfirmed reports of stock missing over the past two years, all in the same area. The disappearances seem to follow a similar pattern. One night when the owners aren't home someone goes in with a truck and pinches the stock. Mainly sheep but there have been reports of cattle. Has to be premeditated and researched – the use of a truck confirms that. I can't see anyone taking a truck into a property that wasn't theirs without prior knowledge of the farm's stock and knowing for sure the owners weren't going to be there.'

'Absolutely. I couldn't agree more,' Dave Burrows said. 'You mentioned that you have a suspect. Have you got a profile on him?'

Geoff passed over a red folder. 'Yeah, although we've got a bit of a problem. The guy we had in mind is dead – but it's too big an operation to be the work of one man. Adam Sinclair – or Sinny as he was known to his friends – crashed his plane on the twentieth of January this year.' He referred back to his notes. 'His wife, Gemma Sinclair, is still running the family station, and we're not yet sure if she is involved or not. When we made some initial inquiries, we went to Billbinya – the Sinclairs' station – and she seemed to be genuinely shocked when we questioned her. Since then, we have interviewed a few other neighbours and found that they believe they have had stock go missing but hadn't reported it because they weren't a hundred per cent certain that they just hadn't mustered a paddock properly or something like that.

'Gemma Sinclair rang us on Thursday of last week. She didn't state what she required; just that she wanted to talk to us. We haven't followed up on that phone call for three reasons. One,' he ticked the reasons off on his fingers, 'before she rang we had an anonymous phone call. We're pretty sure it was a male voice, but it was muffled. Now this guy must have intimate knowledge of what goes on because he suggested that Adam was involved in getting the information of stock movements and passing it on to someone else. Number two, you blokes were due over within a couple of days and we didn't know which way you wanted to play it with Gemma. After this tip-off phone call, she has to be classed as some sort of suspect. Number three is the principal reason we didn't call her back. It is obvious these sheep have been stolen. They've been taken from the yards, so there can't be any thought of miscounting or not mustering properly. Adam Sinclair is dead, so who's doing it?'

Dave crossed his arms and leaned back in his chair, thinking. 'Good point. We need to focus on who is *now* doing the stock rustling and then we'll be able to fit Adam into it, if he was involved. Well, I guess we need to get a feel for the area, people and such. Where is stock mainly sold here?'

'The livestock sales are at Dublin, about three-quarters of an hour out of Adelaide, and the abattoirs are in Lobethal, Murray Bridge and here in Port Pirie. Then there are a lot of butchers that kill small amounts of livestock, just to fill their shops and niche markets. There are a couple of big feedlots in the Spalding and Murray Bridge area. They buy in and feed cattle. I haven't been able to track down any lamb feedlots that buy in sheep. They all breed their own.'

'Okay, is there any more info?' Dave asked.

'No,' replied Ian.

'Craig'll keep a low profile. I'll get him to monitor the live market sales and maybe do the rounds of some abs. I'll stay here and get a feel for the lay of the land and talk to some of the graziers who have been affected,' Dave said.

'Why are you keeping Craig out of sight?' asked Ian.

'Just in case we need him to get in with the locals. Since he's the younger of us and a bit of a magnet to girls with those biceps of his, he can usually infiltrate the pub scene pretty well. Get the trust of the young guys around the place,' Dave explained.

'I'm just the nice guy who gets to have fun with the natives!' Craig smiled, showing his perfectly white teeth, his blue eyes twinkling. Geoff made up his mind to keep his nineteen-year-old daughter away from the pub for the next few weeks.

On Wednesday night, as Gemma was preparing dinner for herself and Patrick, who was due anytime, the phone rang.

'Hello?'

'Gemma, it's Dave Burrows from the WA stock squad calling. How are you this evening?'

'Fine, thanks. How can I help you?'

'Gemma, I'm just doing a ring around of a few graziers in your area to see if we could have a bit of a catch-up meeting sometime in the next couple of days. Just to talk through what happened with the young wethers last week. I'd like to come out and meet you all – put faces to names and just ask a couple more questions.' Dave sounded very laidback.

'Sure, when would suit you?'

'Could I come out sometime tomorrow, or is that too soon?'

'Tomorrow would be fine.'

'How's four o'clock sound?'

'No worries, see you then.' Gemma put the phone down just as the dogs began to bark, alerting her that Pat had arrived. *Should I have told Dave about the wethers in our paddock?* she wondered. No, she decided. Tomorrow would be soon enough for the problems to surface.

'So, sis, what's happening?' Pat's usual greeting came through the door as he pulled off his boots to come into the house.

'Ah, here you are. How's it going at Mum and Dad's?'

'I'm not talking work until you feed and water me. What's for tea?'

'A hearty beef casserole. Does that suit? And I've also tried out my cooking skills on a cake. I think it's even edible!'

'I'll eat it even if it's not. I'm dying for some cake. All Mum had in the cupboard were some shop-bought biscuits. She's slacking off in her old age.'

Their friendly banter continued throughout dinner. It wasn't until they were doing the dishes that Patrick turned to face Gemma and said, 'I've got a fiancée.'

'*What?*' Gemma stopped what she was doing and looked at him in shock. 'Who?'

'Kate.'

Gemma gestured impatiently. 'More information.'

'I've known her since boarding school and I've been going out with her since I've been in Queensland. What's that, about eight years? She's a horse breaker too and we're in partnership.'

'Eight years? Eight years and you haven't told us? What is it with you?' Gemma asked, dumbfounded.

'Well, I didn't want to say anything till I was sure.' Pat shrugged casually. 'We reckon we'll get married sometime next year, but we'll see how the old man is. I'd like him to be there, so if we have to bring it forward then we will.'

'Pat, that's wonderful news. I'm so excited for you. I can't wait to meet her – though you need a flogging for keeping her to yourself for so long. Where will you get married?'

'Probably up there; that's where she's from. Anyway, enough about me. What's going on down here?'

Gemma sighed. 'Let's go into the sitting room with a pot of tea and I'll tell you the whole story.'

Chapter 12

Gemma sat on the couch and tucked her feet up under her. 'I haven't told anyone this, Pat, not even Jess. I've got a queer feeling about it.' She stared into her mug of tea then said, 'When Adam's plane crashed I was there. He was mustering from the air and I was in the ute on the ground and he was radioing me if I'd missed any cattle or whatever. Then he crashed. No warning or call on the radio, which in itself is strange. Anyway, I got to the plane before he died. I tried and tried to get the door open but I couldn't. I could see that his chest was pushed up against the front controls of the plane and he was bleeding from the mouth. He couldn't breathe properly.' Gemma stopped, and took a breath. 'He said something to me and at first I couldn't hear through the windows, but I managed to bash in the little window near the front with the sledgehammer I had in the back of the ute.

Anyway, Adam was gasping and saying that he wasn't going to make it, he was in trouble and they might come after me once he was dead and I was to sell the station. I have searched this place from top to bottom – the house, the sheds and shearing shed – looking for some kind of clue about what sort of trouble he was in, but I can't find anything. Then Ned tells me that Adam had signed a contract for three hundred steers to go to a feedlot. I don't have the steers to fill the agreement, so that's a bit weird. Next thing I know the Kettles, Carters and Smiths have had wether lambs stolen out of their yards, about a thousand of them all up, and I get a visit from the police asking if I've seen a spare thousand floating around. The next morning Bulla tells me he found a thousand wether lambs that weren't ours out in Reimer's paddock. Now I'm beginning to wonder what on earth Adam was involved in. In the meantime, I've got the stock squad coming out here tomorrow to "ask a couple more questions". Doesn't that all sound a bit odd to you?'

Pat raised his eyebrows. 'Bloody oath.'

They were both quiet for a while, mulling over what she'd said.

'So,' Pat said finally, 'why do you think there were a thousand wether lambs dumped on Billbinya? That's the most concerning thing. I mean, giving Adam the benefit of the doubt, he might have just annoyed the TAB man or something. He might not have done anything too wrong – although knowing Adam he'd have been into something. But the wethers on Billbinya puts you in a pretty nasty spot. Are they still here? Did you tell the stock squad guy?'

'Well, no and no. And what do you mean "knowing Adam", anyway? Bulla went back out to Reimer's paddock the next morning to bring the wethers into the yards and they were gone. I was going to tell the stock squad guy tomorrow.'

'Have you told Mum and Dad?'

'No, I've really only realised that something weird is going on since Dad got crook. They were stolen the night of Dad's heart attack.'

'I think you need a lawyer.'

Gemma looked at Pat in horror. 'I haven't done anything wrong!' she exclaimed.

Pat shook his head. 'Doesn't matter, sis; you've had stolen stock on your property. They could put you away for aiding and abetting or something, I don't know.' Pat stood up and started to pace the room. 'I don't think you understand how serious this could be.' He stopped and looked at her.

'I haven't done anything wrong,' she said again in a smaller voice.

'Doesn't matter – unless you can prove that then you're in deep manure. Do you know a lawyer?'

'No! I've never needed one. Believe it or not, I'm usually reasonably law-abiding.'

'Okay, well Jess will. Give her a call in the morning before this stock squad guy gets here, and don't talk to him until you've had some legal advice.' He looked at his watch. 'I'll stay tonight and we'll sort out a plan in the morning. Can I sleep in the spare room?'

'Yeah, of course. I don't think I'll sleep though.'

'Me neither, but we should try.' Pat looked at Gemma. 'Don't worry, sis, we'll get it sorted.' He patted her on the shoulder as he left the room.

Later, in Gemma's spare room, Pat sat on the edge of the bed and thought. Adam was a funny bugger. It wasn't that Pat hadn't got along with him; he had, especially on nights that they had pub crawls planned, or some sort of party in mind. But after he'd moved to Queensland permanently, he really had lost touch with Adam – and when he did come home, the pub crawls and partying weren't the same. Gemma and Adam were married, and up to their ears in debt. Debt was a killer, especially with interest rates as high as they were and stock and wool prices low. The last time he was back at Hayelle and Billbinya, some twelve months earlier, Patrick had sensed a subtle change in Adam. He couldn't really put his finger on it, but it was as if he was slightly cockier than usual. Like he knew something no one else did. Jess had mentioned something about it as well, he remembered. He hadn't taken her concerns seriously at the time. Jess got along with Adam for Gemma's sake, but hadn't ever liked him. Now he wondered if he should have paid more attention.

* * *

The next day Patrick was up bright and early. He and Gemma had breakfast together before Patrick headed back to Hayelle, promising to be back before the stock squad arrived.

As soon as he was gone Gemma bolted for the kennels and then the ute. She had to get away from the house, into the wide open space. She checked the calving cows, then drove out to check the ewes and lambs that they had marked in previous weeks, before heading to the creek. There she sat on a rock in silence, thoughts racing around her head. Patrick and Kate, weddings, Adam, wether lambs and the stock squad. None of these thoughts made any sense to her, they were all too jumbled.

'But Adam. Adam, what had he been involved in?' Gemma looked at the scenery without seeing. Her eyes narrowed, deep in thought. Had he given any clues? Not that she could think of. He was still the caring, loving husband he had always been. Busy? Yeah, they all were. Distracted? Maybe a bit. Trustworthy? Yes. He returned stock to neighbours and always rang if an animal had got through a fence – even if it was a tiny lamb. Gemma shook her head. She hadn't noticed any change in him. He couldn't have been involved with anything illegal. He was too honest.

But soon the fresh air and peaceful surrounds worked their magic, and she could hear the magpies singing and the sheep calling to their lambs. Feeling the sun on her skin, she leaned back gratefully and closed her eyes, letting the warmth seep right through her.

When Gemma arrived back at the sheds at lunchtime, she was surprised to find Bulla waiting for her.

'G'day, I thought you were over on the top part of the place getting cattle in for marking,' said Gemma.

'Haven't seen much of you since before you went away, so I thought I'd better see how things were. Heard anything from the police?'

'Yeah, they rang yesterday evening. Some guy from the stock squad is coming out today at about four, so I'll tell him about the wethers then.'

'Well, Gaz and me will be in the shed if he wants to talk to us. Do you want Jack around?'

'Yeah, I s'pose he'd better be in case this guy wants to ask him where he was on the night of blah at such-and-such a time.' Gemma smiled, trying to make a joke of things.

'No worries. Are you coming up to the yards? We could do with a hand.'

'I'll just grab a sandwich and be right with you.'

Gemma spent the rest of the afternoon chasing calves up into a raceway to where Bulla would push them into a calf-marking crush. The calves were pinned so they couldn't move or kick, then Gaz would deftly slip a rubber ring around the testicles – so they couldn't reproduce – and then earmark them, claiming them as Billbinya bred and owned. Jack then pulled the calf crush open and the calves would jump out with a bawl, then scurry towards the mums who were standing in a big yard bellowing loudly, waiting for their babies to return.

At last the mob was finished and Gemma looked at her watch. 'Shit,' she swore. 'I'm going to be late. See you all back at the homestead.' It was only as she was driving back that she remembered she hadn't rung Jess to find out about a lawyer. She shrugged. Surely she didn't really need one.

She arrived back at the house to find a muddy white four-wheel-drive wagon and a guy leaning up against it. She drove through the gate and stopped behind his car. Jumping out of the ute, she held out her hand as she walked towards him.

'Sorry I'm late. I'm Gemma Sinclair.'

The tall man shook her hand and said, 'No problem. Dave Burrows from the stock squad. Thanks for seeing me.'

'So you found me okay? I did mean to ask if you needed directions. Come on inside.' They turned and walked towards the house.

'Geoff and Ian, the two officers who came to see you last week, gave me the heads up as to where everyone was. It's always hard going into a new area. You learn to read maps pretty quick.' He flashed her a smile.

Making coffee, Gemma glanced at the man sitting at her table. He was wearing a light-blue shirt with the stock squad emblem on it and denim jeans, and he'd left his dark brown R.M. boots at the door. His dark hair was cut short in an army style and his skin was tanned, as if he spent a lot of time in the sun. His notepad lay on the table in front of him and Gemma could see it was full of scribbles from other interviews with her neighbours today. She could see a name written in capital letters and underlined, and as she put the coffee down she was shocked to read, upside down, ADAM SINCLAIR.

Shit shit shit, she thought. Where the hell was Patrick? Gemma pasted a smile on her face and said, 'Would you excuse me a minute?', then headed towards the office. Frantically she dialled Pat's mobile, but there was no answer. Then she noticed the answering machine light flashing. She hit the play button and Pat's voice filled the room.

'G'day, sis. Been held up, had to pull a calf. See you as soon as I can.'

Gemma swore under her breath.

An uncertain female voice followed Pat's message. 'Um, hi Gemma, it's Paige here. I was wondering if you might have time to catch up for lunch or something. Anyway, you've got my number. I just thought I'd say hi. Um, seeya.'

Gemma made a mental note to call her back later and headed back to the kitchen.

'So, how can I help?' asked Gemma, sitting down at the kitchen table and picking up her coffee mug.

'Well, I've just been talking to a few people in the

area and getting some information. Just thought I'd see if you've got anything to add. Really, I'm just here to help everyone and see if we can get to the bottom of what's going on.'

Gemma smiled weakly.

'So, the guys that were here talking to you before said that you were on the road the night that all these wethers disappeared, is that right?'

'Yep, I had a phone call from my mum saying Dad had had a heart attack, so I drove in to the hospital at Port Pirie. I really wasn't concentrating on what was happening around me, so I don't think I can tell you anything more about that night.'

'Is your dad okay now?'

'Yeah, but he'll be in Adelaide for a while. My brother Patrick is over giving us a hand on Dad's farm, Hayelle, so that helps me with my workload.'

'How long have you been living on Billbinya?'

'Oh, coming up nine years. I moved out here when Adam and I were married, and I decided I wouldn't sell when he died. I don't really know anything else other than farming; I need the space. And I'm a local through and through. My parents' farm is about fifty k to the south of here.'

Dave smiled. 'I can understand that. It must be hard though, out here by yourself – and it's not like stock prices are great, and wool prices are in the doldrums.'

Dave was very friendly and Gemma was beginning to relax in his presence. 'No, it's not easy, but it's my life. I was taught that you don't give up just because things are a bit tough. I'm still here, and I hope I will be in years to come.'

'So you've been in the area for a while – have you ever heard of any stock stealing going on around here before?'

Gemma shook her head. 'No, this is a first. I feel so sorry for everyone involved; it would be devastating to lose some of your livelihood that way. And I know the people who have had the stock stolen – they're nice families.'

'Do you know them well?'

'Well, I have known the Kettles ever since I was small. We're not close, but we're neighbourly, if that makes sense. We've had them over for tea occasionally.'

'How recently?'

'Oh, last year I think. I can look in my diary and see if it's written there, but if it was impromptu it won't be. Sometimes Adam used to run into people on the road and would invite them back or just call in to see them and they would end up back here. It was my worst nightmare – I'm not a great cook and never have a huge amount of food in the house.'

'So you'd have socialised with local station owners pretty regularly?'

'Well, about a year and a half ago Adam started up a Best Farmers group. It involved quite a lot of farmers around this area. We used to get together once a month or so and talk about what we were doing on the stations and if someone had a good idea we would look at the pros and cons of it and see if it was worth implementing on other places. So yeah, we had a fair bit of contact with our neighbours.'

'Could I grab your diaries and take them back to the station to have a look at? I'd really appreciate it.'

Gemma shrugged, not really seeing the point of it. 'Sure.'

'So can you think of any information that might help us?'

Gemma shifted in her seat. 'Well, actually I think I may have something. I rang the police about it but no one returned my call.'

Dave looked up from his notes expectantly.

'After I got back from the hospital in Pirie, one of my stockmen, Bulla, told me that there were about a thousand wether lambs in one of our back paddocks.' Dave's eyebrows shot up. 'But when we went to run them they were gone. Like I said, I did try to get in contact with the Port Pirie police – and I want to stress that there is no way anyone on Billbinya could have been invol–'

Dave broke in over the top of her. 'Were they the stolen sheep?'

'I don't think anyone could say. We didn't get them in the yards, so we weren't close enough to see the earmarks. They weren't ours because Bulla would have known our sheep.'

'I'd like to talk to Bulla.'

'Okay, all the fellas should be over in the sheds

by now. We were marking calves this afternoon and they just had to put the mob back into the paddock.'

'Okay, first things first. Do you have a map of Billbinya?'

Gemma went into the office and brought one out. She showed Dave which paddock the sheep had been in and how far away from the houses they were. At his request, she then fetched a district map to point out where the other farms were in relation to Billbinya.

They refilled their coffee mugs and, as the sun went down, Gemma answered a barrage of questions as truthfully as she could.

Finally Dave said, 'Well, I think that's about it. Let me just recap. Three employees and you've given me their names. All three of these guys have access to keys that open the padlocks on your external gates; they also have access to every paddock on the station. You don't know if Jack has a criminal record, but the others definitely don't. Ned Jones from Hawkins and Jones Stock Agents and Merchandise is your stock agent, and there is a new guy, Ben Daylee, who has started coming out a bit with Ned. Now, Gemma, I do need to ask: is there any chance that Adam could have been involved, or known someone who's involved in stock stealing? I'm sorry I have to ask, but surely you can see that Billbinya is going to be a place of interest to us now. I'm not saying you had anything to do with it – I'm not even saying that someone who works here had anything to do with it – but I have to consider every possibility.'

Gemma took a deep breath. 'No,' she replied. 'There's no way Adam would have stolen from his neighbours.'

'Okay, let's go and talk to the others.'

Over in the shed the men were tinkering with vehicles.

After introducing Dave to Garry and Bulla, Gemma looked around.

'Where's Jack?' she asked.

'Crook. He looked like he was about to spew. He went off to the loo.'

'Just what we need, a vomiting bug,' Gemma groaned. 'Well, Dave, I'll leave you to talk to the guys. I guess you don't want me here in case they feel they can't talk freely.'

Dave grinned. 'You watch too many TV shows. I'm not really interviewing, just asking a couple of questions.' He focused on Bulla. 'I'd like to see the paddock the sheep were found in. Is it far?'

'It's too far to go tonight. It's dark and you won't see anything.'

'Okay, how 'bout tomorrow?'

'Fine,' Bulla said shortly.

'What can you tell me about the sheep? Could you see whose they were?'

'Nah, I didn't get close enough. I drove around them, but sheep don't stand still, so I couldn't tell what earmark they had. I do know they weren't Billbinya's.'

'How could you tell?'

'I guess I just know what our sheep look like. I dunno.'

'Okay, why don't I come back tomorrow – I can talk to Jack and we can see the paddock.' Dave looked at Gemma for confirmation.

'Yep, no problem. I'll walk you to your car.'

'See you tomorrow, guys.' Dave waved a hand at them.

Bulla and Garry nodded at him and turned away.

'Thanks for your cooperation, Gemma. It makes all the difference if people are helpful,' Dave said.

'No worries – like I said to Bulla, I haven't done anything wrong, so I have nothing to hide.'

They reached the car and Dave turned to look closely at her. It still amazed him how much a face could give away when you were skilled at reading expressions. Something niggled in the back of his brain. Was she being too helpful? Dave made a snap decision. 'On second thoughts, I might have to give tomorrow a miss. I've got so many notes to write up from today. I might leave it a few days, get my thoughts headed in the right direction, and then give you a call. Would that be okay?'

'Sure,' Gemma said. 'Just let me know.'

Dave started the engine and turned on his lights. 'See you soon. And thanks again for your help.'

'See you later,' said Gemma. As she watched the tail-lights disappear down the driveway she had a sudden memory flash – of tail-lights in the rear-view mirror ...

Hadn't she seen a truck on the road the night she'd driven to the hospital in Pirie? Maybe she should have mentioned it to Dave. Gemma thought hard. She shrugged. It probably wasn't important. She'd tell him next time they spoke.

Jack had stopped vomiting but he felt like hell. Lying in his room he lit a smoke and tried to ignore the cramps in his gut. His mobile phone rang. 'Go to hell,' he said out loud, letting it ring out. It stopped and then started again immediately. Jack picked it up and looked at the number on the screen. Hitting the answer button, he snapped, 'What the hell was in those pills? I have never been so crook in all me life.'

The person at the other end chuckled unkindly. 'Desperate times, desperate measures, I'm afraid, little bro. Anyway, good news – she has plans to go visit town again this weekend. You should be able to get into the house.'

'Okay, gotta go.' Jack threw down the phone and raced to the toilet. The other man shut his phone and laughed quietly. Poor Jack – but it would be worth it in the end. His face hardened as he thought of Gemma and the grief she'd unknowingly caused his family.

Chapter 13

Dave Burrows tapped his fingers against the steering wheel. Gemma Sinclair's revelation that there had been wethers on Billbinya had him stumped. Was she being helpful because she was involved and was trying to deflect suspicion away from her, or did she really have no idea how those sheep came to be on her farm?

One thing was certain. Even without collating all the information he'd received from Billbinya's neighbours, the circumstantial evidence pointed towards Adam Sinclair. Whether that put Gemma in the frame too remained to be seen.

His headlights caught a reflection in the dark. Slowing down, he saw five sheep on the side of the road gazing at him in bewilderment.

'Unbelievable,' muttered Dave. He stopped and turned his car around. His spotlights swept over the road verge and finally rested on an old rusty wire-netting fence that had snapped. There was a mob of sheep standing inside the fence waiting to push through. Dave shook his head. 'And here I am thinking there's a large stock-stealing operation going on. More like an escape operation masterminded by the stock!'

He beeped his horn. The ewes stood and looked at him, frozen in his lights. Switching the lights down to park, he beeped once again and the ewes turned and pushed back through the fence the way they had come. He grabbed the pliers he always carried, hopped out and tried to twitch the wire back together, but it was too rusty and kept snapping.

The engine of the wagon sounded louder than usual in the silence of the night and he walked over to turn it off. Strolling back to the fence he stopped to take in the night. It was quiet and still. He could hear the sheep rustling through the grass and grinding their teeth. His eyes swept across the darkened landscape. If he was going to steal stock, how would he do it? The moon was a quarter full so there was a little light. He couldn't see any lights shining to indicate farmhouses so he assumed there weren't any close by; making noise wouldn't be a problem. It was isolated, so the fear of being caught would be minimal. All you needed was to know where the stock was, a few sheep yard panels, a couple of dogs and a full moon. They would herd the sheep into the panels then load them straight onto the truck. Cattle would be slightly more difficult but could be managed. All in all, stealing stock in this neck of the woods would be easy.

Dave knew from previous cases how easy it was to offload the stolen animals. He'd seen numerous cases of criminals dumping animals straight into the sale yards or an abattoir, receiving the money and mostly, unless the criminals were actually caught at the yards or in possession of the stock, they got away with it. Another way he'd seen recently was grabbing some sheep with a year's worth of wool on them, taking them to a shearing shed, shearing them, selling the wool and returning the stock. Incredibly brazen, but it had happened once or twice.

Giving up on the fence, he returned to his wagon and looked at his speedometer. He'd been recording all the distances he'd travelled today for the time-lines he planned to construct when he returned to Pirie. He hoped he'd be able to use the mileage to work out where he was now and whose farm these sheep belonged to so he could ring the owners in the morning. He turned the key, let his foot off the clutch and turned back towards Pirie.

The phone was ringing as Gemma walked into the house. She let the answering machine pick it up and headed straight to the shower, desperate to wash the anxiety of the day away. About ten minutes later Pat banged on the door to announce his arrival.

'I'll be out in a minute,' she called.

'What's for tea? I'm starving!' Pat yelled.

'I have no earthly idea.'

Gemma walked into the kitchen a few minutes later, rubbing her hair with a towel. 'Jess!' she exclaimed on seeing her best friend sitting at the kitchen table talking intently to Pat. 'It's wonderful to see you, but what the hell are you doing here?'

Jess got up and moved around the table to hug her. 'What, can't I call in and say g'day to my best mate?'

'It's unusual, that's all. Well, since you're here, you can cook tea.'

Jess opened the fridge door and waved her hand towards its contents. 'I've already taken care of it. I made lasagne before I left town. I just need to heat it up and make a salad. So what's happening?'

'I was going to ask you the same thing,' said Gemma, looking from Jess to Pat. Neither one met her eye.

'I'm on holidays,' said Jess. 'I've taken a couple of weeks off and I intend to fill my lungs with country air.'

'I see,' said Gemma, not moving from where she stood at the end of the table with her arms crossed. 'Keep trying.'

Pat gave Jess a look.

'Okay, okay. I'll tell her,' said Jess miserably.

'Tell me what?' asked Gemma.

'Sit down, Gemma. I tried to tell you when I was out here last time but the time never seemed right and . . .' Jess's voice trailed off.

'Well you can tell me now.' Gemma's voice was steely but her face was pale and her eyes held a slight hint of fear. She threw the towel over her shoulders, pulled out a chair and sat.

'Gemma, there are rumours going around Pirie that Adam was part of a stock-stealing ring.' Jess took a deep breath then continued. 'They've been going around for a while and some people are even saying that the plane crash wasn't an accident – that someone had set it up because Adam wanted out of it and they wouldn't let him go.'

'I don't believe it!' Gemma cried. 'My husband's dead, not here to defend himself and everyone is telling stories about him. I know you didn't like him, Jess, but I didn't think that you would stoop so low as to pass on absolute bulldust about him.' Gemma rose from the table angrily and headed towards the door. Pat's voice stopped her.

'Sis, I know this isn't easy to hear, but you gotta listen – there's more. And you're in the poo because of those sheep being put on Billbinya.'

Gemma leaned against the doorframe, tears threatening. 'I have seen my husband die. My father has had a heart attack. I'm trying to run a huge expanse of land with no money and I'm trying to pay back Adam's parents because it's what we started together. If I let go of Billbinya, I let go of Adam. Now my best friend and my brother are telling me, for my own good apparently, that I have to listen to lies about my husband.'

Jess and Pat looked at her in silence. Finally Jess got up and went to Gemma and cupped her friend's face in her hands. 'Gemma, you're my best friend. I don't want to hurt you; I've tried to be with you as much as I could since Adam died, if only in phone calls. You're right: I didn't like him – but this has nothing to do with that, you must believe me. This stock-stealing thing is something completely unrelated and something much bigger. This is serious, Gem, and we need to find out what is going on. Pat told me about the conversation you two had last night and, what with the rumours I've been hearing around town, it doesn't look good.' Jess's eyes held Gemma's as she made her impassioned plea.

Gemma slowly moved away from Jess. Looking hurt and bewildered, she returned to the table and sat down with her head in her hands. 'Okay, tell me what you know.'

Exchanging looks, Pat indicated for Jess to speak. Jess sat down again and started talking in a calm voice.

'There have been rumours flying around the district for some time, Gem. I can't pinpoint when they started, maybe a year ago, maybe more. At first I didn't take any notice. You know how country people are. You and Adam were doing well. You'd taken over his parents' place and were making a real go of it. You had planted all these new varieties of grasses, were running more stock than anyone else in the region, and were making your payments without, it seemed, any difficulty.

'Then came the whisper that a few people had had a small number of sheep disappear here and there. Shearing counts were wrong, and there were not as many sheep at lamb-marking time as there should have been. Calf marking – yeah, missing a few cows. At first nobody thought anything of it. I mean, who doesn't miscount their stock occasionally? Maybe some had strayed through the fence and the neighbours would call when they got their stock in the yards and saw the extra animals. But nobody received any calls.

'Now don't forget, I work in a bank. I'm a loans manager for some of the businesses in town, but also many farmers. I see people's end-of-financial-year figures, and that includes end-of-year stock figures. Some of these people were down ten per cent on their stock from the previous year. That's a huge amount to lose when you're barely making ends meet.'

Gemma broke in. 'So what? None of that implicates Adam in any way.'

'Yeah, I know, but do you remember our conversation that night we were camping about stock numbers not being right on Billbinya? Your sheep numbers were up and you've a cattle contract you don't have the numbers to fill. You have to admit it looks suspicious. Also, someone has contacted the police – an anonymous phone call, but don't ask me how I found out about it because I can't tell you – saying that Adam was involved. And Gemma, you're not going to like this bit. Apparently Brad knew

Adam. It was before I met him, but they must have gone to the pub together a fair bit. Did Adam spend a lot of time at the pub at Dawns Rest without you?'

Gemma shifted in her chair. There had been more than a few nights when Adam had been late home, after meetings with the Best Farmers group. He had always been having 'a couple of quiet ones off the wood with the boys'. Now Gemma nodded reluctantly.

'Yeah, I thought so,' Jess said. 'Well anyway, Brad told me not so long ago that he knew Adam and had heard him brag that getting ahead in farming was easy if you knew the right people.'

Jess's last statement was met with stony silence. After a few seconds had passed Patrick cleared his throat and said, 'Now do you see why we're concerned? And why we think you need help?'

Gemma still didn't comment.

'Gem, we love you very much and we're so sorry to have to be the ones to tell you this,' Jess said softly.

'Mmm,' said Gemma. She rubbed her face wearily. 'Well, it's a good story. I find it really hard to believe, but I can see that there are a lot of things that seem to point to Adam. But I don't want to talk about this now, okay? I need some time to think. I'll make up the other spare room for you, Jess, while you guys get tea.' Gemma pushed her chair away from the table without another word and left the room.

* * *

After dinner, which was eaten in uncomfortable silence, Gemma bade the other two good night and disappeared into the office. The answering machine light was blinking. 'Hi Gemma, Ben Daylee here. I was wondering if you were going to be around tomorrow? I'd like to call in, say hi and see how you're situated with selling some cattle. I've just had a good buying order come in, and thought you might be interested. Um, okay, you've got my number, so could you give me a call when you come in? Thanks.' Gemma pushed the delete button and headed to her bedroom.

Jess and Pat did the dishes, then Jess headed for the bathroom while Patrick went to his room. He threw himself onto the bed but, after lying there for a few seconds, got up again. He was too agitated to stay still. He flicked idly through a couple of books on a low shelf, then opened the wardrobe. It was filled with Adam's clothes.

Gemma must have shifted them out of her room so she didn't have to look at them, he decided. Thinking about Gemma and how she'd have grieved gave Patrick a funny feeling. He was about to shut the door when he had an idea. Pulling all of the clothes out onto the bed, he started going through the pockets. He jumped when he heard a knock at the door. It opened to reveal Gemma.

'What in the world are you doing? What's all the thumping?' she asked.

'Sorry, sis, I couldn't sleep and I . . . um, have you been through Adam's clothes?'

'What? No, I just put them all in here after the funeral and haven't thought about them since.'

'Well, you never know – we might find something.' Patrick turned back to the clothes and began systematically going through the pockets.

Jess appeared in her pyjamas. 'What's going on?'

'Patrick's going through Adam's pockets,' Gemma told her.

'A suit, hey?' asked Pat, holding up a beautifully tailored jacket and matching pants. 'When would he have ever worn a suit?'

'Not too often, but he wore it to Leisha's wedding and stuff like that.'

'You're jokin'? Even I didn't wear a suit to that.'

'But Pat, that's you . . .' Before Gemma could finish the sentence Patrick had fished a black mobile phone out of a pocket in the suit.

'What's that?' she whispered.

'His phone.' Pat turned to look at her and saw the expression on her face. 'Didn't he have one?'

'Oh, he had one all right, but that wasn't it.' Gemma reached out for it and Patrick handed it to her. Pushing the on button, she was surprised that it still had battery power after so many months. Pushing a few keys, she looked through the phone calls dialled and received – no numbers that she recognised. Next she went to the text message inbox, and started to read:

Johnsons. 200 wthrs, 3wks.

Another message.

Tunnleys. 350 preg ewes 2wks.

And another.

Hocks. 20 steers 3wks.

Gemma kept scrolling through the messages, feeling numb. Here was proof that her husband, someone she'd trusted, loved with her whole soul, was not the man she thought he was.

Dazed, she flicked over to the outbox to look at the messages sent.

Johnsons tea pub. sat no one hm. in pad left of house, after 8pm. Come 2 bill after 3am.

Tunnleys. tea bill. Watch fr 2 mch moon. Nth pd of bill b4 2am.

Hocks back pad against rd. bbq footy clb, not hm til 12pm. Reimer's.

Gemma dropped the phone, her face white, and ran to the office. Barely aware that Patrick and Jess were following her, asking questions, she searched through the bookshelves until she came up with last year's diary, which she had forgotten to give to Dave. Flicking through she came to 26 April, a Saturday. Written in Adam's bold handwriting was *Johnsons. Tea-Palace Pub 7 pm.*

'No,' she moaned.

'Tell me what the bloody hell is going on,' Patrick demanded. He held the phone in his hand.

Ignoring him, Gemma kept flicking, this time stopping at 19 May. Again the bold handwriting:

Tunnleys tea, Billbinya, 6.30. Finally she came to 20 September, *BBQ footy club windup, meet Hocks 5.30 pm.*

'Oh Jessie,' she wailed. 'He's done it.'

Chapter 14

Gemma woke to the cheeky *chat chat chat* of a willy wagtail. She felt angry, scared and sad but couldn't remember why. Her eyes felt dry and scratchy, as if she'd been crying.

Chat, chat, chat, chirped Willy from her window sill, his tail wagging madly.

'Nick off,' muttered Gemma as all the discoveries of last night came flooding back. 'Oh Adam, what the hell did you think you were doing?' Tears seeped from the corners of her eyes.

She threw off the covers and dug in the cupboard for her sneakers. Pulling on a pair of trackie pants and a jumper, she quietly unclipped the flyscreen and pushed up the old window and climbed through, landing outside with a hollow thud.

Walking quickly to the track that ran along the creek's edge, she did a few warm-up stretches then started to run. She ran as if her life depended on it, as if she could outrun the questions circling in her mind: *How did this happen? And why didn't I realise what was going on? How could I have been so stupid?* Finally, when she could run no more, Gemma sank onto her knees. Breathing heavily she wiped the stinging sweat from her eyes and retched. She wiped her mouth and waited for her breathing to slow, then she walked to the edge of the creek and leaned against a gum tree, taking in the early-morning glow. The magpies were warbling, their songs echoing in the stillness. A big group of galahs was perched in the gum tree, picking noisily at the small branches. A mob of cattle was still camped up from the previous night, although a few loners had already moved out to graze.

How can this morning be so ordinary when I've just found out my life for the past eight or nine years has been a lie? Gemma wondered. She picked up a small rock and tossed it up and down, thinking. Suddenly overwhelmed by anger, she threw the rock as hard as she could at the trees.

'You mongrel, Adam Sinclair,' she screamed. 'What have you done?' The galahs flew into the sky, squawking with alarm.

One rock after another slammed into the tree, with 'You bastard!' punctuating every throw. At last her arm was sore and she stopped. The anger had dissipated slightly to be replaced with a burning desire to make sure she was not implicated in this terrible scheme. She would not take the fall for Adam.

*　*　*

Pat and Jess were sitting at the kitchen table with coffee and cereal when Gemma returned to the house.

'Morning,' said Gemma, walking past them. 'I'll just have a shower and be right out.' She felt like a stranger in her own home. Her life, an illusion.

The phone began to ring. 'I'll get that in the office.'

Grateful for the reprieve from their sympathetic eyes, Gemma picked up the phone. 'Hello?'

'Hi, Gemma, it's Ben Daylee. Hope I haven't called too early.'

'Don't worry – I'm always up by now. I got your message last night, but a few things came up and I couldn't get back to you. Sorry about that.' Gemma was amazed she could have a normal conversation given all that had happened.

'No worries. How're things out there?'

Without warning a lump appeared in Gemma's throat. 'Ah . . .' She couldn't get the words out.

'Gemma, are you okay?'

The tears threatened again, but she took a deep breath. 'Um, no, actually. I got some pretty bad news last night and I'm still a bit upset by it.'

'I hope it wasn't your dad?'

'Oh no, he's doing fine. No, it was about my late husband. Seems he might have been involved in a few illegal dealings I didn't know about.' There. It was out in the open. She figured she might need Ned and Ben's help to clear her name, so there was no point in hiding what she'd learned about Adam.

'I see,' replied Ben.

'You don't sound surprised.'

'To tell you the truth, I'm not. I'd heard a couple of things, but had no idea how accurate they were.'

'Well, you know the old adage – the one closest is always the last to know. Are you and Ned out this way today? It would be great to talk to you about a couple of things I've found out.'

'I'm not sure what Ned has planned, but if you want to see him, I reckon he'll be there. He's pretty fond of you.'

Gemma smiled into the phone. 'He's been such a huge support to me since Adam died. I'd really appreciate his advice now.'

'I'll see what we can sort out.'

Gemma came to the table looking refreshed after her shower. Jess gave her a hug and handed her a cup of coffee.

'Thanks . . . I've been thinking,' Gemma began softly, 'that if this is as big as you all seem to think it is and Adam was involved, then we need to pool our knowledge. That was Ben on the phone . . .'

'Who's Ben?' interrupted Pat.

'He's the new stockie working with Ned. Anyway, I've asked him and Ned to come out this afternoon so we can tell them what is going on. Ned was here a few weeks ago counting all the sheep and cattle because Adam's stock numbers didn't tally with the numbers on the computer or the numbers Bulla and Garry have. I want to know if he saw anything in our mobs that indicated trouble. I find it hard to read earmarks from a distance whereas those guys who are looking at stock all the time could probably tell me if there were animals in the flock that shouldn't have been.'

'That's a great idea, Gem,' Jess said. 'I think perhaps we should tell them about those wethers that were in Reimer's paddock, as well. You never know what those guys hear. They're walking encyclopaedias on every farm in the district.'

'Jess, I was wondering if you would go through my books and see if you can pick up anything funny. I don't think I'd be able to tell – plus I still need to be looking after things outside. We've got shearing coming up in a week or so.'

'Yeah, of course, Gem. You know I'll do anything.'

'Pat, I don't want to tell Mum and Dad what's going on – I don't want to worry Dad. Okay?' Gemma looked at him with raised eyebrows and stern eyes.

'No problemo, sis.'

'I think we should talk to Dave too, but I'd really like to talk to Ned first.' They all jumped at the sound of a knock at the door.

'G'day, Jack,' said Gemma when she opened it, pasting a smile on her face. 'How're you feeling this morning? The fellas said you were crook yesterday.'

Jack grimaced. 'Yeah, pretty crook yesterday, Gemma. Not feeling so hot today, either – was wonderin' if I could have the day off?'

'Yeah, that's fine, Jack. Do you need anything? I think I've got some lemonade somewhere if you need something to settle your stomach.'

'Nah, I'll be okay, just need to have a camp. I'll catch ya tomorrow.'

'No worries, call if you need anything.'

Jack headed back to the shearers' quarters as fast as his stomach would let him, dialling as he went.

'I wandered over to ask for the day off because I still feel like crap and I overheard something,' he said as soon as the phone was answered.

'Yeah? What did you hear?'

'She had a redheaded woman and a bloke in there with her. I reckon the fella is her brother, down from Queensland to help look after the old man's farm. Anyway, Gemma asked the other woman to go through her books to see if she can spot anything funny in there, and she's asked Ned and that other bloke out to see if they saw anything strange when they were out counting the stock. But Bulla or Garry must have told them that the wethers were here 'cos they were talking about telling Ned about it.'

'Ah, so she does know about that. How's her demeanour?'

'Her what?'

The other man sighed impatiently. 'How did she seem? Scared? Angry?'

'Nah, she seemed fine to me. Offered me some lemonade to help my guts.'

'Right. Good job. Talk soon.' The phone went dead.

After he had hung up, the man stared into the distance for a few minutes. Things were beginning to move. Now, how to handle it? He dialled a number.

'Yes?'

'It's me,' he said.

'I know. I recognised the number.'

'Miss you.'

'Me too. Do you have news?'

'Yeah, Gemma knows about the wethers being dumped on Billbinya and she's asked Jess to go through her books. And Ned is heading out there today to talk to her.'

'Okay, keep me posted.'

'Did you hear anything much at the pub?'

'Refuse to answer until I get a coffee. Otherwise I'll tell Worksafe that I don't have a safe work environment. That you don't supply enough coffee.'

Dave flashed Craig a look and swung into a deli they were just passing. Craig climbed out of the car asking, 'Do you want anything?'

'Better get an iced coffee.'

'No worries. Hey, lookee here, isn't that the two stockies from Jones and Hawkins you were telling me about?'

Dave turned in his seat and saw the white Commodore sedan towing a trailer with lamb scales on board turn into a car park. Ned was driving as usual and Ben was in the passenger seat.

'G'day,' said Ned, heaving himself out of the car. 'Didn't think we'd be seeing you again,' he said to Dave.

'Oh? Why's that?' asked Dave, leaning out of the window.

'Well, I thought you'd get all of your info and then leave town.'

'Nah, mate, I'll stay till the job's done.'

Ben looked curiously at Craig and Dave caught the look. 'Oh, this is a mate from Adelaide. Craig Buchanan. Craig, these are a couple of fellas I met last week, Ned and Ben. Stock agents, I believe. Me 'n' Craig don't get to catch up much so he's up spending a few days while I work.'

'G'day,' Craig nodded to the two blokes.

'Well, you've found the best place in town for B 'n' E sandwiches and coffee,' said Ned, affably. 'I come here every morning, and I look like it!' Ned rubbed his large stomach.

Everyone laughed.

'Well, looks like this is what the doctor ordered then,' said Craig, moving towards the door. 'I'm in need of grease. Bit of a late night, with a few too many beers. Catch you later.'

'Yeah, catch you,' echoed Ned. Ben was yet to say anything. Dave and Ned chatted briefly about the day's plans and then Ned moved towards the shop. Ben nodded to Dave and followed.

'Best bit of grease I've eaten in a while,' mumbled Craig through his bacon and egg sandwich, as they passed in the doorway. Ben grinned. He knew how important grease was after a big night.

Craig hopped in the car and Dave started the engine. 'You're supposed to be keeping a low profile,' said Dave. 'You shouldn't be seen with me if you're going undercover.'

'Well, get me a company car and I'll be happy not to be seen with you. Man you're cranky today. It's supposed to be me that's sore. What's the problem?'

'Let's get to the office and I'll tell you.'

They drove in silence while Craig devoured his sandwich and coffee.

Back at the station, Dave set up his notes and got his thoughts together before he started.

'Why don't you get over to the whiteboard and note down the important facts as I read them out from my notes. I want to look back on this and see if we can find the common thread I think is there.' Dave flicked through his notes until he found the one he wanted. 'Okay, first interview. Brathen Farms, owned by Ken and Judy Brathen. They think they've had about three hundred ewes go missing over the past twelve months. Not all in one lot – just ten here, twenty there. Haven't seen any obvious evidence that the stock was taken. They know Adam and Gemma Sinclair only by sight. The farm is about a hundred k from Billbinya.' Dave looked up. 'I'm sure Billbinya is involved somehow. First there was that anonymous tip-off about Adam Sinclair – that's why I asked all the interviewees if they know Adam or Gemma. Also, it appears Adam started a Best Farmers group about a year and a half ago. It's one of those discussion groups that seem to be springing up everywhere. Gave him the opportunity to visit other stations and farms unannounced. But here's the clincher: yesterday afternoon Gemma informed me that the stockmen think they might have seen the stolen wethers in one of her paddocks.'

Craig whistled. 'That's a lot of circumstantial evidence stacking up. Do you reckon there's any chance of interviewees talking about the fact you've asked about the Sinclairs?'

'As in any interview, I ask that what we have talked about isn't discussed with other people so the case isn't jeopardised. But you know what country towns are like. If the real story isn't known, someone will make it up. Not much we can do about that. Next interview: Pleasant Park, owners Mark and Karen Neverby. They think about three or four hundred young sheep have gone missing over a period of two years. No obvious signs of theft. They don't know either Adam or Gemma Sinclair but have heard of them. Their farm is about one hundred and twenty-five k from Billbinya.

'Third interview: Carter Downs, owners are Jim and Mary Carter. Theirs was one of the farms that had the wethers stolen out of the yard. They're about thirty-three ks from Billbinya. Prior to that they had about ten steers taken about six months ago. Ned Jones, their stock agent, had been out to help them weigh the cattle and had taken a count. When they got them in to load them for sale, they were ten down. Jim drove all over his farm and couldn't find them. He couldn't find a broken fence where they could have got out so he is convinced they were stolen. He knows Adam and Gemma Sinclair, is involved with the Best Farmers group Adam set up and he and his wife have been invited to Billbinya for a meal several times.

'Fourth interview: Sam and Kylie Smith, Glenby. Know Adam and Gemma Sinclair and caught up with them once or twice in the past year. They're about sixty k from Billbinya and had three hundred wethers stolen out of their yards. Not sure if any other stock has gone missing.' Dave took a breath while Craig looked at the notes on the whiteboard.

'So in the last two years all the interviewees have had stock missing, all within about a hundred-kilometre radius of Billbinya,' Craig observed.

'Yeah, and I got another half dozen cases exactly like them,' Dave said, waving his notes. 'But let's ask some questions that we need answers for. If it was

Adam Sinclair, how did he know where the stock was? That's a biggie. One lot of owners didn't even know him, so how did he know the layout of the farm? What stock was in which paddock? I'm sure he wouldn't have risked just driving over the farm. Second, what happened to the stock once it was taken? How did he get onto the farm without the knowledge of the owners? Who did the stealing while he was wining and dining the victims? There are too many variables at the moment. Yep, no doubt he was involved, but how and why?'

'Yeah, I get you. So where do we start?'

'Let's begin by running a criminal history on everyone living on Billbinya.'

Chapter 15

Jess and Gemma were talking seriously about the invoices spread out in front of them when Bulla banged on the door and walked in. Pat had gone back to Hayelle to check the stock and then on to Adelaide to see Jake and Sarah.

'Hey, Bulla,' said Gemma in surprise, then she looked at her watch. 'Hell's bells – sorry, I didn't realise the time. You must want me to help draft the sheep.'

'Nah, you're right. Me 'n' the dogs can do it.' Bulla had superb dogs. 'I just wanted to know if there was anything special you wanted me and Gaz to take care of while you're away this weekend?'

'The weekend? What's today?' she asked. 'Thursday?'

'Friday,' Jess answered with a smile. 'We've got a dinner date tomorrow night, remember? I say we head off tonight.'

'Do you think I can go? I mean, the stock squad guy is supposed to be coming back at some stage.'

'He didn't say when,' Jess pointed out. 'I bet he doesn't work on weekends anyway. I reckon we should take off.'

'Okay, well I've got the shearing contractor organised for Tuesday, Bulla. We're going to need to get the two-year-old wethers in. I think it would be best to start on those. The wool looks great and I guess Ben will bring a shipper buyer sometime in the next couple of weeks, so it'd be a good idea to get all the shearing cuts healed up before they come to look. I was going to go for a drive today and check what sort of feed is out in the back paddock. We're going to need to get some condition on those steers soon. I think they need to go to the feedlot in about October,' Gemma said, turning back to Bulla. 'By the way, I'm sorry I didn't come out to the shed this morning to catch up with you. I found out some really disturbing news last night and I couldn't face you guys. Hang around the sheds this arvo and I'll explain everything, okay? Ned and Ben are coming out as well so I can tell them at the same time.'

Bulla was nodding. 'Yeah, no worries. I saw Jess's ute when I got to the sheds this morning so I sorta figured somethin' was up. Gem, has this got anything to do with Sinny?'

Gemma took a while to formulate her response. 'Yeah, it does,' she said eventually, looking down at her hands.

Bulla nodded and left the house.

Gemma was quiet for a while and Jess busied herself looking at the folders of invoices that Gemma had brought out from the office.

'C'mon, Jess,' said Gemma at last, jumping up. 'Let's go and clean the shearing shed for shearing.'

'What about –?'

'Nah, the books will wait. Let's go.'

They grabbed buckets, scrubbing brushes, brooms and other cleaning paraphernalia and headed towards the shearing shed.

'I don't know what it is about shearing sheds, but I love them,' Gemma said. 'I used to really enjoy going up to the shed at Hayelle after the shearing had been done and just sitting, smelling the sheep smell and reading.'

'Yeah, I know what you mean. I can remember as a kid, Dad used to put me on the wool table and swing me around. We had one of those old round tables that were cemented into the floor and you had to stand in one place and turn the table as you skirted the fleece,' Jess replied.

Gemma nodded enthusiastically. 'Yeah, I remember them. You would stand in one spot and swing it as hard as you could, trying to get the pieces of wool left behind to fly off when no one was looking. Your Dad used to get aggro with you doing that 'cos usually one of the rousies would go to throw a fleece and the table would be spinning! Funny how different we are,' mused Gemma. 'I mean you grew up on a farm too and yet you knew right from when you were little you were never going to stay. The towns have always held something for you and yet you get the best of both worlds, living in town and partying and coming out to the farms when you need a fix of country!'

They arrived at the shed and walked up the steps. The only noise came from Bulla and his dogs out in the yards. 'Go back, Roady, get up, get up. Push 'im up.'

'Woof, woof.'

The flies buzzed near the ceiling, the sun shone in streaks through the windows and the tiny holes in the iron. Other than a piece of tin on the roof, banging in the breeze, the shearing shed was still. Silently Gemma and Jess looked at the shed. It was a tidy shed but all the grease from wool during the last shearing had been ground into the boards, making the floor sticky. It would need to be scrubbed and swept before the next team came in. The cobwebs needed to be swept away, no little wisps of wool lying around or scraps of rubbish in the bins. Adam had joined Flockcare, a quality assurance program, not long before he died and things had to be done to the letter if they were to keep the accreditation. Adam had assured Gemma that by joining Flockcare they would receive higher prices for their wool, but there was a lot more work involved in getting ready for shearing.

'C'mon, townie,' said Gemma, her voice echoing loudly in the stillness. 'Get your hands dirty. I'll go and start the fire to heat up the water, you sweep.'

'You reckon I can't do this sort of stuff anymore, don't you? Give us that.' Jess grabbed the broom Gemma was holding out and started to sweep.

'Don't miss any corners,' Gemma shouted over her shoulder as she went outside to crank up the fire.

'Yeah, yeah,' muttered Jess. 'Give the woman an inch and she'll take a mile.'

The two women scrubbed the shed to within an inch of its life. Even the windows were washed – Jess's idea. 'I don't think the shearers will care, Jess. They don't usually look out of them,' Gemma had said, but Jess had done it anyway. The wool bins were looked over and any fibres of wool found clinging to the wood were removed, the board swept, and finally the water in the old forty-four-gallon drum was boiling on the fire outside. The girls carted buckets of boiling water inside and threw them onto the floor, added detergent and scrubbed. Sweat dripped off their foreheads and they had stopped talking to concentrate on the work. Jack had stuck his head in a few times to offer help, since his room in the shearers' quarters was quite close to the shed, but Gemma had waved him away. 'Have the day off and get better,' she said. 'You'll be needed next week.'

At long last the grease had dissipated and the pine boards began to shine through. Gemma and Jess sat back on their haunches and surveyed their work.

'Well, I reckon if the inspectors come out this shearing, we'll be right,' commented Gemma.

'Excellent,' said Jess. 'Now I'm starving. It's way

past lunch so do you want to finish up here and I'll go and get us something to eat?'

'You turned into the boss or something?' mocked Gemma, her hands on her hips.

'Nah, just hungry,' said Jess with a smile, glad that Gemma was sounding like her old self again.

Gemma in fact had a knot in her stomach. She wasn't sure how she was going to tell Bulla, Gaz, Ned and Ben what was going on and what their reaction was going to be. She had the feeling that Bulla already suspected something after finding those wethers last week but how much, she didn't know.

Craig Buchanan had just about had enough of sitting in the police station. Bending over timelines, maps and computers really wasn't up his street. He did love his stock squad work, but he didn't like the drudgery of the paperwork. Checking out the pubs, that was more his speed. Maybe he'd try the Jewel Bar tonight . . .

He bent over the keyboard of the computer and typed in Bulla's name. *No matches found* flashed up on the screen. Craig sighed and typed in *Jack Charles Marshall, DOB 19/07/70*. Searching, searching. Then *Match found* flashed at him. Craig clicked on the details, expecting to see a drink-driving charge or speeding ticket. He found a little more than he bargained for.

'Hey, Dave,' Craig yelled through the open doorway. 'We've got a hit. Come and look at this.'

Dave responded quickly. 'What've you found?'

Craig read out loud with his partner looking over his shoulder.

'Jack Charles Marshall, jailed for six months in 2003 for stealing. He stole three steers, slaughtered them at an abattoir then sold the meat without permission of the owner. This was in . . . Queensland,' said Craig, searching the computer screen for information. 'And an aggravated assault on a woman in 2005. Hey, hey, what have we got here?'

'Don't get too excited,' cautioned Dave. 'He's only been working at Billbinya for a short time. Still, it does throw a bit of a different light on things. Okay, let's keep that piece of information in the back of our minds. Jack will know that we'll find this out – maybe that's why he disappeared when I went to talk to him yesterday. But the other guys said he was crook and I didn't get the impression they were trying to cover for him. And,' Dave said after a moment's thought, 'I don't want to question him straightaway if he is trying to make a new start. He probably found it hard to get a new job and I don't want to jeopardise that without good reason.'

By 4 pm Ned and Ben were heading towards Billbinya. They spoke little as they drove. Ned had been cranky all day and Ben was really beginning to lose patience with him.

'What's the problem?' Ben had asked more than once. 'Nothing,' had been the curt reply. Ben knew he must be worried about Gemma, so he didn't push it. 'So tell me what you've heard about the stock stealing?' he asked, stretching out in his seat.

At first Ned didn't answer, and Ben thought he was ignoring the question. Then the older man said, 'I heard about some stock going missing about two or so years ago. Somewhere up near Dawns Rest. Think the first people I heard it from were the Tunnleys. They had a thousand and fifty pregnant ewes ready to sell. The vet had preg-scanned them, so they were fairly sure that the count was right. The day I was going to take a buyer out to see the sheep old Clem rang me in a big panic, saying he was missing some sheep. I didn't think much of it. His fences are basically stuffed so I suggested they may have got through the fence. "Not my sheep," he said. So I told him to get them into the yards and I'd count 'em when I got there. Sure enough, he was three hundred and fifty down. I still didn't really think that they had been stolen; I mean Clem probably didn't muster his paddock properly. His place is pretty hilly with quite a lot of tree gullies. We sold the sheep to the buyer I took out there and that was it. Didn't hear anything more about it. Next thing I heard was that someone else had lost some steers. About twenty-odd from memory. Then I started to wonder what was going on. So there were a lot of rumours and gossip flying around. Everyone keen to make the story better than the one they had heard yesterday, if you know what I mean.'

Ben nodded.

'Then a few people heard Sinny sounding off down the pub, big-noting himself about some scheme he had – he always liked a drink and it made him talk a lot. Anyway, someone must have put two and two together and got five. My guess is that's how it all got started. A few months later Adam was killed and here we are. Now, whether Adam actually had anything to do with it, I don't know. I'd reckon not. He was basically a trustworthy sort of fella. Good bloke. The stock squad are gonna hear all this too and my worry is that they might target Gemma as a suspect. Dunno what might happen, but I reckon we're gonna have some exciting times around here in the next few weeks.'

'So there's a lot of circumstantial evidence but not much proof, that right?' Ben asked as they turned into the driveway at Billbinya.

'That's about it.'

As they pulled up at the sheds Gemma came out of the shearing shed loaded up with buckets and brooms. She had dirt smeared over her cheeks and her hair had escaped her ponytail, but Ben thought she looked a treat. He had to keep reminding himself that this woman was a client and he shouldn't even think about her, but it was hard.

Smiling, she waved a hello and walked towards the house to drop off her things.

'C'mon, Jess, it's time,' she yelled.

Ned and Ben got out of the car and walked towards the sheep yards where Garry had now joined Bulla. The sheep had been drafted and were milling around.

'Howdy,' Bulla greeted them.

'G'day. Where's Jack?'

'Crook.'

The guys leaned against the railings without talking. Gemma and Jess walked over.

'Guys, you all know Jess?' began Gemma. The men nodded to her, and Ben flashed her a smile.

'So, here we are . . .' Gemma fumbled for words. 'I really don't know how to start this. I had a visit from the stock squad yesterday.'

Gemma looked at the expectant faces. These people were her friends; people she could rely on and trust.

'Seems that there are some rumours and pieces of evidence pointing towards Adam being involved in some stock stealing. Dave from the stock squad is pretty keen to get to the bottom of it. I have told him everything I know, which isn't much. Whatever happens, I'm not involved - but you guys would know that. Ned,' Ned looked up, 'one of the strange things about all of this is that Bulla found some sheep that weren't ours in one of our paddocks. There were about a thousand of them and they were wethers.'

Ned nodded but said nothing.

'They may have been the ones that were stolen although why or how they got there I don't know. But I think the stock squad is going to base their investigation around here because of those sheep. Did you notice anything strange when we were counting the stock?'

'I can't remember, Gemma. I know I was worried about the feedlot cattle numbers and the contract that Adam signed but I can't remember much about the sheep. I know you said some of the numbers were up after I counted them for you, but I didn't notice any odd earmarks – but then, I was counting, not looking for anything different, so I may have missed it.'

Ned's admission surprised Gemma. He was a very astute stock agent and if there was an animal that wasn't hers, she'd have thought he would have noticed. No wonder the poor bloke needed a holiday.

'Gemma, do you think Adam was involved?' Bulla asked.

'If you'd asked me last night I'd have said no, but – I've found a mobile phone that suggests otherwise. I want to think about it for a bit longer before I say anything else, though. But whatever happens, I want to get to the bottom of it. I don't like that those sheep were dumped here.'

They were all quiet for a while, processing what had been said.

'Anyway,' said Gemma, starting to move, 'I'm taking the weekend off. Jess and I are heading into town for a girls' weekend and we're off out to dinner tomorrow night with some friends.' Gemma looked at Ben as she said this and he couldn't help but smile at her.

'I just really wanted you all to hear it from the horse's mouth. You're all my friends as well as the people I work with. I don't want any of this to rub off on you lot, so you need to know what's happening.'

'Well, shit, Gemma,' said Ned emotionally. 'How can we help?'

'I don't think you can at the moment. It's just a waiting game. Let's hope that there isn't any more stock on Billbinya that isn't ours.'

'And that no more arrives without you knowing,' added Jess as an afterthought.

As Ned and Ben headed towards the car, Gemma said to Bulla and Garry, 'I haven't had a chance to get out to the steers today. Can you get out there sometime over the weekend and have a look at how much feed is in that paddock?'

'Yep, no worries,' said Bulla. 'We'll probably head into Dawns Rest over the weekend and get a few supplies and have a feed at the pub, but we'll be here. I'll put these sheep in the holding paddock so they're quick and easy to get in on Monday for shearing Tuesday.'

'Thanks, guys. Well, I'll see you Monday then.'

Chapter 16

Crouched under the window in the shearing shed, Jack waited anxiously for the group to disperse. He needed to ring the boss urgently. At last everyone went their separate ways. Racing down the steps of the shed, he ran to his room and dialled the number.

'It's me,' he said, lighting a cigarette.

'What's up?'

'The widow knows for sure that Sinny was involved. I heard 'er tellin' all the other blokes she found 'is mobile phone. I'm reckoning there must've still been messages on it.'

'Shit. No, hang on, that won't matter. Those phones were pre-paid. Untraceable. When's she leaving for town?'

'Tonight, I think.'

'Okay, get into the house tonight as soon as she's gone and see if you can find that phone. Get rid of it if you can. The truck-load of steers will take place tomorrow night as planned. This will really set her up. Gonna put them in the same paddock as the rest of their steers?'

'Yeah, but there's a chance they'll get found pretty quick 'cos Gemma is worried about the feed out in that paddock and Bulla's gonna check on it sometime this weekend. It might be all right, though. I reckon Bulla will go out tomorrow and check those steers and then they'll head to Dawns Rest to the pub. So maybe they won't be found for a while.'

'Okay, we'll just have to risk it. I'll come out with the truck tomorrow night. See what you can find in the house tonight, and we can have another go together tomorrow.'

'Aren't ya busy tomorrow night?'

'Not anymore. I'm searching a house with you. Seeya tomorrow.'

When Jack had signed off, his boss hung up his phone and dialled the same number as he had earlier in the day.

'You shouldn't be ringing,' came down the phone in lieu of hello.

'She knows he was involved. We think they found his mobile with the messages on it.'

'What sort of a useless bastard is that half-brother of yours? He's supposed to be finding any evidence left behind.'

'I don't think he's had much of a chance. She's around all the time.'

'Fix it.' The phone went dead.

'C'mon,' yelled Jess excitedly. 'Hurry up. You haven't even packed your bag yet. Let's hit town!'

Gemma threw some clothes in a bag and pulled the door to the Billbinya homestead shut.

'Hey, I've just remembered. I had a phone call from Paige Nicholls a couple of days ago. Do you want to try and catch up with her over the weekend?'

Jess stopped and gave Gemma a careful look. 'I'm not sure. Do you?'

'I think we should make an effort. It's been a long time since the accident.'

'Let's think about it a bit more first. Hey, grab those files with the accounts in them. I might get time to have a look at them. What about we take a vehicle each,' Jess said. 'If you're right to come home by yourself I might stay in town on Monday and check in at work then come out Monday night or Tuesday morning.'

'You just want an extra night in town to be with lover boy!' Gemma teased. Her mood had improved since she'd told everyone what she'd found out. She could feel their support, and the weight was beginning to lift from her shoulders.

* * *

Jack watched the two vehicles crunch down the driveway then ambled over towards the homestead. The dogs gave a warning growl but, knowing that Gemma was safely out of the way and there was a good chance that Bulla and Garry were already on their way to the pub, he didn't stop. He pulled open the screen door and pushed hard on the heavy wooden door that, like all good farm doors, was unlocked. Turning lights on as he went, he systematically walked from room to room, looking for potential hiding places. He searched the wood box next to the fire, the TV cabinet where all the videos and DVDs were kept. He ran his fingers along the top ledge of the shelves in the walk-in robes in the spare rooms and felt under the mattresses. Nothing. He couldn't find anything to indicate an attic and no stairs to point to a cellar, which was slightly unusual in a house this old. He looked for signs that the carpet had been lifted and that a trapdoor might be hidden beneath it, but he couldn't see any indication of one.

Jack really doubted that Adam would have been stupid enough to bring any information into the house. Admittedly, there was the phone that had been found, but he couldn't see any information on payments being anywhere near here. He hadn't found the phone itself yet, but he wasn't too worried. There was always tomorrow night.

As he walked, a thought struck him. What had happened to the plane since the accident? He wondered if Adam would have kept any papers in there since he'd have been the only one flying it. Then he discarded the idea. The plane would have been gone over with a fine-tooth comb, since the investigators would have been looking for a reason for the crash. But still, it may be worth mentioning to his brother.

Jack came to the office and had a quick riffle through the filing cabinets and cupboards but nothing jumped out at him. He found where the bank statements were kept and had a cursory glance over the last year. There wasn't anything there he could see that could cause any problems.

He wandered towards Gemma's bedroom. Hovering at the door he looked in. Jack was beginning to lust after Gemma. He knew the feeling that sometimes got him into trouble was resurfacing and he was doing his best to control it. That was why he had been spending time with the jillaroo. The bed was made, but there were signs she'd left in a hurry – clothes on the bed, cupboard door left open. He entered and breathed in the smell that lingered; the soap she used, the makeup she'd put on, they were all part of her aroma and Jack liked it.

He lay on the bed and rubbed his face into the pillow.

You're a sick wanker, he thought as he felt himself become aroused. But he couldn't deny that Gemma was pretty easy on the eye and he really would like to show her a good time. He reckoned she would go off in the sack. Simmering with desire and anger,

Jack knew she'd never look at someone like him and it pissed him off. He got off the bed and looked through her drawers. Finding her underwear drawer he buried his face in her lingerie and groaned. He shook himself and decided it was time to go and see his piece of fluff down the road. Turning off all the lights, and carefully shutting the door behind him, Jack went straight to his ute and took off. Didn't matter he hadn't looked everywhere; he was pretty sure that there was nothing to find anyway. Besides, he had a need that required attending to.

After a bite to eat at Jess's house, Jess decided they should go to the Jewel for a drink.

'Jess, I really don't feel like it,' protested Gemma. She wanted to curl up and go to sleep, forget everything she'd learned in the last few days. The long drive into town by herself had dampened her mood.

There were so many questions without answers. Adam's involvement in the stock stealing still didn't sit right with her. He was basically a respectable, honest guy. Yeah, he liked to have fun, have a few bets, drink a bit, but Gemma had never known him to take part in anything remotely illegal. In her mind, either he was innocent, or somehow he had got roped in and couldn't get out. But that didn't explain the mobile phone and the rumours that Jess had told her about. And thinking about it, Bulla and Garry didn't seem that surprised when she told them of the discovery. Had they heard something and not told her? There was so much she didn't understand . . .

'Gem, you'll be fine when we get there,' Jess argued. 'You need to have some fun.'

So, reluctantly, Gemma got into the taxi with Jess and they headed out to the Jewel Bar.

Craig had eaten before he'd got to the Jewel and now sat facing the door, chatting to the barmaid. He was nursing a Coke in a spirits glass, so no one would know he wasn't drinking alcohol. He'd gone over the top last night and knew he couldn't do that again. The bar was filling slowly and his new friend had told him that the busiest time was after 9 pm. They had a rush straight after work, as all the banks, accounting firms and businesses shut for the weekend, and then it thinned out when people went home to change and get ready for a night out. Most of the after-work crowd were back by nine, or maybe a bit later.

Watching for familiar faces, faces he had seen in the files, Craig just about choked on his drink when he saw Gemma walk in accompanied by a stunning red-haired woman.

Craig had only seen photos of Gemma, but the minute she entered the room he knew it was her. He wasn't sure who the red-haired chick was, but he thought it might be worth finding out – especially given the way she looked.

'Hey,' he said to the barmaid. He nodded towards Gemma and Jess. 'Who's that?'

The barmaid grinned as she caught sight of Jess. 'That's Jess Rawlings, the biggest party animal in Pirie. She's here most nights with a fella – Brad, I think his name is. Really nice girl but not too many people can keep up with her when she gets the urge to have a good time. She works in a bank and if that's not a contradiction in terms I don't know what is. Not sure who the other girl is . . .' She looked for a bit longer. 'Hey, I reckon that's Gemma Sinclair. Her hubby was killed in a plane crash a while ago. Hey Kath, is that Gemma Sinclair?' she asked her workmate, who rushed past with another order of drinks. Without waiting for an answer, she continued, 'She never comes to town. Heard she's turned into a bit of a hermit since her bloke died.' The barmaid leaned into Craig and whispered conspiratorially, 'The grapevine says he was involved in stock stealing. Seems to be a bit of it happening around here at the moment and apparently he was the guy behind it.'

'Really?' Craig feigned astonishment. 'But how could it be going on still if he's carked it?'

The barmaid shrugged her shoulders and raced off again as another customer snapped his fingers at her.

Jess shouldered her way up to the bar and stood next to Craig. She bestowed a brilliant smile on him as she ordered two glasses of champagne and Craig smiled back, lost in her green eyes.

Jess made her way back to the table where Gemma was waiting and handed the drink to her friend. Craig watched as Gemma crinkled her nose in distaste and tried to lip-read what she said to Jess. He thought it was 'I don't like champagne'. He observed Jess grin and say something back – 'drink up', maybe.

Craig thought that Jess was one of the prettiest girls he'd seen in a long time. Not conventionally pretty, but her green eyes sparkled with fun and her red hair set her freckles off against her pale skin. She looked like 'the girl next door' who turned into a swan after you left town. Given Craig knew how to party too, having Jess in the equation might be interesting.

After a while, and a couple more drinks, he saw Jess look at her watch in irritation and get out her mobile phone. The buzz of the bar had grown a lot louder as more people arrived and Gemma was looking increasingly strained. Craig made his way over to where the girls were and found an empty table.

'. . . ring and see where he is,' he overheard Jess say to Gemma.

'Jess, I'm really ready to head home,' Gemma replied.

'But we said we would meet Brad here.'

'No, *you* said you'd meet Brad here; I don't think he'd have been expecting me. Can I have your keys and I'll go home? You stay, it doesn't bother me.'

'Nah, you're right,' Jess conceded. 'Let's head. Stuff 'im.'

Craig whipped his chair around to face Jess and Gemma's table. 'Hello, ladies,' he said with a grin. 'How's your night?'

'We're just leaving,' Gemma replied, standing up.

Jess looked at Craig's handsome face, and forgot she was annoyed with Brad. 'Hello yourself,' she said with a large smile.

Gemma rolled her eyes. 'C'mon, Jess, let's go.'

Craig stuck out his hand and said, 'The name's Craig, what's yours?'

'Jess,' she replied, shaking his hand. Her pale hand was lost in his large brown one. 'This is my party-pooper friend, Gemma.'

Craig raised his hand in acknowledgement. 'Why don't you hang around? I'll buy you a drink.'

Jess looked at Gemma, who had suddenly found the floor very interesting.

'Can we take a raincheck, Craig? I'd love to, but maybe not tonight.'

'No worries, I'll see you sometime.'

The girls left and Craig waited a few minutes then followed them out the door. It would be worth knowing where they were spending the night.

On the way home Gemma said, 'You can still pull blokes in without even trying, can't you? You're amazing. I've never once been able to do that.'

'Yeah,' said Jess without arrogance. It was the way it had always been, but Jess really didn't think she was pretty. 'I don't know why. Often I don't mean to.'

Gemma looked at her friend and smiled fondly. 'Oh, I know why,' she said. It was Jess's personality. The happiness and friendliness that oozed from her. The way she included everyone, her love of life, and her eyes. 'It's because you're you.'

Jess looked at her strangely. 'You okay?'

'Tired, but fine.'

Back at Jess's house, the girls went straight to bed, but it took Gemma a long time to fall asleep – and when she did, her dreams were frightening.

Chapter 17

Saturday morning dawned cloudy and cold, and Jess could hear the wind outside.

'Go away,' she thought, knowing how bitter it would be at the footy today.

Gemma stuck her head around Jess's bedroom door at an unholy hour.

'Off to do the farm shopping, Jess,' she said quietly.

'Mmm,' mumbled Jess. Now awake, she felt for her phone on the bedside table. Where the hell was Brad? She'd tried numerous times last night, but his mobile alternated between not answering and being switched off. Jess was getting annoyed. Brad had done this before, but not often. It was a bit strange after eight or nine months of rarely missing a beat to do so now. Had he met someone else? She hoped not. With eyes half closed she hit the redial button.

'Hi. You've called Brad Manstead of Manstead Agronomy. Please leave your name and number and I will return your call as soon as possible. Thanks for calling.' Jess took the phone away from her ear and looked at it disbelievingly. The beep sounded.

'Brad, it's me,' Jess's morning voice croaked. 'Where the bloody hell are you? I thought we were catching up last night. If you care to show, Gem, Ben and I will be at the new bistro down on the foreshore at about seven. Not happy, Brad.' Jess pressed the disconnect button and lay back in her bed, fuming.

Almost immediately her mobile rang. Looking at the screen she saw Brad's number. She opened her phone.

'Hello, Brad,' she said coldly.

'I'm so sorry, babe,' Brad's gravelly voice sounded down the line. 'I got held up out at one of the farms and then Justin Downey asked if I wanted to have a beer before I left and one thing led to another. I'm really sorry.'

Silence.

'Jess?'

'You could have called.'

'Yeah, I know. Sorry.' Brad sounded genuine and Jess felt her anger abate. She just couldn't stay angry with him for long.

'So are you coming tonight?' she asked.

'Yep, I'll be there. What are you up to today?'

'Gem's gone down the farm merch shop so I'm just hanging here until she gets back. Then I'll be off to the footy. Gemma isn't up to going.'

Brad's voice dropped to a low growl. 'Will she be gone long?'

Jess smiled into the phone. 'Long enough.'

'See ya soon.'

Jess smiled. He didn't sound like he was losing interest in her.

That evening, standing in front of the mirror, Gemma found it hard to get excited about the night ahead. True, she was looking forward to getting to know Ben better. She had seen him at the farming supplies stores that morning when she'd gone to get the stuff they'd need for shearing, and they had got into a friendly debate about which sires were the best over Angus cows. Gemma had been impressed with his knowledge and enthusiasm about black cattle. She had maintained her passion, but it waned at times, without someone as enthusiastic as she was to throw ideas around with. Ben had even suggested they continue their discussion over pre-dinner drinks.

No, the thing she wasn't looking forward to was Brad. Despite his charm, for some reason she'd felt a bit uncomfortable when she'd met him the weekend before – almost as if he didn't like her. He was probably the jealous type, she'd concluded, and didn't want to share Jess. With everything that was going on in Gemma's life at the moment, she really didn't want to spend time with people she had to try with. And she felt that some of tonight might be spent trying.

* * *

Jack waited for the text message to say the truck was on its way, but instead he had a message from his older brother: *In the shit with the handbrake. Won't make it.*

Jess opened the door to Ben's knock. She'd been pleased to hear about Ben's invitation. 'He's stunning,' she'd said. 'I reckon he's the right bloke for you.'

Gemma had given her a look. 'I hardly know him and I don't want to get involved with anyone. Despite everything, it's only eight months since Adam died and I still love him.'

'Of course you do, but goodness knows why.'

'Jess!'

'Sorry, lovely!'

'Come in, come in,' she said now, grabbing Ben's arm and dragging him inside. 'Now I need to ask you a few questions before you can take Gemma out.'

Ben grinned. 'I promise to not have bad breath, not to drink and drive, and to have her at the restaurant by seven sharp!'

'That's excellent! I was terribly worried about the bad breath. Sorry I didn't get to say hi at the footy. I saw you on the field. Very impressive goal there just before half-time.'

'Brad said you were there but I didn't see you.'

'Yeah, he's stayed down the rooms for a couple of

beers with the guys – he'll meet us at the restaurant. Where are you going for a drink?'

'Just down the pub. We won't be long. I have an argument about cattle I need to win.'

Jess rolled her eyes. 'Good luck. I've never known anyone to win an argument with her about cattle.'

'We could come back and pick you up, Jess, if Brad is meeting us down there.'

'I don't argue with people,' said Gemma as she walked around the corner. For a split second there was silence while Jess and Ben looked at her. She was dressed in a denim panelled skirt with a white shirt and red jacket. She had left her hair down and the little makeup she had on made her look beautiful. She looked lovely, but Jess could still see the signs of strain on her friend's face. With a pang, she wished she could make this whole thing go away – the problem was, she suspected there was worse to come.

'You don't look too bad for a country chick,' said Jess. 'Although, you might need to do something about those hands. You're starting to look like a mechanic.'

Gemma threw Jess a look of exasperation and embarrassment as she shoved her hands in her pockets. 'Just 'cos you sit at a computer all day . . .'

Jess practically pushed them out of the door, saying, 'See you tonight. Thanks for asking, Ben, but I'll catch a taxi down. Bye now!' And she slammed the door.

Ben shook his head in amazement. 'Is she always like that?'

'Oh, yeah, Jess is full on.'

When they got to the car Ben held the door open, which made Gemma blush. *It's been so long*, she thought, fighting the urge to flee back to the safety of Jess's house. *What on earth am I going to talk to him about?* There was an uncomfortable silence as Ben started the car and pulled out. Then he cleared his throat and said, 'Well, I thought we'd go to the pub. That okay?'

'Yeah, no worries.' Gemma fiddled with the hem of her skirt.

'So what cattle –' Ben started.

'Where are you from?' Gemma spoke over the top of him. They laughed and Ben indicated with his hand for Gemma to continue.

'Where are you from and how did you get mixed up with Ned?'

'I'm from a farming family down south and I bought some land twenty-odd k's away from where I grew up. It was great for a while, being my own boss, running the farm the way I wanted. But it's pretty lonely and I decided that I wanted a change without losing the farm. Couple of mates I went to school with said Ned was keeping his eye out for the right bloke, so here I am. I've only leased the farm out, though – not quite ready to give it all up completely, but I really wanted a break.'

'So how long do you think you'll stay here for?'

'I've only just got here – are you looking to get rid of me already?'

Gemma smiled. 'No way, I've got to educate you on the way of cattle and their genetics.'

Ben pulled into the pub. 'Stay there,' he said as she reached for the door handle. He opened his door and ran around to open hers.

'That feels really weird, you know,' Gemma confessed as she stepped out of the car.

'Only because you're not used to it. By the end of the night you'll be fine.' He took her elbow and steered her gently towards the pub.

'What will you have?'

'Rum and Coke, please,' she said, as she settled down in the chair. She watched as Ben walked over to the bar and ordered. He was very good-looking. She felt a twinge of guilt. *I'm married. No I'm not, I'm a widow.*

Their talk flowed easily and Gemma was surprised how much they had in common. Same music – country, of course. They both loved to camp. Ben had done some wonderful trips up to the Bungle Bungles and other places that Gemma had only dreamed of visiting. And they both loved farming.

'Why couldn't you handle farming anymore?' asked Gemma.

'Got too lonely,' admitted Ben. 'Pretty hard when you're on your own. No one to talk things over with, no one who sees things the way you do. I got sick of going to the pub every Friday night and seeing the same old faces – no one with new views on things, no one with any new ideas. And then there were the ladies who just wouldn't leave me alone.' He reddened as he realised what he'd said. 'Sorry, that probably sounds really big-headed, but there were a few single girls who had their eye on me and wouldn't back off. Yeah, I want a partner – but not just anyone.' Ben paused as he saw Gemma nodding her head.

'I know *exactly* what you mean.' Gemma was rushing to get her words out. 'No one to talk to at the end of the day, no one to say, "Was that the right decision or could we do it better next time?" – all that sort of stuff.'

'Yeah, of course you understand.' Ben nodded. 'Sorry, I'd forgotten who I was talking to.'

Gemma smiled sadly. 'Yeah well, that's something I *do* understand.' She looked at her watch. 'We'd better get a move on or we'll be late.'

On the way to the restaurant, Gemma found herself confessing her apprehension about the night to Ben.

'I'm sure I'm just imagining that Brad doesn't like me, but when I met him, Jess was too excited to notice and I'd never say anything.'

'Don't worry about it,' Ben advised. 'Just try and enjoy the night. I haven't had much to do with him. Bit over the top and full of himself, but I think he's mainly all right.'

When they got to the restaurant, Jess was sitting at the table by herself.

'Sorry we're a bit late,' Gemma said as they sat down.

'No problem, I'm still waiting for Brad.' Jess forced a smile. 'So, good time?'

'Yeah, lovely. I still can't convince Ben it's important to use genetics that aren't big on growth in this area. It makes for cattle that grow too big and then you can't put weight on them because we haven't got the feed to fill them up.'

'Like I understand that,' Jess said with a grin. 'Did you talk about anything else other than farming? I'm trying to teach this country bumpkin that there are heaps of different things to do in the world other than farming. Can you help me, Ben?'

'I'm not sure I know that much more! But one thing I do know about that I've heard you like too is camping. What was your favourite camping trip, Jess?'

'Ah, well now . . .' Jess launched into an enthusiastic description of a camping trip she'd taken with her parents about fifteen years before.

'The colours were amazing and there were only certain places you could camp in case you were attacked by crocs . . . The country is so weathered. Everyone says old, but it can't be any older than the rest of the land, can it? Loved every minute. But it was worth spending a couple of quiet weeks with them just to experience the Top End. Never really been anywhere quite like it since. There he is,' said Jess, waving like a maniac to get Brad's attention as he walked in the door. 'Looks like he's had a few. Check out those cute red cheeks!'

Ben and Gemma's eyes met across the table. Ben raised a crooked eyebrow at her and gave her a small smile.

'G'day, everyone, how's it going? Ah, my exquisite woman.' Brad leaned down and gave Jess a kiss on the cheek. Going around the table he shook Ben's hand. 'Good goal you kicked today,' he said.

Brad got to Gemma. 'Mrs Sinclair,' he said smoothly. 'How marvellous to see you again.' He took her hand and bowed over it before kissing it.

Gemma tried to extract her hand gently, while smiling to hide her discomfort. 'Great to see you, Brad. How was the footy match?'

'Not bad, not bad. Think I'll have another drink, We're commiserating another loss. Anyone else?' Everyone declined.

After they'd ordered their meals the talk turned to farming. Brad held forth on what farmers he'd been to see recently, who was a good farmer and who wasn't – his judgement seemed to rest on who took his advice on their pastures and crops and who didn't. The more he talked, the more uncomfortable Gemma felt. She watched Jess, and saw that she was beginning to get annoyed. Ben listened quietly.

Finally, after ordering coffee, Brad stretched his legs and leaned back in his chair. 'So, Gemma, tell me – how are you finding farming now you're on your own?'

'Okay. It's great to have Bulla and Garry helping me. Don't know what I'd do without them.'

'When will you sell?'

'That's none of your business, Brad,' Jess butted in as Gemma said: 'Oh, no. I won't sell.'

'You know, I think you'd be so much better off selling.' The tension around the table was apparent to everyone but Brad, who blundered on. 'You're better to take the money now, before you lose everything. Stop trying to prove you're something you're not.'

Gemma was stunned. She felt Ben's hand come down firmly on her knee in support, and Jess looked ready to explode.

Pushing back her chair, Jess rose from the table, fury distorting her face and her tone icy. 'That was inexcusably rude. I can't think why you would say such things when you have only met Gemma twice. I think we might call it a night. I expect you'll be fixing up the bill, Brad? Good. Then you had better go and sleep off what you have had to drink. I'm not sure you need to call me again for a while. Ben, would you mind driving us home?'

Jess invited Ben in for coffee after the silent ride home, but he declined. Jess had stormed into the house before Gemma had even left the car. Ben grabbed at her hand as she leaned in to thank him for the ride.

'Not everyone thinks like him, Gemma. You're doing a good job under difficult circumstances.'

She smiled weakly. 'Thanks again for tonight. I really enjoyed the first part. I guess I'll see you out on Billbinya sometime.'

'I'll be bringing the wool buyer around next week to look at the wool and then the shipper buyer later,' Ben promised.

As soon as Gemma entered the house Jess said, 'Gem, I'm so sorry, I have no idea what got into him. He's never been like that before. He's usually a very caring, sensitive sort of guy. It was like he was another person tonight. I'm really sorry.'

Gemma waved her apology away. 'Don't worry about it, Jess. The meal made up for it. Wasn't it beautiful? I'm stuffed, so I think I'll hit the hay. Night.'

Gemma lay awake for a long time that night, wondering why Brad had targeted her and what she'd done to deserve his dislike.

Chapter 18

Jack had finally received the text telling him the truck was on its way. He started his ute and left the shearers' quarters. At the top part of Billbinya, off the worn track in a sheltered place by a creek, Jack kept his two dogs, some sheep yard panels and some wire. It was his sheep-stealing kit. He went there most days while he was supposed to be working, fed and watered the dogs and made sure they were okay.

'Get up the back, ya mongrels,' said Jack as he let them off the chain and loaded on the panels. 'We've got work to do.'

The night was cold and the large yellow moon lit the sky. Jack parked the ute near a patch of bush, far away from where the truck would arrive. He would walk to the gateway. It was easier to hide in a bush than to explain why his ute was on the road at a strange time of night, and if someone drove past he didn't want their lights picking up a reflection of his ute.

The shadows of the trees and bushes made eerie movements on the ground and could have caused him to trip, but Jack moved silently through the darkness without stumbling. This was his world.

The dogs' breath puffed white as they moved beside him, occasionally sniffing at a bush or stopping to cock a leg. At the call of a night bird they would stop and listen, then move along as quietly as Jack. They settled down under a bush to wait for the arrival of the truck. The truck would reverse through the gate and the stock would be unloaded. The dogs would mob them together and the job would be done. The only noise that would be heard was the truck, and the sound of running hoofs on the damp ground as the cattle were unloaded.

'Yep,' mused Jack to himself. 'Gemma's about to get those steers she's worried about, for the feedlot contract. It's nice to be able to help out.'

Jack heard the truck before he saw the lights. At the low rumble of the engine, his dogs tensed, cocked their ears and whined softly. He quietened them with a hand on each head and, as the truck drew closer, he went to open the gate. The driver and Jack didn't even acknowledge each other as they unloaded the truck. The steers, wide-eyed with fear, raced off the truck ramp and out into the paddock. Soon the air was filled with the sound of cattle hoofs pounding the ground, as the cattle ran around the paddock trying to work out where they were. Jack sent his dogs around the runners to slow them down and push them into a mob. His dogs worked quietly, herding the mob together. They had done this many times. Soon all was quiet in the paddock.

After the truck left, Jack used a sturdy branch with dead leaves on it to swish away the truck tracks. There wasn't any sign that a truck had delivered these cattle. He knew that it would be obvious that someone had covered them up, but it didn't matter. There wouldn't be any way that the stock squad, if they arrived, would be able to cast tyre prints and match them back to the truck.

Jack squatted under the bush for a while longer, listening to the cattle. He lit a cigarette and the end glowed in the dark. The steers were slightly restless, milling around each other, snorting and sniffing the new smells. There was the odd loud bellow, but they would settle down in the next few hours. They'd be tired from their long trip and, once they'd had a feed, they would sleep. Jack got up to make his way home.

Sunday morning dawned sunny and bright. The cold winter winds had subsided and Gemma was heading home. Jess had apologised again and then tried to convince Gemma to stay and go over the books with her. Gemma had flatly refused, saying it was her last free day before two weeks of shearing.

Gemma's ute was loaded up to the hilt with wool packs, bale fasteners, lice control and dog food. She also had to call in at the pub at Dawns Rest to pick up the food supplies for the shearers' cook. She hoped this year the shearers' cook would be a good one.

Three years ago, Gemma and Adam had been threatened by a drunken cook wielding a broken bottle and demanding a pay rise. Adam had managed to calm the man down just as Bulla and Garry had come into the shed. They had relieved him of his bottle and his duties. Once the man had been asked to leave the property and put on the mail truck back to town, Gemma went to the shearers' quarters to discover all the meat that had been given to the cook was spread out on the kitchen table, covered in maggots. For the two days the team had been there, none of the meat or food had been put in the fridge and the dishes hadn't been done. The shearers had threatened to walk out but were placated when told that Gemma would cook. They threatened again once they had tasted her first meal! Gemma smiled. Her heart ached but the good memories still made her happy.

As she drove, she planned the movement of all the sheep. You couldn't just get sheep out of a paddock for shearing. They had to be off feed for twenty-four hours so they emptied their bladders and bowels. There was nothing worse than shearing a sheep and having it wee all over you. All the mobs had to be kept in their age groups so mobs had to come and go without being boxed into other mobs. Sometimes it was a tricky operation – sheep in the yards, draining out, sheep in the holding paddocks ready for the next day, and shifting sheep from outlying paddocks to ones closer. Then after the shearing was completed the sheep had to be back-lined to prevent lice – which decreased the wool's quality – and then taken back out to the paddocks. It was going to be a busy time.

Once home, Gemma unpacked her supplies and then went over to the shearers' quarters kitchen to put the supplies away there. While she was unpacking, Jack stuck his head into the room and said hi.

'How're you feeling?' asked Gemma.

'Much, much better. Jeez, I felt crook. Haven't had a gut ache like that for a long time.'

'So, are you ready for shearing?'

'As ready as ya ever are for that amount of work. Can I give ya a hand 'ere at all?'

'No thanks, Jack. I'm just about finished. I'll catch you tomorrow, okay?'

Gemma leaned back on her knees after scrubbing out the fridge and wiping off the dust and grime that had seeped through the cracks in the walls. The benches shone, the floor gleamed and Gemma felt exhausted. Jack had kept the place basically clean, but kitchens always needed a woman's touch.

Thinking of the lonely night ahead, she sighed. Having Patrick and Jess around, even though it hadn't been for long, had eased the loneliness she hadn't known she was feeling. There had been movement in the house, people to talk to, have a coffee with. Gemma had found herself listening at night for the sounds of her house guests. Someone heading to the loo or getting a drink of water. Comforting sounds that made her feel less alone. On the drive home, Gemma had been shocked to realise that she didn't really want to go back to Billbinya. It was isolated and, since the stock-stealing investigation had begun, it was frightening.

Gemma knew that the busyness of shearing and all the different people around would lift her spirits, but she was wondering how she could get through tonight. She had an idea.

'Hey, Jack?' she yelled. 'You still there?'

'Yeah,' came the faint reply.

'I'm going to give Bulla and Gaz a ring and see if they want to come to tea. Have a barbecue or something to celebrate the start of a great shearing. Interested?'

'Yeah, that'd be good.'

'Okay, I'll see you tonight then.' Packing up her cleaning supplies, Gemma headed home to ring Bulla and Garry.

Gemma held up a glass of rum and Coke and proposed a toast. 'Here's to a great shearing, an exceptional wool clip and great wool prices. Cheers.'

'Hear, hear,' mumbled the three men. The barbecue was sizzling and the salads were sitting on the outdoor table. Bulla, thankfully, was in charge of the cooking.

Jack stood back and watched everyone. He could see that Garry and Bulla were very fond and protective of Gemma. He already knew he wouldn't be able to break into this close-knit group or glean any information on Adam from them. Adam was barely mentioned in front of him.

Jack was used to feeling like an outsider; he had felt like one for as long as he could remember. He'd never fitted into any group at school and never had any close friends. He'd been so excited when he'd met his brother for the first time. A brother! Someone to go shooting with, someone to drink with. Someone to steal with. By the time his brother had come on to the scene, Jack had already been in trouble with the police numerous times. His mother despaired of him and their father had long since disappeared.

When his brother had first found him, Jack had been overwhelmed to know he had family. Someone who cared. It hadn't taken long for the brothers to forge a strong bond but it was Jack who appreciated it most.

Chapter 19

Craig loved the smell of the sale yards, the hustle and bustle. There was always so much going on. Dogs barking, the stock being herded into their pens, the clanging of the metal gates as they slammed shut behind the cattle, auctioneers talking to stockies before the sale started and, without fail, there would always be two old men sitting up on the rails somewhere, discussing the season and stock prices. He had lost count of how many times he'd heard 'When I was a lad . . .' stories.

Craig watched the cattle being unloaded and herded into their pens. The cattle snorted and bellowed as they ran down the cement raceway, looking for a way out or an open gate. He heard a yell of 'Watch that one, mate,' and turned in time to see a young man leaping for the rails with a Brahman bull close on his heels.

'Looks like that one's come from up north,' said a man standing next to him.

'The bull's just being friendly,' Craig grinned and moved on. He climbed the ladder that led to the walkways which lay across the tops of the yards. Sale yards always had steel walkways across the top so the buyers and stockies wouldn't be stirring the stock up every time they walked past. He walked across, eyeing the stock and making notes in his notebook. As a detective, he was attuned to conversation around him. Interesting snippets could incriminate crooks and blow others' covers. Maybe he would hear something about the wethers here. Keeping an eye on numbers of cattle in each pen, he quietly made his way to the auctioneer to have a quiet word about who was in charge, paperwork, records and the way sales ran in South Australia.

The smell of cooking caught Craig's attention and his stomach growled. Heading over to the food van, he ordered an egg and bacon sandwich and an iced coffee: standard food for cold sale mornings. He was leaning against a tree when he heard someone greet him. Turning, he saw Ben Daylee, also holding an egg and bacon sandwich.

'G'day,' said Craig. 'What are you doing here?'

'Brought a buyer down to look for some feedlot cattle. What about you?'

'Ah, just on my way back to Adelaide and I thought I'd stop in for a while and have a look. Being back in the country made me yearn for a few country experiences, so here I am,' Craig invented quickly.

Ben regarded him quietly then said, 'So how long have you been with the stock squad?'

He raised his eyebrows, searching for an answer.

Ben grinned and pointed at him: 'You've been made, fella!'

'Shit, how the hell . . . ?'

Ben grinned. 'Saw you leaving the motel with Dave heading to the cop shop. Bit of a giveaway that there are two new fellas in town staying at the same motel and hanging around the cops! Not to worry. I've not been in town long and I don't know who to trust about this business either, so I'll be keeping my mouth shut.'

'Decent of you,' Craig managed.

'Catch you round.' Ben was about to walk away then stopped. 'Don't suppose you want to have a beer one night? Might see you down the pub tonight, hey?'

'Yeah, maybe.'

Ben disappeared into the crowd and Craig finished his breakfast, unnerved by the encounter.

'Sale-o, sale-o,' called the auctioneer. 'We're starting the sale now. Thanks to all the vendors who have put in these magnificent animals. Now what am I bid for this line of Angus steers? Start at six hundred, I got six hundred, six hundred now. Six fifty, the bid is with you, sir.' He pointed to a man in a green shirt. 'Six fifty now. Can you find seven hundred? Yes sir, seven hundred. For seven hundred dollars I *sell*.'

The auctioneer clapped his hands together and yelled, 'Sold to Hyland Butchers.' Forgetting about Ben, Craig followed the sale, making notes of all the abattoirs, feedlotters and private buyers that bought at today's market. He'd have quite a list to check out when he returned to Pirie.

Gemma felt a surge of excitement when she saw the first shearer's car arrive. It pulled up at the quarters and she saw a woman get out – the cook. Gemma left the sheep yards where she'd been classing the wethers into fleece types and went to get her settled in. Soon there were several cars parked by the sheds. There were four shearers, a classer, three rousies, a presser to press the wool into bales and a penner-upperer. By five o'clock the sheep were in the shed, the bedrooms at the quarters full and the shearers were up in the shed hanging over catching pens, looking at the sheep to be shorn.

Gemma made her way up into the shed to say hello to everyone. Some of the guys that were shearing had shorn many times at Billbinya so it was like greeting old friends. They were a motley-looking lot – three older men who were losing their hair or going grey and one young learner. The roustabouts were two young girls who looked like they could give back as good as they got and an older woman whose partner was Buster, the second-fastest shearer in the shed. The presser and the penner-upperer seemed as if they belonged in a heavy rock band, with their long hair and goatees.

'Sheep look good, Gemma,' said Kenny, the owner of the contract business and a shearer himself. 'Boys should get their one fifty a day. Should make for a two-week shed. Ya reckon?'

'Sounds right to me, Kenny,' Gemma replied. 'That works out at about three thousand a week, give or take. There's six thousand wethers all up.'

After the inspection of the sheep and shed was finished, the shearers set up their handpieces, comb and cutter containers, and radio ready for the morning, then headed off to the quarters. Gemma, Bulla, Garry and Jack made plans for the next day. Jack was bringing the sheep in from the outlying paddocks to the holding paddocks, which could take all day depending on how far he had to come. Once the sheep were in the holding paddocks, it would be easy for them to be moved into the holding pens the next morning to drain out for the next day's shearing. Garry was doing plant maintenance, so he'd be around the shed to help if needed. Bulla and Gemma would be working in the yards, back-lining the sheep as they came out of the shed then taking them away.

As the stockmen headed off to their house, Gemma went over to the sheep yards. She started up the fire-fighting pump, whose tank had been filled with water, and started to wet them down. Even though it was winter, the earth was dry and dusty. The constant stream of sheep through the yards during the lamb marking had powdered up the manure and dirt and made the dust extremely fine. The hose throbbed under her hands and the mud splashed up into her face. Tomorrow the yards would be muddy, but working in mud was preferable to the red dust. When the working area was wet she turned off the engine and walked over to the shed to lug out four kegs of the lice treatment. Setting them up on the work table inside the covered yards, near the race, she made sure the applicators were in working condition and set at the right dosage. She then walked through all the yards and checked the chains on the gates to make sure they couldn't come open and the sheep escape or get boxed up with another mob.

Up in the shed, Gemma once again went through everything that was needed. Checking the wool press, she made sure an empty butt was in the press, ready for the first fleece off tomorrow. The bale fasteners and wool packs were close by and the presser would be able to reach them easily. The bale hooks for shifting the large cumbersome bales around were hanging on the press and the stencils that stated what was in each bale were hanging on the wall. Her footsteps were muffled on the wooden floor and the shed was silent except for the occasional cough of a sheep and the clicking of their hoofs on the grating.

Gemma looked at the bench, making sure the emery papers were alongside the grinder. That was how shearers ground their combs and cutters every night to make them sharp for the next day. She tested the chains on all the swinging doors to make sure the sheep couldn't get out of the catching pens. There had been times during previous shearings when a shearer or rousie hadn't chained the gate and during the night the sheep had pushed through the doors and ended up on the board. When the doors of the shed had been opened in the morning, they had been greeted with droppings all over the floor, the wool in chaos and bewildered-looking sheep.

Gemma was leaving nothing to chance. This was her first shearing by herself and she was determined there wouldn't be any stuff-ups while she was in charge.

As she walked towards her house Gemma could hear the raucous noise of talking and laughter coming from the shearers' quarters. Looking at her empty house, she made a snap decision. Heading towards the dog kennels, she let off two dogs who danced happily around her feet, licking at her hands. Stopping to fondle their heads and ears she talked to them quietly and then headed to the house for her sneakers. In the twilight, she ran with the dogs at her heels. She ran until she could see no more, then turned and headed towards home.

The next morning, Gemma was at the yards and shed by 6 am, checking that nothing was amiss. The wind was starting to pick up and she was grateful she'd wet the yards down the night before. Her dogs were whining on the end of their chains, waiting to be let off, but they would stay chained until the yard work was about to start. The shearing shed had come to life with noise and action. The team was always chirpy and keen at the start of a shed but by the time the end drew near, the chat and cheek had disappeared as everyone just wanted to finish. Gemma could hear all the shearers giving a rousie a hard time. Apparently she'd been caught with a farmhand in a compromising position at the last shed and the men were paying her out.

Bulla and Garry arrived and Gemma realised that Jack must have already left. His bike was gone from the shed and the gates in the holding paddocks were open, waiting for the sheep to be brought in. Gemma hadn't heard him leave and was surprised he'd got going earlier than her. Still, at least she knew the sheep were on their way – they could be hard to shift in the wind.

They walked into the shed in time to see the first sheep dragged from its pen and handpiece picked up, and hear the whirr of the machine kick into gear. Watching Kenny open up the belly and throw it onto the board for the rousies to pick up, Gemma felt overwhelmed with a strange mix of exhilaration, sadness and anticipation. Here was her main income. This was her harvest. How would it go? Would she make the money she needed to pay Adam's parents and still have some left over for the running of Billbinya? She prayed silently that this shearing would be a successful one.

* * *

Jess had called in to work on Monday but there wasn't any pressing business. She'd returned a couple of phone calls and answered some emails that were important, and left it at that, determined to spend the rest of the day concentrating on Gemma's books.

As she sipped a cup of coffee at her kitchen table on Tuesday morning with Gemma's files spread out in front of her, she felt very concerned. Noted on a pad beside her were a list of questions to ask Gemma. Once again she flicked through the bank statements of the last year. From the reports she'd printed out from Gemma's computer before she left Billbinya, she could see where the money had been spent and the source of income received but there was something very obvious missing. Jess went to the September bank statement once more and checked the amounts debited from the Billbinya bank account. Gemma had told her that the payment to Adam's parents came out in September as one large payment. Once Adam had authorised the amount he had rung the bank to organise a transfer of funds.

It seemed to Jess that last year's payment hadn't been made, yet she was sure that if that was the case, Gemma would have heard about it from either Adam or his parents. So if it *had* been paid, it hadn't come from the Billbinya bank account.

Jess picked up the phone to call Gemma, knowing she'd get the answering machine.

'Hi, gorgeous, how's the shearing going? Can you give me a call at lunchtime? Speak soon. Seeya!'

There wasn't much more Jess could do until Gemma called her back. Picking up her phone again she dialled Brad's number but she hung up before it began to ring. She really wanted to know why he'd been so rude to Gemma. Whenever she had talked to him about her friend during the time they had been together Brad had always seemed genuinely interested, encouraging her to share her concerns. But, she had to admit, he wasn't always so attentive. He'd been late for a few parties that Jess had held and more than once had had too much to drink and made a fool of himself. Not wanting to lose him, she hadn't said anything, but Saturday night was the final straw. Jess couldn't put up with someone who was so rude and self-obsessed. He hadn't rung to say sorry, and if he hadn't rung by now he wasn't likely to.

Stuff him, she thought, throwing her pen on the table. It was time to finish it with Brad. Picking up the phone before she could change her mind she rang Brad's mobile.

'Hi, babe, how's it going?' said Brad.

Jess was incredulous. How could he act normal after Saturday night and then not calling for three days?

'Hello,' Jess replied. 'How's things?'

'Pretty good. I'm heading out to Polkmans to check out their wheat crops for any disease. What are you up to?'

'I'm, uh . . .' Jess faltered. Had she imagined what had happened on Saturday night? Her resolve kicked in. In what she hoped was a steady voice she replied, 'I'm just ringing to say I don't think we should see each other anymore. I was appalled by your behaviour on Saturday night. You not only offended my friend – my *oldest* friend,' Jess emphasised, 'but you offended me as well. You made a fool out of yourself in front of Ben who, considering you work in the same industry, could be classed as your colleague. So that's it, Brad. Finished.' Taking a deep breath she waited to hear what he'd say. Silence. 'Brad?'

'Your loss, babe. Catch ya round,' and Jess was listening to dead air.

You've got to be kidding me! she thought. *How can a relationship of eight months be over just like that?* Jess stared at the table for a while, feeling a bit lost. But after a few moments she tossed her head. 'Well, stuff you, buddy. It's *your* loss not mine,' she said aloud. She started reading through Billbinya's financials for the past year, compiled by the accountant, and brushed away a tear.

Chapter 20

Dave and Craig were making plans to head out to Billbinya.

'We'll head off first thing in the morning,' Dave decided. There didn't seem to be much point in keeping Craig undercover since Ben had identified him at the sale yards.

'I'll ring Gemma today and tee it up with her. We might call in and see a couple of other families on the way. I've got some questions for Sam and Kylie Smith. They seem to have been to Billbinya more than anyone in the last year or so.'

Craig nodded, still smarting from yesterday's failure. Dave clapped him on the shoulder as he walked past, knowing his friend was feeling down.

'Don't worry, mate. You can still go to the sales; no one will know you in Adelaide. It will probably take time to filter through here as well.'

'Dave, you heard of Jess Rawlings?'

'Nup, should I have?'

'Maybe. Remember how I told you I saw Gemma Sinclair and a friend at the Jewel on Friday night?'

Dave nodded.

'Well, the friend was a girl called Jess Rawlings who lives here in Pirie.'

'Why don't you ask around about her? I don't know if she is going to make any difference to our inquiries though, do you?'

'I didn't think so at first, but the barmaid told me Jess works in a bank. I've been thinking about that. I don't know what her job is, but it might be worth finding out.'

'Yep, good thinking. Banking, hiding money ... yeah, definitely worth following up. What's she like?'

Craig was lost suddenly in the green eyes and stunning smile.

'Um, tall and skinny with red hair. Amazing green eyes.'

'Must have been up close and personal to check the eyes out, mate!' Dave joked. 'Good detective work.'

'Yeah, yeah.'

Dave was about to leave the room, but stopped at the door. 'Out of interest, let's do some more criminal checks. Let's check Adam and Gemma, the stockies – Ned Jones and Ben Daylee and they've got another partner in that office ... Bert Hawkins, I think? This Jess Rawlings and all of the interviewees. Let's see if we come up with something there.' He went into his office and picked up his phone. Dialling Billbinya's number he thought over what Craig had just told him. If Adam and Gemma had inside knowledge from a friend in banking, it would be easy to hide money that was coming in from stolen stock and bring it back into the system as legal money.

'Gemma, Dave Burrows here from the stock squad. It's, ah, Tuesday morning. My partner and I'd like to come out and see you tomorrow. If you don't get this message until after hours my hotel number is on the card I left with you the other day. We'll probably be out first thing in the morning.' Dave hung up, and sat staring at the phone blankly. It was amazing how little snippets of information could bring down a huge operation. Adam . . . large station . . . plane . . . Jess . . . banking . . . money. *There's got to be something there,* he thought. *We've just got to find it.*

Gemma watched in awe as the shearers flew through the sheep. Her dog Scoota sat quietly at her feet, watching intently in case a wether tried to make a getaway.

The shearers made hard work look so simple. Gemma's dad had told her once that a good shearer was one who made it look easy. Kenny hardly raised a sweat. He dragged a new sheep out from the catching pen and opened up the belly. Throwing it on the floor he then proceeded to the crutch and onto the side of the sheep, where the long blows started. One of the rousies, Paula, who was working the flat blade paddle, swept up the belly and threw it into a wool butt. Manoeuvring the paddle next to the sheep's rump, she expertly swept out the crutch and then went on to the next shearer.

Kenny's sheep hadn't moved out of position. He held it firmly between his legs, putting on small amounts of pressure when the sheep moved to let it know who was in charge. Jamie, one of the younger, less experienced shearers, found the big wethers hard work. They struggled and didn't like sitting on their rear. Whenever he accidentally loosened his grip, the wethers took full advantage, thumping their hind legs on the board and throwing their heads, ending up on their backs with Jamie swearing.

Lisa, the young blonde rousie whom the shearers had been teasing, swooped down on the fleece that had been left on the floor. She jiggled the wool around on the board until she found the legs, scooped it up in her arms and ran to the wool table. She flicked her wrists and the fleece flew up into the air, landing perfectly flat on the wool table, where Jackie skirted it quickly and decided which line it belonged in. The little pieces of wool that didn't stay attached to the fleece floated onto the floor like soft snowflakes. Paula scraped her paddle across the floor, sweeping up all the excess wool.

The radio was blaring and the engine that drove all the handpieces was humming loudly. Kenny bent over and said something to Jamie that Gemma couldn't hear, but all the shearers burst out laughing and Jamie, already red in the face from exertion, looked up and gave a mouthful of cheek back. Kenny laughed, clapped him on the back and went to grab another sheep.

Lisa danced across the board, in her short shorts that showed off her tanned legs, a tank top that left nothing to the imagination, and sandshoes. Her blonde ponytail was swinging to the rhythm of her body. She sang along to the radio, picking up fleeces, sweeping up locks and never standing still. The golden rule in the shed was never, ever stop to lean on the paddle.

Gemma watched the other members of the team – the third rousie, the presser and the penner-upperer. Those three were different from the rest. They were younger by quite a few years and had a sullen air about them. To Gemma they looked like unsavoury individuals, but she also knew it was hard to get people to work in shearing sheds and the rural industry full stop. It was hard, tiring work and it seemed that people were shying away from the industry. The money offered to shearers, farm employees and station managers didn't seem to be as good as the mines, and many young people were heading to where the big money was. Gemma supposed that Kenny couldn't be picky when it came to getting a team together. The important thing was, the shed seemed to be running like a well-oiled machine so Gemma, singing the words to one of her favourite songs that was on the radio, bounced outside to the yards. She went to the count-out pens to let the wethers out so she could back-line them. As they ran from the dimness under the shed they were suddenly blinded by the bright sunlight and stopped, piling up on top of one another until their eyes adjusted and they could see the open gate heading into the yards. Gemma's reaction was similar, her eyes responding to the iridescent whiteness of their bodies now the wool had gone. It made her blink a couple of times until her eyes adjusted to the brilliance of the skin.

'Push 'em, Scoota,' Gemma said. Her black kelpie ran forward and barked at the sheep. Turning, they ran in the direction of the open gate and piled in through it. 'Good boy. Siddown now.' Gemma closed the gate and pushed the sheep towards the race. Whistling to Scoota, she filled the backpack with chemical, hoisted it on her back and gave the instruction to 'pack 'em in'. The wethers, feeling energised without the wool on their backs, jumped and bucked as they ran into the race. They ran fast until they realised there was a gate at the end and tried to stop. The first three went crashing into the gate while the others ran into the backs of the sheep in front of them with a domino effect. Gemma shut the gate behind them and started walking along the race, squirting the bright blue liquid on their backs. When they were all done, she opened the front gate and let them into the big yard where they would wait for the rest of the mob, and started on the next lot of wethers.

Gemma made her way back to the homestead that night weary but happy. The sheep had cut about six kilos per head and the amount of wool they had baled for the first day was above her expectations. She'd been working out prices per kilo a bale in her head all day, knowing the amount she needed to achieve to make all the payments she had coming up, and so far she thought she might be above what she needed. How good it would be to actually have a bit left over after paying everything! Gemma felt a surge of optimism for the future. Going into the office, she listened to her messages, writing them all down so she wouldn't forget any phone calls she needed to return. Jess was the first one, Dave Burrows the next. Two from Patrick.

Gemma made her way to the bathroom and washed, then thought about some tea. While she was preparing everything she grabbed the cordless phone and started to return the calls, starting with Dave, who confirmed that he and his partner Craig would be out tomorrow to look over Billbinya, and she agreed to let them camp on the property for a couple of nights. She dialled Patrick at Hayelle.

'Hey, Pat, what's happening?' she asked when he picked up the phone.

'Ah, it's the sister. How're you going?'

'Shearing went brilliantly. I'm so excited. We cut about six kilos per head.'

'That's great.'

'How's everything in Adelaide?'

'Oh well, probably not the best. Dad's a bit down in the dumps, reckons he's gonna cark it any minute. Mum's scared he's going to and is watching him like a hawk, and Leisha is finding them all a bit hard to cope with. I think they'll sort it out over time but at the moment it's a bit hard.'

'Yeah, right. I guess it's natural to be a bit scared after a heart attack. Brings mortality to the front of your mind. Did they all dump on you? Are you coping okay?'

'Pleased to get out of the city,' Patrick conceded. 'Tell you what though, those two little girls are just great. If they don't bring a bit of sunshine to their grandparents, I don't know what will.'

Gemma smiled. She could imagine the chaos of two active kids, a fraught pregnant mother, a sick grandpa and an overwrought grandma.

'I bet they've grown since I saw them last. They were brilliant then. Do you want to come over tomorrow and stay for a bit?' Gemma tried to keep the hopefulness out of her voice.

'Nah, sis, I can't. Dad has given me a list of jobs as long as my arm. Don't know why, when he couldn't care less about the farm at the moment, but gotta do these things. Dutiful son and all that.'

'You wanting out, Pat? Ready to head north again?'

'Sometime soon I reckon. Need to get a bit of sun and see Kate. I'll hang in here a bit longer though and see what happens with Dad and how things shape up for you.'

'Well, Dave Burrows from the stock squad and his partner are coming out tomorrow for a look around. They're going to be camping on Billbinya for the next couple of days, so hopefully this mess will be sorted out by the end of the week and I'll be able to go to Adelaide and see Mum and Dad myself. And once everything's back to normal I can cope with Hayelle and Billbinya with the guys' help,' Gemma assured him, hoping it was true.

They said their goodbyes, and Gemma turned her attention to stirring the pot full of tinned spaghetti and turning the toast. She'd call Jess after she ate. Barely had she sat down at the table when the phone rang.

'Hello?'

'Hi, Gemma, it's Paige Nicholls here.'

'Hi, Paige,' Gemma said warmly. 'You were on my list to call tonight. Sorry I haven't called back; we've just started shearing so I've been a bit busy over the past few days. How've you been?'

'Oh, that's okay. I know you're busy. Yeah, I'm good. Busy with work and stuff. You know how it is.'

At Gemma's prompting, Paige told her a bit about what had led her into nursing.

'It's so fulfilling,' she enthused. 'You get to help people, and often when people are really sick and you're the one that makes them better, the gratitude is amazing. I love it.'

'That's great, Paige. I'm so happy that you found something that you love. Working is just a means to a pay packet for so many people; to really enjoy your work is such a bonus. I know when Adam died I found that work wasn't as much fun as it had been when he was alive. But it's getting better and I've just had the most brilliant day with shearing. It's so great to know that I've managed it all by myself and there haven't been any problems. That gives me a buzz!'

'Oh, of course it would. How are you managing with the workload since Adam . . . ?' Paige trailed off.

'Died? It's okay to say it, Paige. The workload's hard, of course, but I'm so lucky. I've got the two most fabulous stockmen who've been here since Adam's mum and dad ran the place. They've been so helpful since the accident. I ended up having to put another guy on just in the last couple of months. He seems okay with all the work I give him, he can handle it all, but I think he's a bit weird. Bit of a loner or something.'

'Well, I'm glad to hear everything's going okay. I've been thinking about you. I heard there were a few exciting things happening with stock out your way,' Paige said.

Gemma suddenly remembered that one of the things she'd never liked about Paige was her gossipy nature. She seemed to be one of those people who felt important and fulfilled if they knew everyone's business. Had this phone call been all about milking her for information so she could talk about it around town?

Gemma considered her next words carefully. 'Yeah, there has been a bit of excitement. Don't know much about it though. Think the police have been around asking questions, but I haven't come across them at all.'

'Well, that has to be good,' Paige answered. 'Okay, if you're shearing again tomorrow I'd better let you get some rest. Maybe next time you're in town we could have lunch?'

'Sounds good, Paige.' Gemma was suddenly desperate to get off the phone. 'Talk soon, okay? Bye.' Sighing, Gemma hung up the phone with a sense of relief. She picked at her now-cold dinner and finally pushed it away in disgust. Cold spaghetti on toast. Yuk.

Tucked up in bed with a hot chocolate, Gemma finally dialled Jess's phone number. The answering machine kicked in and Gemma felt a stab of disappointment. She'd really wanted to hear Jess's upbeat voice and laugh with her for a while. Leaving a message to say she'd called, she pressed the disconnect button. Maybe Ben would be home . . .

Chapter 21

Dave threw his swag up on the roof-rack next to Craig's. Roping them both down, he rechecked the oil and water while Craig loaded food supplies and investigative gear into the four-wheel drive.

Opening the stainless-steel chest full of equipment, Craig checked through it. 'Okay, we've got the video camera, sat phone, NLIS wand for scanning the tags if we need to, binocs, night-vision goggles . . . How long did you say we're goin' for?'

'Maybe two nights, depending on what we find.'

'Looks like we're goin' for bloody weeks.'

'I think our mobiles will work out there anyway; shouldn't really need the sat phone,' Dave conceded.

'Better to be prepared though, hey? Just in case we hit a black spot or something. Jeez, it's cold.' Craig rubbed his hands together and blew on them.

'Wait until we get out to Billbinya. You'll know

what cold is then. So, you right? Can I back into the trailer now?'

'Yep.' Craig directed Dave as he backed up to the trailer that held a quad bike in case they needed to muster any stock. After attaching it to the tow ball and hooking up the lights, he jumped in the passenger side. He adjusted the squelch on the CB radio and asked, 'Have you been listening to the CB as you've been driving?'

'Yeah, I haven't heard anything that indicates unusual stock movements. I've heard the truckies telling others that we're around, though, so it's common knowledge that we've arrived.'

As they drove towards Billbinya, Dave discussed the program he had in mind.

'I want to try and do a stocktake of all the animals that are on Billbinya. So we'll get Gemma's stock numbers and a map, work out what stock is in which paddock. We'll check out those animals. You can check the earmarks and I'll see if I can get a count of the mobs we come across. If we don't get it all done by tomorrow we'll stay another night. If we find anything untoward we'll ask to see the paperwork. Weigh bills, stock sale invoices. Gemma told me that Ned has done a full stock count for the 30 June figures, so they should be pretty up to date.'

'I reckon talking to Ned and Ben would be a good idea too,' Craig suggested. 'Theoretically, they should have copies of all the contracts to do with stock from the past few years, that way we can cross-reference it with Gemma's paperwork.'

'Yeah, that's true,' Dave said. 'That might be worth following up when we get back. You didn't find anything criminally interesting on any of the players, did you? Jess or Ned? I assume you would have said if you had.'

'Nah, nothing of interest; Ned's had a couple of DUIs, but that's about it. Do you think Gemma is involved?'

Dave thought for a while. 'You know, I'm not convinced she's guilty. I think there's enough information to indicate that Adam was somehow involved. Now whether he was the mastermind or just a participant, I'm not sure. There's no way he could have managed it all by himself. But having Gemma as the accomplice just doesn't sit right with me. I'm really not sure. I'm thinking we might have to go into their bank records and see if there is anything incriminating there, but we've not had any indication where – or even if – the animals have been sold, so that could be a dead end. I'd have thought that Ned would have told us if there had been stock sold through the Billbinya name that wasn't owned by Billbinya. Do you see where I'm going?'

Craig nodded. 'Absolutely, I agree. If they'd tried anything like that Ned would have spotted it. You know what I don't understand? In every other investigation I've been involved in, farmers aren't that happy about giving out too much information, yet this time it's been flowing very easily. I mean, let's start with the anonymous phone call. That gave us information on how the stock stealing is happening. Then you've gone to heaps of different farms, been welcomed with open arms and had information spewed at you. It's really weird.'

'Yeah, you're right. It's not the way it normally happens – but I think in this case, people are pissed off at having their stock nicked. Don't forget, this is their income you're talking about. Times are pretty tight so I guess no one wants to see their dollar notes walking out the front gate. It's pretty obvious that they are being taken and the alleged culprit is dead, so they don't think anyone will get hurt. Although,' Dave said as an afterthought, 'I'm not sure how they think Gemma is not being hurt somehow – innocent or otherwise.'

They drove in silence for a while, Craig thinking about Jess. She'd filled his head for the last few days and he was hoping to meet her again. She really was stunning ...

'You dreaming?' Dave asked.

'What?' Craig's mind cleared.

'What are you dreaming about?'

'Nothing much. Just wondering about Jess Rawlings and how she might fit into it all.'

'Is that right?' Dave gave his partner a knowing look.

'What?' Craig asked again.

'A word of warning. You remember what happened last time you fell for someone who was involved in an investigation? Turned out she was guilty, didn't it?

I know nothing happened between you, but, all the same, don't let your tool rule your head again, okay?'

Craig didn't answer. He hated to even think about that incident, let alone have it pointed out to him. He nodded slightly to let Dave know he'd heard, but turned to look out of the window, ending the conversation.

The dirt road kicked up a purplish-coloured dust and he looked at the low scrubby bushes that were the colour of kangaroos. The fences were old wire netting and looked like they had seen better times.

'Not surprising stock goes missing with these fences,' Craig said.

Dave nodded in agreement. 'I told you about coming back that night and the sheep being on the road, didn't I?' he asked.

Craig nodded, looked out the window again, and silence reigned.

Gemma's phone rang at 5.30 am, startling her from a deep sleep. Wondering who on earth could be ringing, she leapt from her bed, praying her dad was okay.

'Hello?'

'Morning, Gem.' It was Jess.

'Jess! What are you doing awake at this time of the morning?' Gemma asked, completely thrown.

'Needed to ask you a few questions and I knew that you'd be leaving early. How's the shearing going?'

'Yeah, really good,' said Gemma and proceeded to tell Jess all about the wool cut and her hope that there would even be some money left over after paying her debts.

Jess listened, toying with the pen and paper she had in front of her. 'Sounds great, Gem. Now listen, I have some questions about your financials – have you got time to answer them?'

'Yeah, go for it.'

'What time of the year do you make the payments to Adam's family?'

'Um, I think it's in September sometime, depending on when shearing is completed. We need to have time to sell the wool and work out what we've made before we can make the payments to them.'

'Okay. And was there a payment made last year?'

'Yeah, as far as I know. I'm sure they would have said something to us if they hadn't received it. Why?'

'Well, I've been looking through the bank statements and the monthly reports of expenditure and I can't see that there has been a payment of substance made. How do you make the payment? Cheque? Or do you give them some of the wool to sell in their own name? That would explain why I can't find a large payment.' Jess waited, hoping that was the case.

Gemma answered slowly. 'As far as I know the payment came directly out of the bank account. It was set up so that Adam would authorise the payment when we knew how much we had made.

If prices were good, we would pay more than the agreed amount of fifty thousand a year, but if the wool was down, we were able to drop it to twenty thou.' Gemma played with the phone cord and waited for Jess to deliver what she assumed was going to be bad news.

'Okay.' Gemma could almost hear Jess thinking. 'Look, Gem, I'm certain that there hasn't been anything near those amounts coming out of the Billbinya account for at least two years . . .'

'Two years?' Gemma screeched. 'You're joking. Ian and Joan wouldn't have let Adam get away with not paying for two years.'

'No, the payments have been made. I've been through the financials that you gave me and the payments have definitely been made and the debt reduced. I'm wondering if there's another bank account, or shares, or some sort of investment that Adam could have been making the payments from?'

'Not that I know about,' Gemma stated firmly.

'Okay, well maybe that needs a bit more research. The payments have been around the sixty k mark over the past two years. That's a lot of money to be made just from wool. Gem, I know you're not going to like this, but he must have been getting the money from somewhere else. It just isn't coming out of the Billbinya bank account and there is insufficient money going through that account to make those kinds of payments. In fact, I'm not sure how the hell you're managing to survive. It's a lot worse than you've ever told me. And how you're going to be able to convince the bank to lend you more money next year, unless you have a great wool clip, I don't know.'

'Jess, don't take that banking tone of voice with me,' Gemma interrupted. 'I *know* how bad things are, okay? I live it every day. But the wool clip is going to be good. Didn't you listen to what I said at the beginning of the call?'

'Sorry, lovely, I'm used to being stern with the clients! But seriously, you're going to be in the shit if you don't make some changes. I've got some ideas about making extra income that I'd really like to talk to you about when I come out later in the week. Okay?'

'I'm always open to ideas, you know that.'

'Good. Now, going back to these payments. Steel yourself, because you ain't gonna like this one bit. I think that Adam must have been getting money through this stock-stealing business. We do know he was involved somehow. We found the phone to prove it.'

Gemma grimaced. To say yes now meant actually admitting that she thought her husband was guilty. She remembered the text messages and knew that really there wasn't any doubt, no matter how much she wanted there to be.

'Gem?' prompted Jess.

'Yeah, okay,' Gemma sighed. 'Yes, I think you're right.'

'I wish I could give you a hug, lovely,' Jess said, her voice full of compassion. 'I'm sorry to do this to you over the phone, but it has to get sorted. I need this info before I leave town.'

'Don't worry, I'll be fine. I'll be so busy I won't have time to think after I get off the phone from you,' Gemma said weakly.

'Can you think of anywhere Adam would have hidden information? Would he have kept the documents to say he'd made the payments or would he have destroyed them?'

'Oh, he'd have kept everything,' Gemma said in a sure voice. 'I have never known anyone to keep things like he did. But, Jess, I've been through the house thoroughly looking for something – I just don't know what. I thought I knew everything about Adam. Then there were these discrepancies with stock numbers, followed by Ned telling me about this contract for cattle I don't know how to fill, and now the stock squad are involved and they're coming back out here today. Everything I thought I knew about my husband has turned out to be lies. I don't know anything anymore. I mean, the phone confirms Adam was involved, but I can't help wanting to defend him – I still love him. He was my husband for nine years!'

'I know, Gem, I know,' Jess's voice was quiet. 'But forget about Adam for the moment – what's concerning me is that the stock squad thinks you're involved somehow. Having those wethers on Billbinya has really put you in the spotlight. We need to clear your name. That's what you have to focus on, okay? So to do that, we need to find these papers. Think, Gem, where else could he have put them?'

'Well,' Gemma said slowly, 'the plane would have been the obvious place, I guess. He was the only one who ever flew in it. I don't like small planes. But there wasn't anything found that I know of. They gave me back some of his things that weren't destroyed, but there weren't papers among them. I really don't know where they could be, Jess. I'll have to think about it and have a look around.'

'Okay, sounds like a plan. Now, you said the stock squad are coming out today, that right?'

'Yep, Dave rang yesterday and said he wanted to have a look around, check out the lay of the land.'

'Don't give them the phone, Gem. We need to get more evidence against Adam before we talk to them. Every time you see them remember that they probably think you're a suspect. Don't tell them anything.'

'Jess, are you sure that's really necessary? You seem to forget I haven't done anything wrong. The facts will speak for themselves.'

'Gem, listen to me. The fact that those payments have been made to your in-laws implicates you. It's going to be obvious to anyone who looks at your books that Billbinya is under financial strain. Adam took steps to ensure he didn't lose the farm to the bank. There is nothing to say that you didn't know anything about this. There is heaps of circumstantial evidence implying that you knew exactly what was going on. I mean, I'm not trying to be cruel, Gem, but most farmers' wives would have known that the payments hadn't come out of the operating business's account. It's just that Adam liked to do all the books himself so you didn't see the discrepancies. You trusted him and signed anything he put in front of you. You could be in serious trouble.'

Gemma felt the floor reel under her. How could she be in so much trouble when she hadn't done anything wrong?

'Okay,' Gemma managed. 'I think I need to go now. It's nearly time for me to be over in the shed.'

'Gem, I'm only telling you so you understand.'

'I know, Jess. Thanks.'

'Where's Adam's phone now?' asked Jess quickly, before Gemma could hang up on her.

'In the suit that it was found in.'

'Keep it safe, okay? When we know which way the stock squad are going to go, we'll either give it to them or take it to a lawyer.'

'You've thought a lot about this, haven't you?'

'It's all I've thought about since I started looking at the books. Now listen, I think I should talk to your accountant, see if I can track down this money that Adam seems to have been paying his parents with. I need your authorisation to do that. Is that all right with you?'

'Yep, that's fine. It's Rodney Woods in Adelaide. Do you know him?' Gemma asked.

'No I don't. Can you fax through a letter explaining

the circumstances and tell him I will be in touch today?'

'Yeah.'

'Okay, lovely, hope shearing goes well today. Take care,' Jess said and she was gone.

Gemma hung up the phone in a daze. Hiding places. Gemma looked around the kitchen, hoping to spot something she hadn't seen in her nine years of living there. Dropping the phone she ran from room to room, looking for something she hadn't noticed before. A hidey-hole, a hidden compartment in a chest of drawers. She pulled all of the drawers out of her dressing table and upended them, leaving a trail of clothes behind. She checked underneath every piece of furniture, looking for papers taped to the bottom and behind the pictures on the walls. Nothing. What about the bathroom? Nothing. There wasn't a cellar. There wasn't an attic. Old houses were supposed to have those things. Maybe this one did and she didn't know. With rising panic she crawled along the floor of the corridor, pulling at the edges of the carpet to see if it came up easily. It didn't. Moving into the lounge room she looked around wildly. Ah, the manhole into the ceiling. Maybe there was something up there. Racing outside to the laundry, she grabbed the ladder and hauled it back inside. Just as she was propping it up against the wall, there was a knock on the door. Panicking, she jumped and the ladder clattered to the floor. She straightened up and tried to control her breathing. The knocking sounded again.

'Coming,' she yelled. What on earth was the time? Was she late for shearing? Amazed, she realised it was only six fifteen. Shaking her head to clear it, she went into the kitchen and opened the door. It was the shearers' cook.

'Good morning, Helen,' Gemma said, trying to appear normal. 'How are you? Things okay?'

'Morning, Gemma. Actually I've run out of milk, have you any powdered stuff?'

'Yeah, I have. Come in and I'll grab it for you.' Rummaging in her pantry she found the tin and handed it to Helen. 'Do you want me to get some fresh stuff out today?'

'Nah, you're right. I just forgot to get enough out of the freezer last night and get it defrosted in time for brekkie. I'll give you my list on Friday for next week.'

The bluntness and practicality of the cook settled Gemma and enabled her to focus on the day. Realising she was still in her pyjamas she said, 'Well I guess I'd better get on. Running a bit late this morning.'

'Yeah, me too – the fellas will be looking for their brekkie. Thanks for this.' She held up the tin. 'Catch ya later.'

'Seeya,' Gemma replied. Going back into the lounge room, she lifted up the ladder and leaned it against the wall. It would have to wait until evening. She needed to get to the shearing.

Chapter 22

Gemma was in the yards, back-lining the wethers, when she saw a plume of dust coming up the drive. Watching nervously, expecting it to be Dave Burrows and his partner, she was relieved to see Ben's car. With everything that had happened that morning, she'd forgotten he was coming today with the wool buyer to inspect the wool. She met them at the steps of the shearing shed and led the way inside, hugging to herself the smile that Ben had bestowed on her. He'd been pleased to see her, and she him. Their phone call a few nights ago had been a welcome distraction.

Watching the shearers peel the wool from her sheep, she felt that surge of optimism again. There was going to be good wool and lots of it. Even Jackie the classer had told her it was some of the best wool she'd classed in this area this year. The wool buyer looked over all the bins. He took out samples, looked at their length, measured them against his finger and then moved on to the next bin. He stopped to speak with Jackie, who showed him the wool and specification books that detailed what the wool was like, how many bales had already been put out and at what weights.

Ben took Gemma aside. 'How're you going?' he asked, with such concern in his voice that Gemma almost cried.

'Terrible,' she answered honestly. 'Jess rang this morning with some bad news about the books. Hopefully she's coming out in the next couple of days and we'll go through a few more things then. Dave and his partner from the stock squad are coming out today to have a look over Billbinya and camp for a couple of nights.'

'Has Jess sorted things out with Brad?'

Gemma looked aghast as she said, 'You know, I forgot to ask. Oh, I'm such a bad friend at the moment. Completely wrapped up in my own problems. How thoughtless of me.'

Ben put his hand on her arm. 'Don't worry. Jess is perfectly able to cope with that incident herself. In fact, I'm really pleased that Brad was the subject of her wrath, not me!' He smiled encouragingly at her but left his hand on her arm. Gemma glanced around the shed to see if anyone had noticed the contact and moved closer for a moment, relishing the feeling of comfort and security, before gently removing herself from his hold.

'Looks like you've got company,' Ben said, gesturing towards the door. Dave stood there, waiting to be noticed. Behind him stood another man who must have been his partner.

'I'll be back in a minute,' Gemma said, looking at the pair apprehensively.

'Want me to come with you?' asked Ben. Gemma hesitated, tempted by his offer of support, then squared her shoulders and shook her head.

'I'll be right,' she said, and headed over to greet the men.

After introducing her to Craig, Dave explained, 'I want to go into each of your paddocks and see if your stock figures tally with what's there. We're going to have a look at the earmarks, do a rough count. If we find anything that's a bit off, we take photos, videos and so forth. The other thing that you need to be aware of is that in the unlikely event we do find some stolen animals on Billbinya, we will need to access your weigh bill books, stock sale invoices and financials.'

'Yep, that's fine. What's the motorbike for?'

'If we find some stock that we don't believe belong here, we muster the paddock and bring them into the yards. Depending on what we find with them – you know, if you tell us you've bought them, then we will need to see proof: a signed contract or something like that, or if they aren't yours then we will impound them and return them to their rightful owners.'

Gemma nodded then turned towards the yards. 'Hey, Bulla?' she yelled. When the older man raised his head she motioned for him to come over. 'I'll get Bulla to give you all the details. I have the wool buyer in the shed and I need to talk to him.' Turning to her stockman, Gemma said, 'Bulla, would you mind getting a map of Billbinya and making a list of which stock are in what paddock? Let Dave and Craig know how many are in each mob and answer any of their questions. They're going to do a run around and see if anything is amiss. Oh and you better tell them where Jack is getting the sheep in from so they don't get a fright if the sheep aren't in a particular paddock or they run into him somewhere in their travels. Okay?'

'Yeah, no problems,' said Bulla.

Gemma turned back to Dave and Craig. 'If you've got any problems, talk to Bulla. I'll be a bit freer this afternoon if you want to come back and talk to me then.'

'Okay,' said Dave. 'Thanks for your help. See you later.' Craig nodded and Gemma left for the safety of the shearing shed, wondering where she had seen Craig before. The men followed Bulla over to the machinery shed to get the required information.

Craig and Dave watched as Bulla noted all the stock movement and numbers in slow, deliberate handwriting. Looking up, Craig saw Ben, the wool buyer and Gemma coming out of the shed.

'Be back in a tick,' he said.

He walked to within thirty metres of the group,

hoping to catch Ben's eye. When Ben saw him he muttered his excuses and walked over.

'How's it going?' asked Craig.

'G'day mate. You don't look so undercover now.'

Craig grinned ruefully. 'Nah, that went by the board when you made me. Had to tell the boss.' He nodded towards Dave, who was now reading a sheet of paper and asking questions of both Bulla and Garry, who had materialised from the depths of the machinery shed, holding a spanner in his hand. 'We're camping out for a couple of nights, but I was wondering if I could catch up with you when we get back to town?'

'Sure. Want to have a beer?' Ben asked.

'Yeah, sounds good. I might have to tackle you on some stock sale invoices and contracts, if that's okay.'

Ben nodded regretfully. He'd known he'd be interviewed, but he was hoping to avoid handing over those sorts of documents. If he thought for one second Gemma was involved in stock stealing he'd have handed her to the police on a platter. But he'd seen her face when Ned had told her about the contract and about the extra stock numbers. There was no way she could have faked that shock. No, he was positive she was innocent.

Jess looked up Rodney Woods' phone number in the book, picked up her phone and dialled.

'Rodney Woods and Associates,' answered a crisp voice.

'Good morning,' answered Jess, in her most professional tone. 'This is Jessica Rawlings calling for Rodney Woods.'

'One moment and I'll transfer you.'

Tick, tick, tick.

'Rodney Woods,' a voice growled down the phone.

'Jessica Rawlings here, Rodney,' Jess began. 'I'm calling on behalf of Gemma Sinclair. I'm her auditor and I have her authorisation to ask you some questions.'

'I'm unaware of any authorisation.'

'Gemma is busy shearing and she's assured me that she'll fax you as soon as possible. I'd like to talk to you about payments made to Ian and Joan Sinclair for the purchase of Billbinya Station.'

'I won't answer anything until I have heard from Gemma,' Rodney stated.

'I understand that. Perhaps I could tell you what information I require? Then, once you have received Gemma's fax, maybe you would consider calling me back with the information?' Jess's voice dripped with sweetness.

'I'd rather wait until I have the fax,' the accountant said stubbornly. 'Now I have a question for you. Why does Gemma Sinclair require an auditor?'

'I'm afraid I can't answer that question at this stage, Rodney, but I'd be happy to talk to you properly once the information is available.'

Silence.

'Touché, Ms Rawlings. What information do you require?'

'There have been payments made in September of the last two years to Ian and Joan Sinclair towards the acquisition of Billbinya Station. I have sent a fax with the dates of these transactions to you. The problem is, I'm having trouble tracing where this money has come from.'

'Ah,' Rodney said, his tone full of meaning. 'Could you perhaps give me a brief rundown on why you need this information?'

'Gemma has requested that I look through Billbinya's books, and I'm having trouble accounting for these payments.'

'Your number, Ms Rawlings?'

Jess recited her home phone number, thanked the accountant for his time and then hung up. 'Pompous prick,' she muttered under her breath. Well, there was nothing to do now but wait and hope Gemma remembered to fax the letter of authorisation through at lunchtime.

Dave and Craig headed to the northern part of Billbinya, Craig studying the map while Dave drove. They followed a two-wheeled bush track that weaved its way through cassia trees and creeks, then opened out onto wide empty paddocks. The green grass covering the stony red ground was about two inches high. Dave knew that this was harsh country, even though it was productive. Temperatures in summer soared above the forty-five-degree mark and plunged to frosty minus ones and twos during winter.

The barley and spear grass waved gently in the breeze as Dave pulled up at a windmill, tank and trough. Looking around near the trough Dave could see fresh sheep tracks. One thing he'd learned during his time with the stock squad was how to track animals. The department had employed an Aboriginal tracker who taught all the detectives. Getting out of the car, he surveyed the land. Today the sun shone brightly and made the sky seem a vivid blue that was rarely seen in the cities. Against the ruggedness of the hill range that went through the top part of Billbinya, it seemed like a timeless land.

'Looking at these tracks I'd say the sheep have already been in for their morning drink,' Dave commented. 'It's not that hot, so they may not come back in again tonight. Maybe if we head over towards that creek line, they might be camped up in some shade.'

'Windmill looks like it's working pretty well and the trough is clean. I'd say someone has been by recently to clean it out,' Craig observed.

'Garry does all the maintenance on the bores and machinery, apparently. Geez, I reckon you could have a disaster out here in summer if things weren't maintained. Stock running out of water and so forth.' Dave shuddered at the thought of thirsty animals hanging around empty troughs in forty-degree heat.

'I think Jack is the lackey who cleans out the troughs, does boundary fence runs and all that sort of general work. Bulla seems to be the head stockman and the other two lend a hand with the stock when it's needed.' Dave lifted his binoculars to his eyes and surveyed the gum-tree-lined creek. 'Can't make any sheep out over there, but we'll go and have a look.' They climbed back into the car and Dave eased it into gear. Craig took control of the binoculars, scrutinising every inch of the landscape.

'Hey, look over at eleven o'clock, Dave. Looks like there's an old building that's been let go to ruin. Want to have a look?'

Dave swung the car towards the ruins.

'Look at those stones. They're huge.' Dave shook his head. 'I don't know how the early settlers tamed this land.'

The men walked around the ruined house marvelling at the way it had been built. The pug looked like it had been made with mud, clay and water, without a setting agent. The sheep were making themselves at home around the ruins, Dave observed, looking at the sheep manure that was dotted through the two rooms.

Walking over to the creek Dave looked up at the towering red gums. They must have been hundreds of years old. The galahs on the branches were squawking to each other, and Dave could hear sheep bleating in the distance. Turning to locate the sound, he saw a mob of sheep walking down the creek towards them. He quietly made his way back to the ruins, where Craig was still poking about, and settled himself behind a crumbling wall. Motioning to Craig, he put the binoculars to his eyes and watched. Craig sat beside him with his own pair trained on the sheep. Quietly, one by one, the sheep followed a well-worn path at the edge of the creek, unaware of the watching men. Some of the lambs ran ahead and some stayed with their mothers. Some ewes followed nose to tail with the one in front and others seemed to be more individual and strayed off the path, but not by far. They walked quietly except for the occasional bleat of the mums to ask where their lambs were. Dave couldn't believe how easy it was to count them. Two, four, eight, ten, fifteen. As the tail of the mob sauntered past, Craig said, 'What the bloody hell is five hundred and thirteen plus eighteen?'

Dave grinned as he stood up. 'Well at least I know you got the same count as me. Five thirty-one. All the earmarks on the ewes match as Billbinya's earmark, same with the lambs, and the numbers match what Bulla has given us. No problems in this paddock.'

'Dave, have a look at this.' Craig pointed to a cigarette butt. 'Looks like someone else has been here recently too ...'

Dave squatted down and looked at the butt, then looked around, trying to ascertain where it could have come from. 'Probably nothing – one of the stockmen. Let's poke around a bit more and see what we find . . .' He stopped as Craig indicated a half bottle of rum stashed in a hollow mound of rocks. 'Interesting,' he said with raised eyebrows.

Chapter 23

Jack saw the police officers before they saw him. They were sitting around a fire eating big steak sandwiches. Jack had a choice. He could pretend he hadn't seen them and push his mob further to the west, or he could introduce himself. Probably time for introductions, he thought. He'd be able to get away with not staying long since he was shifting a mob of sheep. Leaving the animals he rode towards the men.

'We seem to be in the right places at the right times,' said Craig.

Jack pulled up and took off his helmet. 'G'day, I'm Jack Marshall,' he said. 'I guess you're the fellas Gemma told us about checkin' out the stock.' He stayed astride his bike, not offering his hand. The other two men stayed sitting as well, their hands full of food.

'G'day. Yeah, Dave Burrows and Craig Buchanan from the stock squad. Shifting a few sheep?' Dave nodded towards the grazing animals.

'Yep, on their way back to Reimer's paddock. These fellas are hungry and lookin' for their paddock. Prob'ly should get 'em there. Catch ya anon.' Jack nodded to the men and put his helmet on.

'A mob of yellow tags haven't long headed down the creek line,' called Craig as Jack started the bike. Jack waved his hand to show he'd heard and rode back to his sheep, knowing their eyes were still on him.

It was nearly five o'clock and Jess was pacing the kitchen floor when the phone rang.

She snatched it up. 'Jess Rawlings.'

'Ah, Ms Rawlings. Rodney Woods here. I've received the authorisation from Gemma Sinclair and I have files containing the information you requested here in front of me. If you would like to ask your questions, I'll do my best to answer them.'

'No problem, Rodney. I think I should explain the situation. Since you're situated in Adelaide, you may not have heard that there have been allegations made that Adam Sinclair was involved in stock stealing –'

'Absolutely preposterous,' Rodney broke in. 'That man was as honest as the day is long.'

Jess raised her eyebrows. 'Well, actually, there does seem to be some evidence to the contrary. However, that isn't the main issue since Adam has passed away.

It seems that there are some inconsistencies in the payments to his parents. The payments were coming from the Billbinya operating account until the last two years. It seems that since then, the payments to Ian and Joan Sinclair have still been made, but not from the business operating account. My hypothesis is that Adam became involved in stock stealing due to financial hardship. He had to find a way to make the payments and, somehow, this opportunity presented itself. He then was paid for his services, the money was put in a separate account and the payments to his parents were made from that. I need to know how these payments were made and from where, so if Gemma comes under investigation – and it appears the police do suspect her of some involvement – we are armed with all the relevant information. This is why Gemma requested my audit.'

There was a long silence as Rodney Woods digested this information.

'I'm shocked,' the accountant said finally. 'I thought Adam was a sterling young man. So much vim and vigour. As for forward thinking, he had an exceptional knack for predicting things in the stock industry. However . . .' Rodney cleared his throat and Jess could almost hear him straightening his tie and shifting in his seat ready to deliver his findings. 'Um, yes, however, I do believe there are bank records not accounted for and I do know that the payments to Ian and Joan were coming out of this particular account.'

Jess felt like dancing, but held her breath. Surely it couldn't be this easy.

Rodney cleared his throat again. 'I'm sure you're aware that, as an accountant, I would make notes of bank account details, share reference numbers and the like. When Adam visited me two years ago to tell me he'd been bequeathed a large amount of money, I made a note of the bank the account was held at and the amount of money deposited there, however I neglected to record the account number. I have since regretted not having this detail.'

'Hang on a sec,' Jess interrupted. 'Are you telling me that Adam received a large amount of money through an inheritance and he's been using this money to make the payments to Ian and Joan?'

'That's correct. And because it was an inheritance – and therefore tax free – it wasn't necessary for me to see the statements, hence I didn't pursue further details. I asked about accruing interest and he told me he wouldn't receive any interest on the money for four years as it was tied up in an investment scheme. I asked to see the paperwork regarding this peculiar investment, however he failed to produce any documents.' The accountant sighed. 'As much as I'm having trouble believing that Adam was involved in something illegal, your hypothesis could very well be correct given the lack of information I have regarding this particular bank account.'

Jess had been writing furiously on her pad while

Rodney was talking. Before she could say anything, Rodney spoke again.

'Miss Rawlings, I have a great deal of respect and admiration for Mrs Sinclair and what she is trying to achieve. I'd be very uncomfortable if she was having problems such as you've described.'

Jess felt herself softening. He did have a heart, it seemed. 'Thank you for the information and your candidness. I'll start some research and question Gemma about this alleged inheritance. I may need to speak to you again. Would that be okay?'

'You're more than welcome to call me at any time.'

Jess hung up the phone absently, her mind whirling. Well, that was a bombshell. Looking at her watch, Jess decided it was too late to go to Billbinya tonight, but probably too early for Gemma to be in the house. *I'll leave a message*, she thought.

To Jess's surprise, Gemma picked up the phone on the second ring.

'Hi, Gem,' Jess said. 'What are you doing in already? I thought you'd be slaving away in the sheep yards.'

'Jess!' Gemma sounded pleased. 'How's things?'

'I've spoken to Rodney. Now tell me, what'd he do? Swallow a dictionary?'

Gemma let out a peal of laughter. 'And so posh sounding, hey? We inherited him from Ian and Joan. Not sure where they picked him up from, but he advised us on the best way to succession plan so we just kept using him when Adam and I took over Billbinya. It saved having to explain everything from scratch to a new accountant. He is actually a tremendously nice guy. Very gentlemanly and all that. Did he have anything interesting to say?'

'Well, once I could understand him, yes, he had some extremely interesting information. Has Adam received an enormous inheritance from some rich old relative in the last couple of years?'

'What? Don't be stupid.' Gemma laughed at the notion. Then she stopped. 'Why?' she asked.

'Well, I was right. There is another bank account that we haven't got access to. Adam explained it to Rodney by saying that he'd been the beneficiary of a large inheritance. He was using the money to make the payments to his parents.'

'Well, he hasn't received any inheritance that I know about. Although, I'm not sure I'm the right one to ask, since I don't seem to know him as well as I thought,' Gemma said bitterly.

'I think he's been putting the money from the stock stealing into that account and using it to pay his parents that way.'

Gemma said, 'Well, that's all very interesting, but I doubt there was ever an inheritance, so I guess that means we're back to finding the source of this other income – which seems to be pretty obvious, I guess.'

'Yeah,' Jess said.

There was silence until Gemma said, 'I suppose I'd better go and shed up tomorrow's sheep. Had a really big dew here this morning so it was a good thing we'd put the sheep undercover overnight. Can't shear wet sheep and all that.'

'I was going to come out tonight, but I think I'd like to try and track down this other bank account. It's at the Inland Development Bank. You don't happen to have seen a statement from them?' Jess asked.

'Pretty sure I haven't. We've never banked with them at all that I know of.'

'Righto, I'll get onto it tomorrow. Too late to do anything about it now.'

'Hey, Jess, did you sort out that man of yours?' Gemma asked tentatively.

'I got him sorted all right. Gave him the flick.'

'Oh, Jess. I hope you didn't do that because of me.'

'Nah, time for a change anyway. Can't have fellas bagging my mates. Plus he had begun to annoy me. Just little things, you know? Like not turning up at the Jewel the other night. Or he'd turn up at a party three hours late and stuff like that. So Saturday night was just the final straw. Nah, stuff him. Don't like tardiness. I gave it to him over the phone on Monday.'

'You did it over the phone? Jess, that's so heartless.'

'It didn't seem to bother him. Anyway, I'd better get going. I'll talk to you tomorrow. Seeya.'

Jess hung up before she revealed how hurt she had been by Brad's casual dismissal. Gemma had enough to worry about without feeling like she had to comfort Jess.

* * *

226

Dave and Craig had set up camp for the night. They had made it through five other paddocks and none seemed to have any problems. The stock looked happy and healthy and all had the same ear mark. Dave was stretched out on his swag with a beer in his hand looking at the stars. Craig held a beer in one hand and with the other poked at the fire with a stick. The flames warmed his face as he stared into them. Shaking himself, he jumped up. 'Off to see a man about a dog,' he said.

Away from the fire, the night was pitch-black. No moon tonight. Craig had to walk cautiously through a landscape he didn't know well. He relieved himself, zipped up his strides and stood silently listening to the sounds of darkness. A mopoke call and the bark of a fox. Some cattle bellowed in the distance, but the sound stopped as suddenly as it had started. He was just about to turn and go back to the camp when a new sound caught his attention. Craig listened carefully until he was sure of what he'd heard. Looking around, he saw no sign of any lights or movement. Heading quickly back to camp he couldn't contain his excitement.

'Dave. Hey, Dave. Get off your arse and come and listen to this,' Craig whispered hoarsely.

'What's the matter?' Dave said sleepily.

'Come on!'

'All right, all right.' Dave stood up, grabbed the torch that was next to his swag, and followed Craig into the darkness.

About fifty metres from where they camped, Craig stopped, stood still and listened hard.

'Can't hear anything,' Dave complained. 'You're joshin' with me.'

'I'm not. Shut up and listen.' They stood quietly for a full five minutes and then they both heard it. Dogs. Barking. Dave and Craig were camped too far away from the Billbinya homestead and Bulla and Garry's house to hear the dogs from either place. According to the map, this was the most isolated part of the property.

'Okay, let's have a look.' Dave's tone was urgent now. 'I think they are only a few k away by the sounds. Might be a bit further, noises can carry a lot further, especially when it's cold and clear like it is tonight. Can you dig out the night-vision goggles and evidence kit? And make sure you grab the GPS unit so we don't get lost. I'll get the camera. Got your gun?'

They grabbed their tools, made sure the fire was safe and walked out into the night. Pulling the night-vision goggles on, they made their way swiftly through the open paddocks and into a creek bed, following the sound. Every so often they had to stop and listen. The dogs didn't bark all the time. Craig stumbled, fell and swore as he grazed his knee.

'Shh,' grumbled Dave. After about fifteen minutes of solid walking, the barking was closer. Dave held up his hand to signal a stop and they waited. The barking seemed to be only a few hundred metres away. Looking around, Craig could see a patch of thick bush nestled into a gully coming down off a hill, near the creek they had followed. He motioned towards it.

After careful surveillance, Dave said, 'I don't think there's any stock stealing going on here. I wouldn't think you could get stock through bush that thick. So it's either wild dogs or someone is keeping dogs in there. Go steady and cover me.'

They walked quietly into the bush, their guns pointed towards the sky. Craig kept glancing behind and around them then back to Dave. Dave suddenly crouched down and Craig followed suit. Looking over Dave's shoulder, Craig saw a man-made clearing. Two dogs sat in a roughly made yard, surrounded by sheep yard panels, coils of wire and a bundle of steel posts. This was someone's stock-stealing kit. Craig breathed deeply, his heart pumping.

One of the dogs lunged towards Dave as they caught the smell of the two men and then both brindle-coloured dogs started a frenzied bark that echoed through the silent night.

'Shit,' swore Dave. He took a couple of deep breaths, then raised the camera again, motioning for Craig to video the scene. They moved slowly around the site, keeping well clear of the dogs. Seeing a cigarette butt, Dave gloved his hands, reached into his back pocket and found an evidence bag. From his other pocket he pulled out a pair of tweezers and picked up the butt. Behind the dog run there was a half-empty bottle of rum. Dave held it up for the video camera. Craig zoomed in on it while Dave fossicked in one of his many pockets for a ruler. Placing the bottle on the ground he held the ruler up against the bottle so they could see the size. 'Want to fingerprint it?' Craig whispered. Dave shook his head.

After about five minutes of videoing they began to back out slowly. The dogs were still barking and Dave was keen to get out of the area before their owner turned up. One thing he was certain of: whoever owned these ferocious dogs didn't camp here. There wasn't any sign of a swag, fire or cooking equipment. It really looked like the dogs fended for themselves and someone came by every so often to feed them.

'Want to try and take the dogs?' Craig whispered after they were out in the open again.

'No bloody way! They're vicious those things. Nup. We'll go back to camp and leave the scene the way it is at the moment. I don't want to alert whoever owns those dogs that they've been found. When we go in, the Pirie boys will have to bring a dog handler with them and they can check for fingerprints then. C'mon, let's get back to base camp.'

'Wait, Dave, I've got an idea. Why don't we watch the area? Let me do some surveillance on it tomorrow to see if anyone rocks up to feed the dogs.'

'You know, you might have something there. We've got the video and photos, so if there is some sort of stuff-up, at least we've got visual evidence.

Yeah, let me sleep on it and we'll make a final call in the morning. How's that?'

'No worries.' Craig was happy as they followed the GPS signal back to camp. He loved this part of the job.

Chapter 24

Gemma opened her eyes sleepily and looked at her clock. It was 5 am. Man, she was tired. Shearing was always exhausting and combined with everything else that was going on she could barely keep her eyes open by the end of the day. She'd cleaned up the mess she'd made in her frantic search when she'd returned home after shearing yesterday, and had decided to get up early to try the ceiling.

Heaving herself out of bed, she quickly dressed and headed for the kitchen. After a hit of caffeine she went to the lounge room.

Taking a deep breath she climbed the ladder to the manhole, clutching a torch in one hand. She pushed at the manhole cover. Stuck. She pushed again and it moved, releasing a pile of dust onto her hair. She climbed to the topmost rung of the ladder and peered into the darkness. Her torch lit up spider webs and dust. It didn't look like anyone had been here for years. Gemma climbed down, blinking back tears of frustration. Another dead end.

Dave had decided to go with Craig's surveillance plan, so early morning found Craig camped under a river red gum about a hundred metres away from the clearing, with food, a two-way radio, a camera with a zoom lens, and a video camera. In the pockets of his overalls he also had an evidence kit.

Craig looked around carefully, then stood up and stretched. It was time to go stake out the clearing.

Craig moved slowly out of his hiding spot and made his way towards an outcrop of bush. On the other side of a stand of cassia trees and black oaks he found a sheep track. The path looked well worn and Craig surmised that either sheep walked through here quite often or whoever was feeding the dogs came in this way, not breaking through the scrub like he and Dave had the night before. Ducking under branches he followed the path until he came to the clearing. He was grateful for the breeze blowing his scent away from the dogs who slept on, seemingly unaware of his presence.

Craig scanned the area for a hiding place. Seeing a clump of saltbush plants off the track, he moved behind the thick vegetation. Satisfied he was now well hidden from all angles, he got out his camera and waited.

Sometime later Craig jerked awake. Shit. He looked at his watch. Midday. He saw the dogs were now sitting up to attention, their ears cocked as though they were listening. Straining his ears, Craig wished his hearing was as good as theirs. At last he thought he heard the growl of a motorbike. He clicked his radio button twice, paused, and then clicked twice again, signalling to Dave that the job was on. Hardly daring to breathe in case the dogs heard, Craig picked up his camera and held it ready, hoping to get photos of the whole encounter.

The motorbike roared closer and the dogs began to bark in welcome. 'Shuddup, ya mongrels.'

Craig's heart pounded at the voice. It was Jack Marshall.

'How many bloody times have I told ya to shuddup,' he snapped. As Jack came into view, Craig started clicking madly, hoping desperately that Jack wouldn't let the dogs off for a quick run. He had a cigarette in his mouth and was carrying a white garbage bag that looked like it was leaking blood. Ducking under a branch, he passed Craig's hiding spot. The dogs were straining at their chains, whining in anticipation.

'What's goin' on?' He put the bag down and bestowed a whack that was supposed to be a pat on each head. Jack opened the bag and took out two hind legs from a sheep, still covered in wool. Craig zoomed in. Maybe he was killing Billbinya's sheep for dog tucker as well as stealing.

'You're a bit lucky,' Jack was saying to the dogs. 'Wouldn't have got out here today if it wasn't for a problem with the fence between here and the neighbours. The widow wanted me to check it out so I thought I'd feed ya since I was out 'ere. Strung up one of the wethers for ya on the way.'

The dogs were dribbling with expectation and finally Jack threw the meat to them. He wadded up the plastic bag and stuffed it in his coat pocket. Checking their water he looked around. Happy that everything seemed to be as he left it, he grabbed the half-empty bottle of rum and took a couple of swigs.

'Catch ya, boys,' he said as he stubbed out the cigarette on top of the kennels.

Craig had caught the whole scene on camera. 'You're gone, buddy,' he thought as Jack glided through the bush and out of sight. As soon as he heard the bike roar away he got to his feet, knees cracking.

Back at his base by the creek he called Dave on the CB.

'When you're ready, mate,' he said, and settled under a tree to wait for his ride.

Gemma felt the wind pick up and looked across the sky. Towards the north thundery clouds were building. She yelled to Bulla, who was working in the yards, 'Reckon we'll get a storm?'

Bulla scanned the sky and nodded. 'Might do. Let's get these shornies up closer to the shed in case.'

Shifting the sheep that had been back-lined into the race leading under the shed, she went back to finish the ones that still needed spraying. She heard and smelled the rain before she felt it. When Gemma scanned the horizon, she could see the rain pouring down in columns, moving quite quickly towards the yards. A loud crack of thunder galvanised them into action. Bulla jumped over the sheep yards in a bound and ran towards the sheep, whistling at his dogs as he went.

'C'mon, Roady, go back,' he commanded.

Gemma called Scoota to her, knowing he'd be in the way, and sprinted to open the gate so the sheep could flow freely under the shed. The bewildered sheep baulked at running into the darkness but, with Roady's gentle persuasion, started trickling under slowly. By the time the sheep were under the shed both Bulla and Gemma were soaking wet, the rain still pelting down. They both dashed for the shelter of the shearing shed.

There were only three sheep left in each pen and the shearers had downed tools to watch the storm.

'Good thing it's Friday afternoon, hey, Gem?' Kenny said as she walked in. Gemma wiped the rain out of her eyes, swept her soaked hair back off her face and grinned. 'I'm never going to say no to rain, mate,' she said.

The shearers tore themselves away from the window and picked up their handpieces again.

'The creeks'll come down,' shouted Buster. 'We should get finished and get goin' or we'll be stuck here for the weekend.'

'We'll be able to get out tomorrow if we can't go tonight.' Paula shrugged. 'Cookie'll have enough food for us all.'

'Bull, want to grab a couple of cartons of beer out of the coolroom? I reckon these guys can have a wet day cut-out since it looks like they might be stuck for the night.'

'No worries.'

'Better check that Jack and Gaz are okay, too. Jack'll be drenched on the bike.'

Bulla brought back two cartons of beer just as Jamie pushed the last sheep down the shoot. Everyone made a beeline for the carton and then to the window to watch the rain that had subsided into a slow drizzle. Gemma shivered and pulled her jumper closer to her chest. It had become quite cold with the change. She cracked her beer and held it up. 'Hey, listen up, you feral lot. Here's to a great week's shearing and a better one to come. Thanks to the Big Fella upstairs for the rain.'

'Hear hear,' everyone yelled. Lisa reached over to the radio and turned up the volume. Kenny and Buster looked at each other and groaned. The three youths who Gemma had thought looked like shady characters decided to brave the rain and go to the pub in Dawns Rest, but the rest of the crew were happy to kick back at Billbinya.

Before long everyone was laughing and talking loudly and Gemma felt her cheeks begin to grow warm from the alcohol. Jack and Garry had joined the impromptu party, both wet from running through the rain.

Lisa suddenly grabbed a paddle and yelled into it. 'Okay, everyone, welcome to *Billbinya Shearing Shed Idol*. Thanks to our judges, Buster, Garry and Jackie, you'll be scored out of ten. The rules are everyone has to sing to a song that comes on the radio, or you can choose a CD.'

She was drowned out by cries of dismay. 'I'm not doing that.' 'Bloody stupid woman.' 'Get a life, would ya?' 'On ya horse.'

Gemma stood up, laughing. 'Ah, come on, ya wusses, have a go, I've got some CDs in the ute. I'll grab them and you can decide which songs you're gonna try and kill,' she said and disappeared out the door.

'Woo hoo,' yelled Lisa. All the others looked at each other in horror. Lisa sidled up to Kenny. 'Watchya gonna sing, big fella?'

Kenny looked at her, bemused. 'You're bloody mad, woman.'

'Oh, have another beer. Hey, Jamie, I reckon Chisel should be up your alley!'

'Oh yeah, and what are you gonna sing, songbird?' he yelled back. Lisa bopped over to the carton of beer and grabbed a sixpack. Handing a beer to everyone she said, 'Here's some Dutch courage. Drink up!'

By the time Lisa had belted out a surprisingly tuneful rendition of Melissa Etheridge's 'Romeo' and Kenny had received twelve out of ten for his deep melodic version of 'Old Rusty Ute' by John O'Dea, Jack was on his seventh beer. He'd been watching Lisa. She'd be all right in the sack, he thought, legs were pretty tight. Not a patch on Gemma though.

He looked at Gemma, whose face was glowing with laughter and beer. Her hair had long since dried and she'd taken it out of its ponytail. It hung over her back and Jack could imagine it tickling his face. Tonight, he thought. Tonight he'd make a move. Then he could check the steers, see if the stock squad had found them, and head to the young jillaroo's place. He'd hole up there for the weekend. But before all that, Gemma was gonna be his tonight.

Idol continued while the beer flowed. Eventually, after much indecision, Kenny was awarded a sixpack of beer and declared Billbinya's Idol, and it was time for a feed.

The hungry hordes made their way to the shearers' quarters for some tea, with Gemma and the Billbinya stockmen invited by Helen to join them.

An hour later, full and content, Gemma stood to go home. She'd had more than her fair share of beer, fun and food. It was definitely time for bed.

'Catch ya in the morning, guys. We'll check the creek out and see if you can get through.' She left to a chorus of goodnights.

No one noticed Jack slip out behind her.

Chapter 25

Dave and Craig had been battling the elements. It was nearly 9 pm and they had just made it to the track that led to the Billbinya homestead. After Dave had picked up Craig and looked at the photos, they talked about the startling discovery Dave had made earlier in the day. Sitting around the fire having afternoon smoko, he relayed how he'd found some cattle that looked out of place.

'The problem seems to be up on the boundary paddock,' Dave said. 'I've found one hundred and fifteen Hereford steers. Now, as we know, Gemma only runs Angus cattle. I've been over the map that Bulla gave us and there's nothing to indicate that there should be Hereford cattle here. The earmark is different, too. I need to talk to the Department of Ag and get access to the stock brands register. I want to find out who owns those steers.'

'Let's go and have a look,' Craig said. They packed up their camp, and drove towards the boundary paddock.

As they drove around the Herefords Craig saw what Dave had been talking about. They definitely didn't belong to Billbinya.

'Gemma would have said if she'd bought in cattle recently, wouldn't she?' Craig asked.

'Yeah, I reckon she would have.'

'Well, let's muster them into the cattle yards now. We'll confront her with them tomorrow.'

Dave scanned the sky. 'Dunno, that's a pretty black cloud over on the horizon. We could be in for a storm.' Craig waited for Dave to make the decision. 'Ah, we might as well, I guess. The cattle yards are only in the next paddock, aren't they?'

Craig nodded.

'Righto. Let's get the quad off the trailer and you can start the muster while I go open the gates.'

Craig rode until he reached the fence then started to circumnavigate the paddock, keeping an eye on the storm clouds building on the horizon. The light had started to fade as he gathered the cattle into a mob. The steers were skittish and anxious and started to run in the opposite direction. They weren't keen on the noise the bike made but Craig had managed to contain them. With Dave back from opening the gates and flanking one side, they carefully drove them towards the yards. A big gust of wind blew and then the wind whipped up in earnest. As the rain started to fall, the cattle tried to canter away from the men. Craig, knowing if they lost the mob now they would be harder to muster the next time, revved the bike and stood up on the foot pegs as he cracked his whip. He managed to get the cattle turned and headed back towards the yards. Running now, the cattle didn't realise they were caught until the two men had herded them into the yards and the gate clanged shut. Dave wrapped a chain around the gates, padlocked it with a stock squad padlock, and then stretched yellow crime-scene tape around the yards. Craig pushed the cattle into a covered pen that had a trough and an old bale of hay. In the morning they'd send a truck to take the cattle to the closest sale yards for safekeeping.

The rain was pelting down, stinging Craig's face. After a shouted conversation, they decided to leave the bike under a tree near the yards and head straight back to the homestead in the four-wheel drive. They would have to be quick in case any of the creeks came down.

As it happened they didn't make it in time to avoid the last creek running. They sat on the edge for a couple of hours waiting for the waters to subside, watching the muddy water swirl around the bottoms of the river red gums and surge past them. Once it had fallen slightly, Craig, since he was wet already, tested the depth of the creek by walking slowly out into it. Satisfied that they could get through, and not really wanting to spend the night on the creek's edge, they inched their way through the gushing waters and then along the muddy, slippery tracks. When they arrived at the homestead, they were surprised to find lights blazing everywhere and Bulla and Garry backing the utes out of the shed.

What the hell is going on here? Dave wondered.

Jack listened outside Gemma's bedroom window. He realised she was going for a shower and quietly made his way around to the kitchen door to let himself inside. Sliding through the darkness of the kitchen and into the lounge room, he positioned himself so he could see every move Gemma made when she came out. In the darkness he waited, breathing quickly with need. He almost groaned out loud when he saw Gemma move into the passage, naked and drying her hair with a towel. When she got into the bedroom, he watched her reflection in the mirror as she brushed her hair and rubbed moisturiser into her hands, legs and face before pulling on a nightgown. When she walked into the kitchen to get a drink, he moved into the light and said, 'Hello, Gemma.'

Spinning around to see whose voice had come out of the darkness, Gemma let out a little scream. 'Shit, Jack, you scared the crap out of me. What's wrong? Is there a problem?'

'Yeah, you could say that,' he said, one hand stroking the bulge in his jeans.

Startled, Gemma's eyes flew to his movement. Then she bolted for the door with Jack at her heels.

Bulla saw Dave and Craig pull up and flew out of his ute to talk to them.

'Gemma's been attacked!' he yelled. 'She's in the shearers' kitchen with Helen and Lisa. It was Jack, the bastard. He's bashed her good and proper and shot through. We're all going out looking for him.'

Dave and Craig looked at each other.

'I'll check everything out here,' Dave said quietly. 'You find out what is going on in the quarters.' Craig nodded, and they both got out of the car.

Dave walked over to Bulla and Garry, who were obviously shocked and distressed. 'Okay, calm down and tell me what you know.'

'Calm down? Get stuffed, we need to get out there and look for him. He'll be gone otherwise.' Bulla moved towards his ute.

'Bulla?' Dave's tone was firm. 'How about we let the coppers do that, okay? You tell me what's happened and I'll get some Pirie uniforms out here pronto.'

'We don't really know what happened,' broke in Garry. 'We had a few beers in the shearing shed and then we all stayed and had tea. Gemma went home and a while later she stumbled in through the door cryin' and screamin' and stuff. She had blood all over 'er face and her nightie had been ripped. She was screamin' that Jack had ambushed her in the kitchen. I dunno if he did anythin' . . .' Garry's voice trailed off as he realised what could have happened.

Bulla took up the commentary. 'We went to 'is room and it looks like 'e's done a runner. Can't find his clothes or anythin' and his ute is gone. Dunno why we didn't hear him leave.' Bulla looked around wildly, as if hoping to see Jack lurking in the darkness nearby.

'I'll get on the phone to Pirie. We'll get some uniforms out here. You both can come with me while we go and have a drive around. Do you know if Jack carries any weapons – knife, gun?' Dave looked from one to the other.

Bulla and Garry shook their heads. 'Not ever seen him with anything like that,' Bulla said.

'Righto, I'll have to come with you guys. Craig will take Gemma to town. Give me a description of the ute and I will pass it on to the blokes in Pirie.'

'White Ford ute with Victorian number plates. Don't remember the number but ya won't see many Vic plates round here. Oh, he's got a really obvious naked woman sticker on the back and a couple of Bundy Bear stickers on the side windows –'

Craig emerged from the shearers' quarters just as Dave hung up from the Port Pirie police.

'What's the go?' Dave asked.

'She needs to get to a hospital. He's bashed her pretty good. Looks like a bunged-up nose – don't reckon it's broken, though – couple of black eyes and a fat lip. She's holding her arm quite tenderly. She said he tried to drag her back into the bedroom.'

'Okay, you take her. I'm going to have a quick look

around here with Garry and Bulla. Seems Jack has taken his ute and some things from his room. Don't reckon we'll find him, but you never know – he may have headed out to get his dogs. Keep an eye out on the road for a white Ford ute with Victorian plates and a sticker of a naked woman on the rear window. I'll ring you with the plate number when the uniforms get back to me.' Dave glanced over at Bulla and saw he was listening. 'Why don't you rustle up a spotlight, mate, and I'll be right with you.' Dave waited until Bulla was out of earshot and then said quietly to Craig: 'Ask the hard questions without causing too much distress. But make sure you ask the hard questions, okay? Let me grab the camera before you leave.'

'No worries.' Craig hopped into the driver's seat and pulled over as close to the shearers' quarters as he could. Dave and Bulla paused in hooking up the spotty and watched as Helen and Lisa walked Gemma out to the car and gently helped her in.

'Stop dallying,' Bulla grunted at Dave and got into the ute.

'Okay, here's the deal,' Dave said to Buster and Kenny. 'You blokes don't need to come with us. Go inside and keep your eyes open. Call us on the two-way if he comes back but pretend you know nothing. Do not – and I mean this – do *not* try and take him down yourselves. And don't go into his room. I want to look it over and dust it for prints. Just sit tight, okay?'

'Okay,' Kenny said.

'We'll be back shortly.' Dave jumped into the passenger side of Bulla's ute, with Garry in the tray operating the spotlight. Bulla let out the clutch, spun the wheels and headed down the driveway.

'Bulla, I want you to go out to the top part of the place. Jack has some dogs tied up out there, hidden in the bush. He'll probably try to get to them before he leaves the property.'

'You found dogs? Jack can't stand dogs. Why did he have them tied up in the bush?' Bulla asked.

'I can't really comment on that now. Can you tell me what happened tonight? Have you got any ideas about why Jack would have attacked Gemma?'

Bulla told Dave about the rain, the beers, the singing competition and tea. 'Then Gemma said good-night and took off to her house. I didn't see Jack leave. I *can* tell ya that he'd mouth off occasionally about Gem to us.'

'Mouth off? What do you mean?'

'Well . . .' Bulla looked uncomfortable. 'He thought she might be good in the ah, ya know . . .'

'Bedroom?'

'Ah, yeah. Suggested once or twice that Gaz 'n' me were on with her.'

'And are you?'

'No! She was our boss's wife and now she's our boss. We love Gem, but not like that.'

'So any ideas why Jack would have attacked Gemma, or do you think it was purely sexually motivated?'

'Well, I guess it looks like that. I know he thought she was a bit of all right, but I never thought he'd go as far as that. I did tell Gemma to lock her doors, but she never worried about it. Too trusting and naive is our Gemma. 'Bout lots of stuff, not just lockin' doors and that.'

Slipping and sliding through creeks and washed-out tracks they arrived at the bush near the clearing. Garry flashed the spotlight around and picked up some impressions that looked like they'd been made by a vehicle, but they had been smudged with the rain. Dave searched the edge of the bush with his torch and found some fresh footprints.

He took photos while Bulla held the torch and then they moved into the bush, looking for the dogs. When they got to the clearing the dogs had gone. The chains lay in the dirt, glistening in the torchlight.

'We've missed him,' Dave said.

Jack pushed his old ute as fast as it would go. He knew he'd have to take the back roads to Pirie so he didn't run into any cops. They'd be out at Billbinya quick smart with the two stock squad guys already out there and all the other people around. Someone would have called them as soon as Gemma was game enough to come out of her room.

'Bloody bitch,' he thought. 'I really thought she'd like it a bit rough.' Jack grinned as he thought of the way she'd moved under him while he was trying to push her nightie up. Bloody shame he'd taken his mind off the job of controlling her for a couple of seconds. He looked at his wrist and grimaced. She packed a fair bite. Hurt the crap out of him and made him lose his grip on her hair. He still couldn't work out how the hell she'd got hold of the gun and where it had come from.

Sighing with frustration, Jack knew he'd really stuffed things. He couldn't go back to Billbinya now. He lit a cigarette and toyed with his mobile phone. This was one call he didn't want to make. Reaching into the duffle bag beside him, he came up with a full bottle of rum and unscrewed its top. Feeling the liquid burn his throat he thought about how he was going to break the news to the boss. His brother was not going to be happy. Dialling the number, he took another swig.

'How goes it?' asked a very drunk voice at the other end.

'Had a few, bro?'

'Yeah, partying with a very nice little lady I met in a bar. Bit busy. I'll call ya back.'

'Reckon ya might wanna hear this.'

'Shit,' his brother muttered. 'Hey babe, hang off on that, I want to watch. Gotta talk here for a sec.'

'I've had to shoot through.'

'What? What the hell happened?'

'Ya know me weakness. She got under me skin. Had to try and get it on with 'er. Sorry 'bout that but . . .'

'What did you do?' The other man's voice was steely and it sounded like he'd sobered up extremely fast.

'Got a bit frisky with her. She didn't like it much. The cops'll be out pretty soon, so I'm taking the back roads to Pirie. I'll camp the night with you and see if we've got a plan from there. Whaddaya reckon?'

'Is she badly hurt?'

'Nah, just a bit bloodied I think. Bloody bitch pulled a gun on me.'

'You're a bloody idiot. Just typical of you to stuff up at a critical time. Unbelievable. Don't come to my house. I'll meet you at the normal place, give you some money and you get to Adelaide. Lay low there for a while. We're going to need you soon – I've got plans to make a big hit on the bitch soon so we'll need you in the truck. How far away are you?'

Jack looked around. 'About fifty minutes away.'

'Okay, I'll see you there.' Jack's brother hit the button to end the call.

Chapter 26

Craig watched the road carefully. Gemma sat beside him, trembling. Occasionally he could hear a stifled sob but when he glanced over Gemma shied into the corner of the vehicle.

'I'm not going to hurt you,' Craig said quietly. 'I'm the good guy, remember?' There was no answer so Craig didn't push it.

A little while later Gemma spoke. 'Why did he do it? I didn't do anything . . . I had no idea he thought . . .' She broke off, sobbing. It was obvious she was in shock. Craig brought the car gently to a standstill.

'What are you doing?' Gemma asked fearfully.

'I'm getting you a blanket from the back of the car. You're in shock and you need to be kept warm, okay? I'm not going to hurt you.' He handed her the blanket through the window of the car, careful to keep his hands away from hers.

'Is there someone I can call to meet us at the hospital?' Craig asked, getting back in the car.

Gemma nodded. 'Jess Rawlings.' She recited the number in a monotone.

Gemma looked out the window, grateful for the blanket but still shivering. She turned her head when she heard Jess screech through the phone and listened to Craig's reassuring words. She leaned her head up against the glass and thought about all that had happened.

'I'm going to be sick,' she said suddenly, and bolted from the car. Craig stood back until she was finished and then made sure she got back into the car safely.

'I can still feel him,' muttered Gemma.

'That will happen for a little while,' Craig said softly. 'Victims often feel their attackers for some time afterwards. But that will pass. It just takes time. Who attacked you, Gemma?'

'Jack. Jack Marshall. He's been working on Billbinya for the last few months.'

'When did he attack you?'

'What do you mean? It was tonight but I don't know the time.'

'Can you tell me what happened?' Craig asked gently.

'I don't really know. I went to the kitchen to get a drink and he was just there. He said, "Hello, Gemma" and he was . . . he was touching himself. I just knew I was in trouble. I tried to run but he chased me. He dragged me back to the . . .' Gemma took a shaky breath, 'to the bedroom. I tried to get away. I tried. Couldn't, couldn't get him off . . .' She began sobbing uncontrollably. Craig was silent. No matter how much training you were given, it didn't prepare you to get through an assault victim's first interview. Every interview Craig had done was difficult. The devastation etched in each victim's face broke his heart every time.

'Gemma, did he manage to penetrate you? I'm sorry, but I have to ask.'

Gemma shook her head violently. 'I pulled a gun on him,' she said.

Craig looked at her incredulously. 'You what?'

'I pulled a gun on him. He'd thrown me onto the bed and was trying to get my nightie up . . . I bit him on the wrist and then – ever since . . .' She took a halting breath. 'Ever since Adam died I've always kept a gun under my pillow or near my bed. I'm scared most nights. I've never told anyone, but I hate being in that big house by myself. I hear every groan and creak. And sometimes I think I hear his footsteps. The gun, it helps. When I pulled it out, Jack backed off and ran to the door. Then he looked back and said, "Ever get the feelin' you're being set up, Gemma Sinclair?" And then he left.' Gemma was shaking so violently now that Craig was beginning to get worried, but he had to follow up on Jack's remark.

'What do you think he meant by "set up"?' Craig asked.

'How the hell should I know?' Gemma cried. 'My life has turned to shit over the last year. I don't know anything anymore.'

'Gemma, have you double-crossed Jack somehow? Is that why he attacked you?'

Gemma looked at him, fury eclipsing the pain and desolation. 'No, I haven't. I suppose you're talking about the stock stealing? How dare you! I have nothing to do with this stock stealing. I've told Dave and now I'm telling you. I am not involved. Don't try and get me to say something just because I'm in a vulnerable state. I'm *not involved.*'

As they walked into the emergency department Jess darted over to them.

'Oh, my sweet. What has happened to you? Poor baby.'

'Jessie, I'm so scared.' Gemma fell towards Jess and hugged her.

Craig stood back watching, taken by Jess's warmth and compassion. She really was something else. The friendship between these two was amazing. They were both so loyal, so supportive of each other.

Gently Craig said, 'We really need to get Gemma seen to, Jess. You can come with us, but please don't touch her anymore. We need to look her over for evidence.'

Jess quickly stood back from Gemma but didn't let go of her hand. 'C'mon, lovely, let's get this over and done with. Then I'll take you home. You'll never believe who the casualty nurse is tonight – Paige Nicholls. Amazing how that woman keeps popping up.'

'I'm going to see you to the doctor, Gemma, and then I need to check in with Dave. I won't be far away if you need me.'

Gemma nodded and they walked towards the casualty ward.

'Hi, Gemma,' Paige said when she walked in. It was obvious she'd been briefed on what had happened and was prepared for Gemma's bloodied face. 'Won't be long and we'll have you all fixed up. Just sit on the edge of the bed. I'll call the doctor now that you're here.'

Craig made his excuses and beckoned to Jess. 'I just need to ask a couple of questions, Jess,' he said, when Jess looked reluctant to leave Gemma's side.

'Go, I'll be fine, just come back quick,' Gemma said to her.

Jess followed Craig into the waiting room.

Craig flicked open his notebook. 'Do you know Jack Marshall?'

'I've heard Gemma talk about him but I've never met him,' Jess answered.

'Has Gemma ever indicated that he'd tried to hurt her before?'

'No. She said he was a bit odd, but that's all. We don't talk much about the guys that work on Billbinya when we catch up.' Jess was tapping her foot, anxious to get back to Gemma.

'Jess, is it possible that Jack was seeking revenge on Gemma for some reason?'

Jess stopped tapping, narrowed her eyes and crossed her arms. 'And what does that question mean, Detective?'

Craig looked at her flashing eyes and was lost. 'Uh,' he stammered, trying to regain his thoughts. 'Is it possible Gemma could have double-crossed him at all?'

'Detective, have we met before?' Jess asked.

Thrown by the question, Craig blinked. 'Umm, possibly,' he answered. 'Maybe.'

'Yeah, I thought so. Last Friday night at the Jewel, wasn't it? Keeping an eye on us, were you?'

'Nothing like that. Had to go somewhere and have a drink.' Craig was beginning to get cross.

'Well, you listen to me. No matter how hard you try, you aren't going to be able to pin this on Gem. She didn't know what Adam was up to before he died and the only reason she knows now is because you bastards are hanging around like a bad smell. Now was there anything else? Because if not, I'd like to get back to my friend, who has had more than enough kicks in the gut in the last few months to last her for the rest of her life.' Jess started to walk away. 'Oh, and Craig – it's Craig, isn't it?'

Craig nodded mutely.

'When you get this bullshit about Gemma being a thief out of your head, I'd love to have that drink with you.' Jess flashed him a dazzling smile then turned on her heel and walked away, leaving Craig staring at her back, open-mouthed.

Dave had been through Jack's bedroom and hadn't found anything to indicate where he could have gone to. He'd collected an empty rum bottle from under Jack's bed and samples of hair from his pillow.

His phone rang, startling him.

'How are you going there?' Craig asked.

'No sign of him, and the dogs are gone too. Forensics are out here dusting for fingerprints and I've found an empty rum bottle – same brand that we found in the dogs' yard, and at the ruins – and a few hairs off his pillow. I've instructed the local officers searching for him to use unmarked cars, and to follow him rather than apprehend. I'd rather follow him and see if he leads us to anyone else or the stock. What do you reckon?'

'Sounds like a great idea. I just hope we can find him. He's done a real job on Gemma. She's scared witless. She pulled a gun on him in the end. She keeps one near her bed since Adam died. Her injuries are superficial mainly, but her arm'll be pretty sore for a while – pulled all the muscles in it when he was hauling her back to the bedroom – and she'll have some lovely black eyes from the bang on the nose. I spoke to both her and Jess, who met us at the hospital, and they have categorically denied any involvement or knowledge of stock stealing. And I have to say, I'm inclined to believe them.'

'Okay. Take down her statement, then you get back out here. We'll take a closer look at that dog enclosure tomorrow and impound the sheep yard panels. We can bunk down in the shearers' quarters.'

'No worries. See ya in a few hours.'

Chapter 27

Ben liked being in the office at night. It was peaceful and he was able to achieve a lot more when nobody else was around. Ned had given him his own car and a few clients over the past few weeks and Ben was finding that his workload had increased since taking on these extra customers. But it was better than riding around with Ned all day. Ned had become increasingly edgy and grumpy, and had told Ben he'd been having trouble with his stomach due to stress. Ben had noticed the older man had a tremor in his hands and there seemed to be a rash on his arms. It could be stress, but Ben was worried that it might be something more. He wondered if Ned was seriously ill.

Ben walked down the narrow corridor to the storeroom where the old files were kept. The feedlot contract that Adam had signed dated back three years, Ned had said. So that was four contracts he was looking for – the three that had been filled and the one that was due to be filled in the next few months. He wanted all the information at his fingertips when he met with Craig.

Running his fingers over the dates and sale numbers he found the first two without any trouble. Looking at the contract, Ben could see nothing amiss. They were signed by the state manager, Ned and Adam, and it appeared the cattle had been delivered and paid for. The third one proved much more difficult to locate. It should have been at the top of the archive box but Ben couldn't find it. Shifting a couple of heavy folders out of the way, he found another filing box pushed to the back of the shelf. Leafing through the contract and sale papers, he finally found the one he was after. He was surprised that it hadn't been filed correctly. Barb, the office manager, was usually meticulous about filing. Ben shrugged. Must have had a temp in at some stage who stuffed up.

Taking all three contracts back to his desk, he then went in search of the current contract. That one would be in Barb's office since it was still to be filed.

Flicking through the pages of the contract file, he found the one he was looking for and unclipped it from the folder and took it back to his office, thinking of Gemma. He kept seeing her face, hearing her voice. No woman had ever affected him this way. Ben couldn't wait to see her again. He was sure he hadn't imagined her moving closer to him in the shearing shed. *Next time*, he promised himself, *I'll kiss her.*

Shaking his head to clear it he sat down and carefully read through the contract. Trying to decipher the scrawled signature, Ben's heart almost stopped when he realised it was a woman's writing. Pretty messy for a woman, but it had the round loops that women often used in signatures. Looking closely, Ben saw a distinct G. Surely Gemma hadn't signed it. She'd looked so shocked when Ned had told her about the contract, but here was her signature in black and white: G.R. Sinclair.

Ben put the contract down and rubbed his eyes. There must be an explanation.

He picked up the earlier contracts and examined Adam's signature. His writing was virtually illegible; Ben didn't think there was any way he could have forged Gemma's name.

Ben put the four contracts in a large yellow envelope and headed out the door. He wanted to confront Gemma with these. He couldn't help her if she wasn't honest with him. He'd go and see her tomorrow.

Once Gemma was finished at the hospital, Craig took her statement. He was as sympathetic and compassionate as he could be but by the time everything was finished, Gemma was exhausted. She alternated between crying, being very angry and just wanting to go home.

Jess drove her to her house, insisted she take the sedative that Paige had given her and Gemma fell into bed. Jess sat with her until she fell asleep. Tomorrow they would go out to Billbinya.

The amount of traffic that Ben passed on the way to Billbinya the next morning amazed him. The quiet country dirt roads seemed to have turned into a drag-racing track. Two police cars had come up behind him, passed him and disappeared into the distance. Then he'd passed Dave and Craig and four other cars he didn't know heading back towards town. A truck carrying some Hereford cattle went past. The presence of the police cars made him wonder if some more stock had been stolen. Ben put his foot down and got to Billbinya as fast as he could.

When he arrived he saw Bulla at the shearing shed, letting out the sheep that had been left under the shed the night before. Bulla nodded and carried on with his work.

'Where is everyone?' Ben asked, jumping over the fence to give Bulla a hand. The stubborn sheep had decided they didn't want to come out from underneath the shearing shed and even Bulla's dog,

Roady, had been baled up against the railing by an angry wether.

Bulla swore and threw a rock at the sheep. 'Gem's in town,' he answered.

'Oh, I was hoping to catch her,' Ben said.

'She'll be out with Jess this afternoon. Some pretty bad business went down last night and Craig had to take her in to hospital. C'mon, you stupid bastards, get out from under there.' Bulla crawled in under the shed. 'Go back, Roady.' He let out a piercing whistle and from nowhere a black and white collie dog flew over the fence, under the shed and started barking. 'Fetch 'im up, Mac, go back there.'

Ben watched as together Mac and Roady worked their way to the back of the shed and teamed up to push the sheep towards the small gateway. His curiosity got the better of him and he yelled under the shed: 'What happened?'

Bulla didn't answer straightaway. He worked his dogs quietly and quickly and within a couple of minutes the wethers realised they were beaten and ran through the opening. The two dogs followed the sheep out and accepted their pats from Ben with big grins on their faces. Bulla struggled out from under the shed and stood up. He groaned. 'I'm getting too old for this,' he muttered. 'Bloody Jack got to Gemma last night,' Bulla said, looking Ben in the face for the first time. 'He bashed her up a bit and Craig took 'er in to the hospital. Jess rang this morning and said she was up and about feelin' pretty sore but they'd be comin' out today. The bastard did a runner last night and the cops are on the lookout for him.'

Ben felt sick. 'Right, well then I guess you're a man down. I'll give you a hand until Gemma gets back. I need to stay and talk to her anyway. Garry about?'

'Nah, he's gone to town to get the supplies for shearing.'

'Righto, hand over the back-liner. I can do this if you want to get the other sheep back out into the paddock.'

Bulla looked at Ben for a second.

'I own my own farm, Bulla. I know how to do this.'

Bulla indicated with a nod of his head to where the backpack and spraygun were lying on the bench. 'There you go, sunshine. Hook in.' As he turned to walk away, he stopped. 'You're a bit keen on our Gem, aren't ya?'

'Yeah, a bit,' Ben answered candidly.

Bulla nodded. 'You'd be good for her.'

Ben shook his head. It didn't matter if he was keen on her or not. If she was involved with the stock stealing, he wouldn't touch her with a ten-foot pole. But, deep down, he still couldn't believe she was.

Jess had had the prescription given to Gemma at the hospital filled, then stocked the car with comfort food and alcohol. 'Right, Gem?' she asked as they pulled into Billbinya's driveway.

'Yeah,' Gemma answered softly. She didn't feel okay. She was scared. She didn't want to go back to the house. But Craig had said that was normal and Jess had promised to stay for a while. Pat would come and stay too, and Bulla and Garry would camp at the shearers' quarters if she asked them to. Plus, the shearers would be around for another week.

'Looks like Ned is here,' Jess commented as the shed and yards came into view.

Gemma looked. 'No, I think that's Ben.' A warm feeling shot through her stomach. 'I wonder what he's doing here on a Saturday.'

'Checking up on you, I'd reckon.' Jess smiled slyly. 'Think he's got the hots for you.'

'Uh huh,' said Gemma, shifting painfully in her seat.

They pulled up at the yards and got out of the car. Ben looked up and took a quick breath when he saw Gemma's face and bandaged arm. He finished the race of sheep, let them out, hung up the backpack and walked over to the girls.

'Been in the wars, Gem?' he asked, touching her gently on the shoulder.

'Yeah, a bit.' She smiled up at him, basking in the warmth of his concern. 'How come you've been roped in here?'

Ben's face sobered as he recalled the reason for his visit. He moved away from Gemma and turned back towards the yards. 'I came to talk to you and found that Bulla was a bit short-staffed so I offered to help while I was waiting for you.'

'Oh.' Gemma was confused by his sudden withdrawal. 'Well, thanks. I think I might be out of action for a little while with this arm.'

Ben spun around to face Gemma with an intense look on his face. 'Gemma, tell me truthfully: are you involved with stock stealing? Do you know anything about any of it? Any tiny little thing?'

Gemma recoiled and Jess moved in closer. There was a heartbeat of silence then Gemma's eyes narrowed. 'I thought you were different, Ben,' she choked out. 'I thought you believed in me. Well, stuff you! I'm not even going to dignify that question with an answer. We don't need your help. You can leave any time you like.' She stumbled back to the car, tears filling her eyes.

Jess stared at Ben. 'I must have pegged you wrong,' she said. 'I thought you were one of the good guys.' She turned to go to Gemma.

'Jess, I've found something with Gemma's signature on it that would indicate she is involved. If you guys want me to help you, I have to know everything. If Gem's involved then I need to know. I can't help if she is involved, but if she isn't then let's have a crack at working out what the hell is going on around here.'

Jess watched his face carefully. 'Finish up here and I'll have the kettle on at the house when you're ready to come and talk to us.' She turned and walked away.

Ben let out his breath and ran his hands over his face. Shit, what a bloody awful position to be in.

The girls were sitting at the kitchen table when Ben entered the house. Gemma had her back to him and wouldn't look him in the face when he sat at the table.

'So what have you got, Ben?' Jess asked. 'Why are you giving us grief?'

Ben opened the yellow envelope. Addressing Gemma he said, 'These are the contracts for the cattle that have been going to the feedlot. Craig asked to see all the sale contracts early next week. I particularly went to find these because I knew Gemma didn't know anything about the feedlot cattle. The first two are fine. They have Adam's signature on them, they've been filled, money paid, no problem. It's the last two I have a problem with. Gemma, your signature is on the last two contracts, but you told me and Ned that you didn't have any idea about them. Did you lie about not knowing about the contracts?'

Gemma's good hand shot out. 'Let me look.' Ben passed the contracts over to her. 'That's not my signature,' Gemma said without hesitation. 'Jess, can you pass me that pen and paper?' Gemma signed her name with a flourish and pushed the paper towards Ben. 'That's my signature – want me to show you my credit cards? That one,' she said, pointing to the contracts, 'is not mine.'

Ben looked at Gemma's signature and Jess took the contracts from Ben's hand to look. It was quite clear the two signatures didn't match. Ben smiled.

Jack was holed up in a cheap motel in Adelaide. It was off the main drag and he didn't think there would be much chance of anyone finding him here. Another five days and this would all be over. His brother had told him about the last big job they were going to pull when they had met the previous night. He wasn't needed until Friday so to have a week in a motel with nothing to do but drink rum and watch TV sounded great to him.

He'd snuck the dogs into his room. They didn't care about the luxury they were in – they were just pleased to have their master with them.

Jack couldn't stop thinking about Gemma though. He kept remembering the feeling of her close to him, the screaming. Jack couldn't understand why women's screaming and fear turned him on. He really had tried to control those feelings – until he'd met Gemma. She'd been too irresistible to ignore.

Jack shrugged. It would be over on Friday. He'd made plans to head bush and spend some time in stock camps with just the fellas. He needed to stay away from the ladies and the law for a while.

* * *

Gemma, Jess and Ben had moved to the lounge room to discuss what they all knew. Jess was in full flight. 'We need to find those bank statements. It's the only way that we can prove Gemma wasn't involved. I'd bet my last dollar that her name isn't on the statements.'

Ben listened to a rundown of the latest developments without comment. Jess finished by saying, 'The other thing I have found in the books is that the proceeds from the feedlot contracts haven't been going into the Billbinya operating account. I'm beginning to think that the money from that is hitting the bank account that we don't have access to.'

'So what we need to do is find the bank account the money went into and who owns it. See if the payments match the transaction history – is that right?' Ben asked.

'Hit the nail on the head,' Jess said. She nudged Gemma. 'See, I told you this one was smart.' Gemma rolled her eyes; they were about the only part of her that didn't ache at the moment.

'Well, I can do that without any problems,' Ben declared.

Gemma raised her head to look at him. Ben's eyes met hers and it was all Gemma could do to stay sitting on the couch and not throw herself into his arms for comfort.

'How?' she asked.

'Well, you know Barb, our office manager?' Ben asked.

'Yeah,' Gemma said as Jess suddenly whooped.

'Of course!' she shrieked. 'Why didn't I think of that? Oh Ben, you are clever – well done, mate.'

Gemma looked confused. 'What've I missed?'

'Ben can trace where the money was paid to, can't you, Ben?' Jess was almost dancing with delight.

'Yeah. I can ask Barb about last year's transaction. Although I'll only be able to get the account number and name – I can't track the transactions or anything like that. But it will give you something to work with.'

'Absolutely,' Jess said, her mind working overtime. 'I have a contact in the head office of the Inland Development Bank. I'd rather try and find the statements of Adam's than use her, but I'll call on her as a last resort.' Jess stood up, stretched and looked at her watch. 'Drinks all round, I think,' she said, and then looked at Gemma. 'Oh, except for you, Gem. Can't drink with your painkillers. Want a beer, Ben?' she called over her shoulder as she headed to the kitchen.

'I should probably be getting home. It's a long drive.' Ben got up from the couch. 'I'm really pleased we've sorted that contract, Gem.' He smiled down at her and reached out to touch her shoulder. Gemma brought her hand up to cover his. His hand stilled and he looked at her longingly until they heard Jess coming back and dropped their hands.

Jess stood in the doorway with a Scotch and Coke, looking knowingly at them. 'Well, Ben, thanks for your help. Will you give us a call on Monday when you've got the account number?'

'Yeah, no problem.'

Gemma got off the couch and swayed slightly. Ben quickly put his arm around her waist to steady her. 'You stay here, Gem,' he said softly. 'I'll be back soon.' He squeezed her waist, helped her back to her seat and sauntered towards the door.

When Gemma woke the next morning, she felt better. She was up and tottering around the kitchen when Pat burst in. Without saying anything he strode over and picked her up in a bear hug.

'Ow, Pat, my arm!'

He released her immediately, looking sheepish. 'Sorry, sis. You okay?'

'Much better today. Coffee?'

They sat at the kitchen table and talked about all that had happened in the last few days.

'The weirdest thing,' Gemma concluded, 'was that as Jack was leaving he turned around and said, "Ever get the feeling you're being set up, Gemma Sinclair?" What am I being set up with?'

'Morning all,' said Jess from the doorway. 'Is there any more coffee?' Gemma handed her a cup.

'So how can I help?' asked Pat.

It was Jess who spoke. 'We need to search this place high and low and find those bank statements.'

'Jess, I've already done that. I didn't find anything,' Gemma said.

'Where did you look?' Pat wanted to know.

'Um, in the ceiling, all through the drawers, under all the furniture in case something was taped there . . . Nothing.'

'What about outside? Have you looked in the sheds?' asked Pat.

'No, I've only done the house.'

'Worth a shot then, eh? You girls take the machinery shed and I'll do the shearing shed.'

'Dunno how we're going to find anything here, mate,' Jess said. 'There's crap everywhere. Do you actually use everything in this place?'

'Mostly. There's so much stuff needed for fencing, fixing machines, utes and all that. And it's a bloody long way to go to town if you need something. Better to keep it all on hand if you can.'

'Where do you keep all the manuals for the machines?'

'Over there on the bench in that tin box. Garry likes them at his fingertips.'

Jess walked over and opened the box. She sifted through the contents while Gemma looked behind the boxes of parts, tins of oil and jerry cans full of petrol.

Pat wasn't faring well in the shearing shed. Hours had passed, during which he'd searched through the drawers where all the stencils and wool books were, pulled open cupboards and run his hands along the tops of the thick wooden wool bins. He'd already searched through the wool packs, lifting each one up to make sure nothing had been slipped in between them; there weren't any hidey-holes or sneaky corners.

Sweat began to trickle down the back of his shirt. It was humid after the storm and the shed didn't let any breeze in. Sighing, Patrick switched off the light and the shed fell dark. The echo of the tin slider door reverberated around the shed as he left.

He walked into the machinery shed and burst out laughing. Jess was up a ladder looking behind the shadow board. Her hair was covered in cobwebs and her hands were filthy. She'd obviously been sneezing and had rubbed her nose, smearing dirt and grease across her face. Her clothes were dirty and she must have sat in some oil at some stage as her shorts were stained black across the rump.

'Bet ya look like that every day after work, Red,' Pat said. 'Suits ya.'

'Nick off, Patrick,' Jess retorted mildly.

Gemma came out of the smoko room. 'Find anything?' she asked hopefully.

'Not a brass razoo,' Pat said. 'There's nowhere to hide anything in a shed like that. No nooks or crannies. Guess you haven't found anything yet either?'

'Nup.' Jess started to climb down the ladder. 'I haven't been through that section over there, Pat,' she said, indicating the corner where the fencing gear was. 'Can you do that?'

They worked quietly together for the next couple of hours, sifting through dust, cobwebs and old machinery parts. Finally, Jess stood up and said, 'I've had enough for today. My back's killing me and it must be time for a Scotch. Whaddya reckon?'

Gemma looked at her watch. 'Far out, today has gone quickly. I'm stuffed – but at least my body isn't as sore today. I think I'll give the painkillers a miss and have a drink instead!'

'Good idea,' Jess said.

Patrick's head appeared from behind an old rusty combine. 'Did I hear the word drink? Lead me to the fridge!'

Gemma felt better as the ice-cold rum slipped down her throat. Hearing a dog bark, she got up off the couch and looked out the lounge-room window. She could see a mob of woolly sheep being herded down the laneway by Bulla's faithful kelpie, Roady. 'Lucky for me I've got those two,' Gemma murmured.

'What's that, lovely?' Jess asked.

'Lucky,' Gemma said, turning towards Jess and Patrick. 'I'm very lucky. I've got two wonderful stockmen who would do anything for me, I've got a brilliant friend who would do anything for me, a brother who is basically okay and most likely would do anything for me . . .' She grinned and poked her tongue out at Patrick, who raised his rum glass back at her. 'And maybe a guy who likes me. I just know that we'll find those papers.'

'I'll drink to that,' said Jess, raising her glass in a toast. 'Now how 'bout I get us some tea?'

Pat finished his dinner and pushed his plate away. 'Right, I'm sick and tired of you girls twittering away. I'm off to have another crack at the shed without you lot getting in my way.'

He grabbed a torch and went back over to the machinery shed.

The spotlights flooded the shed and a couple of frightened mice scuttled back under the fencing gear. Pat poked around the smoko room and walked the perimeter of the shed. Scratching his head he looked around. He really didn't know where to start. It seemed they had already been everywhere today. Maybe Adam didn't keep anything; maybe he didn't keep the papers here. Maybe he had a safe deposit box somewhere and they didn't have a hope of finding anything. Too many maybes, yet the outcome if the papers weren't found was too worrisome to comprehend. 'Think like Adam,' Pat muttered to himself. Lifting his gaze to the tin roof he couldn't see anything worth investigating – until his eyes fell on the cavity above the smoko room's ceiling.

Jess would have looked up there, Pat thought. *No point. Wonder how she'd have got up there though. Too high for a ladder.* He looked around and at the edge of the shadow board four pieces of wood caught his eye. One of them had a jimmy bar hanging on it but as Pat looked up he could see that they could be used as rungs to get to the cavity. If he climbed up them and walked across the rafters, he'd be able to look on the roof. 'Nah,' he thought. 'Too hard for Adam.' After fossicking in the shed for another hour, he looked again at the pieces of wood that could make the rungs of a ladder. *Can't see anything better to try,* he thought and grabbed his torch. He hoisted himself onto the bench and placed his foot onto the bottom rung to test it with his weight. Slowly he climbed to the top with his torch tucked under his arm and looked over the ceiling of the smoko room. Dust, cobwebs and dirt covered everything. 'Should've known it wasn't worth it,' he muttered as he directed the torch's beam around the small space. He was about to start his descent when the torchlight caught the glint of something shiny towards the back of the cavity. Stopping, Pat squinted towards the glimmer. He climbed onto the rafter and crawled over into the hollow.

Gemma and Jess sat next to each other on the couch, each with a drink in hand. At the sound of the dogs barking, Gemma got up and went to the window. She watched as a set of lights came up the driveway and pulled in at the shearers' quarters. Shearing again tomorrow. Thankfully some normality would return to life.

Jess asked, 'So you think someone is setting you up?'

'It looks that way.' Gemma was upset. 'I don't know who it is or why, and it's getting really scary. What do they want with me? What could I possibly have done to them? I mean, for Jack to talk about a set-up makes it sound personal.'

Jess listened thoughtfully then jumped up. Grabbing Gemma's hand she said, 'C'mon. I've got an idea. Our research methods could do with updating – poking around in sheds is *so* twentieth century.'

'What? What do you mean? Where are we going?'

'I've got one word for you, Gem: Google.'

They went into the office and Jess fired up the computer. She opened the internet browser and typed in the address of the search engine. 'Okay,' she said. 'What should we look up?'

'How about "Jack Marshall"?' Gemma suggested.

Jess typed in the name, then groaned. 'There's over nine hundred hits. I'm going to need another drink to get through that lot. Want one?' she asked, leaving the office.

'Sure,' said Gemma absently, taking Jess's place at the computer and starting to type. 'Bloody hell, Jess? Jess, get in here!'

Jess came running back into the office. 'What's wrong?'

Gemma was staring at the screen in horror. 'I added stock stealing to the search term,' she explained.

Reading over her shoulder Jess read: *Rustling Charges Dropped.* As she read the newspaper article from outback Queensland, her hand flew to her mouth.

The Queensland Stock Squad have today decided not to pursue the case against Brad Manstead and Jack Marshall, who had been accused of stock stealing.

Following a three-month investigation it appears there is insufficent evidence to charge the brothers.

Brad Manstead said in a statement, 'Although I am pleased with the outcome, I'm very angry that we have had to submit to this fruitless investigation. Neither myself nor my brother are guilty of the alleged crime.'

Bob Pergot from the stock squad believes there still is a case to answer. 'Unfortunately we just can't find the evidence we need to lay the charges. This case won't be closed, but we are scaling down the inquiry.'

The investigation started when station owner Gordon Green reported 400 cattle missing from his property in northern Queensland. An investigation established the stock had been trucked south, but the stock squad lost the trail soon after the truck crossed into New South Wales.

Mr Marshall had been working on Mr Green's station at the time the cattle went missing.

His brother, Mr Manstead, admitted to owning a part share in an abattoir in South Australia, but categorically denied any involvement. 'The fact that Jack is my half-brother and I have a part share in BJN Abattoir is circumstantial evidence at best. We are innocent of all allegations.'

The girls stared at the screen, speechless. The kitchen door slammed and they heard Pat's footsteps coming towards the office.

'What's goin' on in here?' Pat asked as he stuck his head through the door. He looked at their faces. 'What's the problem? You both look like you've seen a ghost.'

Gemma waved her hand at the computer screen.

Jess's face grew red. 'That bastard,' she spat. 'That lying mongrel bastard. Print it off, Gemma.' She turned and stormed out of the room.

Pat approached the screen. 'Well, bugger me,' he said. 'So that's the Jack who worked here then, eh?'

'Yeah,' Gemma said faintly. 'And Brad is Jess's ex-boyfriend. She dumped him on Monday after he was horrible to me at a dinner on Saturday night. A little coincidental, wouldn't you say?'

'You're jokin! She's been going out with this Brad?'

'Mmm.' Turning to look at Pat, she realised he was holding something. 'Have you found something?' she asked hopefully.

'Y'know, I reckon I might have,' Pat said, looking

very pleased with himself. 'Although maybe you should go see how Jess is.'

Gemma found Jess sitting in the lounge room with a fresh drink.

'The bastard,' Jess spat again as her friend entered the room. 'I can't believe it. He's done this before. He must have got together with me to get at you for some reason. I'm trying to remember all the questions he asked about you. I thought he was taking an interest 'cos you're my best friend. He owns a bloody abattoir and you've got a dead husband and stolen stock on your property. He's a bloody crim.' Jess leapt off the couch and began to pace the floor.

'Pat's found a box,' Gemma said.

Jess paused in her pacing. 'You little ripper,' she said. 'What's in it?'

'Haven't opened it yet. Thought Gem should do that,' Pat said, walking down the couple of steps into the lounge room. He set the box on the coffee table and they all looked at it silently.

'I know what that box is,' Gemma said suddenly as recognition hit her. 'Tim Milton gave him that box. He made it for Adam's twenty-first. It was before Claire's accident. Adam was going to ask Tim to be best man at our wedding but he was dead by the time we got married. Where did you find it, Pat?'

'It was in a little cavity up above the smoko room.'

Gemma reached forward and pulled the lid off the box.

Taking out the contents, she handed a stack of envelopes to Jess. 'These look like bank statements. You'll know what you're looking for.'

Jess took them and opened the flaps. Gemma looked at what was left. The letterhead of Ned and Bert's stock firm topped a list of sale summaries for the cattle that went to the feedlot. That was one question answered. She kept looking. There were letters that Gemma had written to Adam while she'd been on holidays with Jess, postcards from Alice Springs and Darwin. There was a letter from Adam's dad saying how proud he was of his son for finishing year twelve. At the bottom of the box was an envelope with her name written on it. The sight of the familiar scrawl caused Gemma's stomach to contract. Taking a deep breath she opened the envelope and took out a sheet of paper. Another, smaller envelope fell out marked POLICE ONLY. Underneath, in smaller letters was written, *Gemma do not read*.

Gemma put it on the table.

'What about I get some coffee? Reckon we could all do with some.'

'Good idea, Pat,' Jess said quietly, still looking at the bank statements.

Gemma unfolded the piece of paper she was clutching and started to read:

Dear Gemma,
The first thing I need to say is that I'm sorry and
I love you very much. You are the best thing in

my life and what I'm about to tell you will hurt you. I'm so very sorry.

Three years ago I was having trouble making the repayments to Mum and Dad. You know as well as I do how tight things were back then – no rain, no feed, the wool quality was crap and so were the prices. There were times I didn't think we would be able to make it through the year, let alone keep farming the next one.

I felt so trapped, Gem. Everywhere I went people wanted a piece of me. The bank, Mum and Dad, the Best Farmers group I started. Everyone. Even you, Gem. I felt as if I was losing control of everything.

I met a bloke at Dawns Rest one night and he offered me a way out: stock stealing. I'm assuming you have gone looking for this box because of something that has happened or is happening, so you must know a little bit about it.

Billbinya has been used as a holding paddock for the stolen stock.

All the details are in the enclosed envelope for the police. I have told them how it worked, the people who are involved and that you didn't know anything about it. This is your insurance. Gem, I never meant for this to go on for as long as it has. I want to get out, but I don't know how. The people who are involved are nasty pieces of work. They will stop at nothing to keep this ring going. You need to be careful.

Once all of this is sorted out, please, Gem, sell Billbinya. It's too hard for you to try and make a living from the way we are farming. Take the money and run. At least you will be set up and not want for money again.

I do love you, Gemma. I'm sorry for all the hurt I have caused you. I'm sure you will be okay though. You always were stronger than me.

Love,

Adam

Tears ran down Gemma's face as she reread the letter then handed it to Jess and Patrick to read.

'What do we do now?' asked Pat as Jess folded the letter carefully and put it back in the envelope. Gemma held the envelope for the police. Her fingers itched to open it, but she knew she couldn't.

'We call Dave and Craig and ask them to come out tomorrow. We give them the phone, the bank statements and the letters, tell them about the forged contract signatures and let them handle the rest. I haven't got the energy for anything more,' Gemma said.

Jess nodded in agreement. 'Yeah, I reckon that's the best way to go too. There's more than enough evidence to clear Gemma. Good old Adam, fancy thinking to leave a letter absolving Gem. He wasn't such a complete bastard after all.'

'Jess . . .' Gemma said tiredly.

'Sorry, lovely!'

'Oh, I'm so tired. I've got to get to bed or I'll be useless for shearing tomorrow.' Gemma rose and stretched.

'You'll be useless anyway. You can't do anything with that arm,' Jess reminded her.

'No, but I can drive a ute and Jack isn't here, remember, so someone will have to get the sheep in and out. What's the time? Is it too late to ring Dave?'

Jess looked at her watch. 'Yeah, I think it might be, but we'll call him first thing in the morning. Give me all this stuff. I'm going to sleep with it under my pillow.'

'Don't dribble on it and smudge the writing!' Pat said as he left the room.

'You're lucky there isn't a coffee cup following you,' Jess called to his back. Turning to Gemma she gave her a hug. 'How do you feel?'

'You know, I'm shocked, stuffed, sore and my eyes feel like I've been crying forever, but I feel like a big weight has been lifted off my shoulders. What about you? What about Brad?'

'Oh I dunno, Gem. Men . . .' She shrugged. 'Who can possibly understand them?'

Chapter 28

Monday morning dawned cloudy and cool in Port Pirie. Craig was standing outside the police station eating an egg and bacon sandwich and waiting for Dave. He felt quite jumpy and wanted to get on with the day. He and Dave were going back to Billbinya that morning. They needed to question Gemma about the cattle that had been found on her station.

Craig felt awful about questioning her again after everything she'd been through, but the stock squad's work didn't just involve animals; they had to deal with anything outside of the law when they came across it, and he hated the assaults, the beaten women and rapes.

Dave came out of the station with his notes and files and they set off.

* * *

Within a couple of hours, Dave and Craig were sitting at the kitchen table of the Billbinya homestead facing Gemma and Jess. The stock squad officers had been surprised by the warm welcome – and Gemma's claim that she had been about to call them.

'When was the last time you were out in the northern paddock, Gemma?' Dave asked casually.

'Oh, I don't know.' Surprised, Gemma stopped to think. 'Jack had been covering that part of the place since he arrived. Probably two weeks, I guess. There's sheep out there so between Jack and Bulla they would have been watching them pretty closely.'

'Haven't had any problems reported to you then?'

'No, everything seems to be going pretty well.'

'Do you or any of your neighbours own any Hereford cattle?'

'I don't,' Gemma said. 'And my neighbours don't either. Not boundary-fence neighbours anyway. Why?'

'Well, we found quite a few Hereford cattle in your northern paddock while we were out looking around. Are you saying they aren't yours?' Dave asked quietly, while Craig looked at the table, avoiding Jess's eyes.

'No, they aren't mine,' Gemma said calmly.

'Well, we are going to have to ask you to come back to the Port Pirie police station and make a statement to that effect. This matter has become quite serious. There was nearly a hundred grand worth of cattle on your property that wasn't yours.'

'Did you find anything else that shouldn't have been on Billbinya?' Gemma asked.

'We did find a stock-stealing kit – panels, a couple of dogs and some wire – that we believe belongs to Jack Marshall.'

Gemma's mouth fell open. 'Really?'

'Yes. We have photographic evidence that they were his. That doesn't clear you, Gemma. You own Billbinya and therefore you're responsible for what is found on your station.'

Gemma nodded. 'Absolutely. I don't have a problem with that. However, I have come across some information that I believe you will find quite interesting. Can you get it, Jess?' Gemma asked and turned back to the men.

'On Saturday after I came home from hospital . . .'

Dave interrupted. 'Gemma, would you have any problem with me taping this conversation? Bear in mind this tape will be used in our evidence file. You won't be able to retract anything you say.'

'No worries, Dave,' Gemma said confidently.

'Okay, what did you want to tell me?' Dave asked when he hit the record button.

'What I know about this stock-stealing ring.'

Dave raised his eyebrows. 'Do I need to caution you?'

'No. I'll happily tell you everything I know. Okay, it started when the wethers were taken out of the yards . . .'

'Hang on, for the benefit of the tape we are in Billbinya Station's kitchen. Present are Dave Burrows, Craig Buchanan, Gemma Sinclair and . . .' Dave looked inquiringly at Jess, who had returned to the room carrying a large paper bag.

'Jess Rawlings,' Craig supplied.

'Jess Rawlings. Time is 11.27 am and we are taking Gemma Sinclair's statement.' He indicated for Gemma to begin.

Gemma started with how Bulla had found the stolen wethers on Billbinya. She told about Patrick finding the mobile phone and reading the text messages and handed over the diary for back-up evidence. Then she explained about how she asked Jess to go through the books and they had found that payments to Adam's parents had been made, but not from the Billbinya operating account, and the payments for the feedlot cattle had gone into the operating account. It was through Jess's phone call to Rodney Woods that they had found that Adam was making the payments from another bank account Gemma hadn't known about. They surmised that this is where the proceeds had been credited to.

Gemma stopped and got herself a glass of water.

'Then on Saturday, when we arrived home, Ben was here with the feedlot contracts for the last three years and the one for this year. The last two years have been signed by a G.R. Sinclair, but the signature isn't mine. It's been forged.' Once again she handed over the evidence. She then told of how she, Jess and Patrick had decided to search for the bank statements from this new account and how Patrick had found them.

'We'll need to see where,' Dave interrupted her.

'No worries. While Pat was searching Jess and I looked up Jack Marshall on Google and we came up with this article.' Gemma nodded to Jess who produced the printout. 'Jack was working here and Brad has been going out with Jess for the last eight months – to get information about me, it seems. Possibly to find out how much I knew, if anything, about the stock stealing. I'd assume that's why Jack ended up applying for the job. He must have seen it advertised and thought it was a good way to find out if I knew anything. Then we opened the box.' Gemma stopped. This was the hard bit. This was where her husband turned into the person she didn't know. Swallowing hard, she continued. 'The box was a bit of a keepsake thing of Adam's. It was made for him by one of his good mates who committed suicide some time ago and in it were the bank statements we were looking for. Also there was a letter to me admitting his guilt, and an envelope addressed to the police.' Jess put the paper bag on the table and pushed it towards Craig. 'Everything that we know is in there. I can't tell you anything more.'

Dave scanned the newspaper article while Craig looked at the text messages on the mobile phone. The tape player clicked off and they all jumped, having forgotten it was on. Dave checked his watch. 'Interview suspended at 13.02,' he said absently.

'Can you open the letter while you're here?' Gemma asked hopefully. 'I want to know how it all happened.'

'We need to follow a few procedures first, like fingerprinting it, making sure it isn't a fake. I'd also like to take Adam's diaries for the past two years. You've only given me last year's.'

'I'll get them.' Gemma got up and went to the office. She returned holding two leather-bound diaries with Adam's initials embossed on the covers in gold. Handing them to Dave she said, 'This does clear me, doesn't it?'

'I won't be able to say for sure until I look through all of this info and analyse it. Can I get Craig to fingerprint you, Jess and Patrick so we can eliminate your fingerprints on all of this?'

'Sure, although Patrick isn't here – he went back to Hayelle this morning.'

'If you give us directions, we'll call in on the way back.'

Craig went out to the car to fetch the finger-printing kit. He fingerprinted both Gemma and Jess, gently holding their fingers and rolling them on the evidence cards. Jess looked around to see if Dave was watching, hooked her blackened finger around Craig's top button and pulled him towards her. She whispered, 'How's about that drink soon, Detective?' and released him before Dave turned around. Craig flushed and nodded ever so slightly.

Dave and Craig climbed back into their four-wheel drive and headed to Hayelle. Gemma rang and left a message for Patrick to let him know they were coming and why.

Gemma watched the dust settle in the drive after the vehicle had left. Jess came and stood by her.

'Reckon it's sorted?' Gemma asked.

'Guess we won't really know until the last arrest has been made, but I think so. Changing the subject completely, that Craig is a bit of a hottie, hey?'

Gemma rolled her eyes.

Brad lay on his bed with his wife, the woman he loved. They had met unexpectedly and Brad had been immediately struck by her – especially once he had discovered that they shared certain goals, and a determination to stop at nothing to achieve them. It didn't matter to either of them that the other was unfaithful at times. If it had to happen, it was all in aid of making more money, making sure that the people who were helping them had more to lose than they themselves did.

It had been his idea to start the stock-stealing ring and she'd agreed it was a brilliant plan. They had been involved in this business for many years now and, although they preferred to steal stock from the far northern reaches of Australia, where the owners never knew exactly how many cattle they ran, and there were parts of those stations no one went to for months, that option had gone out of the window when Brad and Jack had aroused the interest of the Queensland stock squad about six years ago.

The downside of these full-scale operations, Brad reflected, was that he and his beloved didn't get to spend much time together. They had decided it was too risky.

But now they were together, discussing the big operation they had coming up – by far the most daring they had tried to pull off. His woman had a history with Gemma Sinclair, and she wanted Gemma hurt – and, with any luck, behind bars.

'Are you sure she doesn't suspect anything?' his wife asked. 'You haven't got a line in there now that Jack has stuffed up and you're not seeing Jess anymore.'

'I'm sure the stock squad would have found those cattle while they were looking around and I'm pretty sure that they would be talking to her very seriously if not arresting her. She hasn't got a leg to stand on, you know.' Brad stopped to enjoy the beautiful smile spreading across his woman's face.

'How wonderful,' she murmured. 'Jail is the only place she deserves to be after everything she did. It was all her fault, you know.'

'I know, darling, I know.' Brad put his arm around her and kissed her soundly. 'This last job will be perfect. Who would imagine that Gemma Sinclair, Miss Perfect, would steal from her own parents? Especially when her father is so desperately sick and unable to do anything about it.' They laughed together.

* * *

Dave was on the phone to his superior in Perth as they drove back towards Pirie.

'Yeah, I understand that, but we need some more uniforms on the ground, okay? We need twenty-four-hour surveillance on two persons of interest. Jack Marshall is still on the run. We haven't managed to track him down yet.' Dave listened then said, 'Thanks mate.' He hung up. 'Beauty, we've got the extra manpower.'

'Want me to do the background on these other two and follow up some of the other facts from Adam's letter to us?' Craig asked. Dave glanced across at him, his eyes taking in the fingerprint ink on his shirt.

'Yeah, we'll do that first. Let's not go half-cocked. Slip with the ink, did ya mate?' Dave nodded towards the stain. Craig's face flamed and Dave laughed. 'Wish ya would learn to play poker better when it comes to personal things, mate!'

'Let's concentrate on the job at hand, shall we?' Craig asked primly. He hadn't had a chance to think about Jess and how he was going to handle the situation. All he knew was he wanted to get to know Jess better.

They pulled into the station. With his partner's assent, Craig headed to the computer and phone while Dave headed to Geoff Hay's office to give him an update.

Some time later, as Dave was walking back into Craig's office, he heard Craig on the phone.

'Yep. I understand. Sure we can get a warrant for the information.' Pause. 'I'll see you on Wednesday. Thanks for your help.'

'Got anything?' Dave asked.

'Yeah, reckon I have. It appears that Brad Manstead attended a psychiatrist's office in Adelaide. He saw Dr Tom Dyason for three years from 1995 to 1998. Dyason won't give me any info until I get a warrant. This may be where he met the other person of interest. I'll go see the judge for a warrant today and I've organised to see Dr Dyason on Wednesday. I also checked out BJN Abattoir; the shares were left to Brad by his father. Jack is his half-brother – different mothers. That clarifies the piece of info that was in the letter. What's interesting, though, is that BJN has a silent partner, so I want to know who that is. I have a feeling it will confirm the other piece of info in Adam's letter. Just need to get onto the company records department . . .'

Dave clapped his shoulder. 'Good work. Right, get that warrant application drawn up and we'll go and interview this other POI. I've been on the phone and he's getting ready to leave the state on an extended holiday.'

'Is that right? When does he leave?'

'Wednesday apparently, so we've got two days – well, a day and a half – to break him.'

Dave and Craig walked up the pathway of a nice-looking house. The garden was well tended and it looked like the house had been freshly painted. Knocking on the door, the two men looked around, hoping to see something that indicated this man had more money than his wages accounted for.

A well-dressed mature lady opened the door with a smile. 'Hello? Can I help you?'

'G'day.' Dave held up his ID. 'I'm Detective Dave Burrows from the stock squad and this is Detective Craig Buchanan.' As he was talking Ned Jones appeared at his wife's shoulder.

'G'day, fellas. Still investigating I see.' Turning to his wife he said, 'I'll fix this up, love. It's got to do with the stock stealing that's been happening out Gemma's way.'

Rosemary smiled and excused herself. 'I've got heaps of packing to do,' she said. 'We're going to the Northern Territory for a big break. We've never had a long holiday, have we, Ned? I've never been able to get him off the phone – too busy with the stock business! Well, I'll see you later.' She disappeared into the house.

'Can we have a chat about some of this business then, Ned?'

'Yep.' He stood there with his hands in his pockets, rocking on his heels. Defiant.

'Want to do it here or down at the station?' Dave asked, just as bold.

Ned stopped rocking and sighed. 'Okay, let's go. I'll just tell Rose.'

The interview room was cold, even though the wintery sun shone. Ned shivered and zipped up his jacket. Craig was setting up the recording equipment and Dave had placed a cup of coffee in front of Ned. Wrapping his hands around it, Ned asked, 'So why do you need to record this again? I don't know anything more than what I've told you. Do I need a lawyer?'

'Why would you need a lawyer, Ned? You haven't done anything wrong – you just said so. Nah, we just want to clarify a few matters that have come to light recently. We like to record interviews so we don't miss anything. Are you ready, Craig?'

'Yep. Let's go.'

'We are interviewing Ned Jones at . . .' Dave went through the spiel of identifying everyone for the tape and then said, 'Ned, can you clarify your relationship with Adam Sinclair?'

'Ah, he was a client of mine for many years, until his death. His father was also a client before him.'

'And what do you do for your clients exactly?'

'I source markets for their stock and sell them for a commission. I can also organise the trucking of the stock. If the client wants to buy stock I usually know of animals that would suit the enterprise and can purchase the stock on the client's behalf.'

'Are you a full partner in this firm?'

'Yes I am. Bert made me a partner fifteen years ago.'

'Pay well?' Dave leaned back, looking interested.

'Yeah, I get three per cent of everything I buy and sell. I've been very lucky.'

'Have you always lived in Pirie?'

Ned suddenly looked uncomfortable. 'Why is that relevant?'

'Just curiosity really. Trying to get a picture of your life.'

Ned relaxed. 'No, Rose and I lived down in the south-east of South Australia for a few years when our kids were little. That's where I trained as a stockie. Naracoorte. We were there for eight years before I got offered this position with Bert, and I'd been here about three years before Bert offered me a partnership.'

'Marriage happy?'

Ned's face broke into a smile. 'Oh yeah. Rose is great. We've had times like everyone I guess – 'specially when the kids were small – but we're very happy together.'

Dave smiled. 'That's great. Nothing better than a good marriage. Gives you so much security, hey? Now listen.' Dave leaned forward with a serious look on his face. 'We really need some help. This is why you're here. We're struggling. Can't find much info but we keep getting snippets and stockies are on the ground all the time. We know that you guys know what's going on around most farms, so we're hoping you can help us.' Dave paused, wondering how to phrase the next part. 'We were out at Billbinya last week and there are some cattle there that aren't Gemma's. Have you sold any to her recently?'

Ned looked quite comfortable with this line of questioning. 'No, I haven't.'

'Do you think she'd have used another stock agent?'

'No, she's always used me . . . Well, Ben now, since he's taken on her account. But not another firm.'

'Okay. On Friday night, while we were out on the property, she was attacked by Jack Marshall. Do you know him?'

Ned started at this piece of information. 'Attacked? What do you mean attacked?'

'She was bashed around a bit. She's okay, but hurt badly enough to require medical attention.'

'Shit. Oh, bloody hell.' Ned's face had started to grow red and his hands had begun to shake.

Dave looked at him and said, 'Hey, take it easy, buddy. She's okay. No harm done. Do *you* need a doctor?'

Ned shook his head and took a deep breath.

Dave watched him carefully. 'You like Gemma then?'

'She's like a daughter to me. I've been watchin' out for her ever since she was a little kid. Her parents deal with me too, you see. I've watched her grow up to become this amazing woman who is managing beautifully when no one thought she could. She's been through so much with Adam dying and now this stock-stealing business. Her dad – you know about her dad having a heart attack, don't you?'

'So who do you think could be trying to hurt her with this stock-stealing stuff then? Do you know Jack Marshall?'

'I only know Jack from Billbinya. I don't know who is trying to hurt her, but I wish I did.' Beads of perspiration had broken out on Ned's forehead and he mopped at them with a handkerchief.

'Ned, I'd like to get you a doctor. How about we do that?'

'Nah, I'm fine. Let's get this over with.'

'Okay, do you know any of these people?' Dave placed three photographs that Craig had downloaded off the web earlier in the day in front of him.

Ned glanced down. 'Well, obviously I know Jack. He worked at Billbinya. As for the other two – I have seen this fella around town. He's an agro, I think – Brad Manstead – but I don't know him personally. Haven't ever seen this one before.' Ned pushed the third photo to the side.

'Well, you see, Ned, that's where we now have a problem.' Dave leaned back again. 'We have a letter from Adam. It has only come into our possession today but it names names. Tells the whole story. And guess what, mate? You're in there. Want to tell us about it?'

Ned's face grew redder and his sweating became more profuse. He toyed with his empty coffee cup and then got up from his chair. He paced the room for a time, while Craig and Dave sat in silence. This was a man wrestling with his conscience.

Finally Ned sat back down and started to talk quietly.

'It started about a year ago. Bit more maybe. I was approached by this young man.' Ned tapped the picture of Brad. 'He started to blackmail me. Said if I didn't supply information on stock that were killable in the district he'd reveal my secret. I tried to talk him around. I've always been a fairly honest guy. I like fun, but not stuff like this. He didn't tell me why he wanted the stock but I did some research and found out that he owned an abattoir. I guess they were killing the stock there and making money that way. I was to supply Adam with the information by text message. He'd then case the farm, try and get the owners off the place and the trucks would move in. Jack did most of the stealing and would travel with the truck to the holding paddock. That was Billbinya. They wanted to paddock the stock for a few weeks until the heat died down, you know? Then they'd shift the stock to the abs.' Ned reached for his coffee cup but found it empty. 'That's it. There you go. I passed on the info to Adam and Brad. But I was being blackmailed. I couldn't risk Rose finding out my secret. I love her too much to hurt her and I'm so ashamed of past events.'

Dave said gently to the ill-looking man: 'Doctor yet?'

Ned shook his head again.

'Can you tell me what the blackmail was about? I can't help you unless you do.'

Ned stared at the scratched wooden table in front of him and murmured softly, 'He said he'd tell Rose about the daughter I had with another woman.'

Silence hung in the air. Craig shifted slightly, trying to get Dave's attention. He made a hand sign like a phone. Dave looked curiously at Craig and then realisation spread across his face.

'Ned, did you make the anonymous phone call to the station after the wethers were found?'

Ned nodded. He could barely control his hands now and he had a heavy feeling in his chest.

'Who is your daughter?' Dave pushed gently. To Craig he said, 'Get a doctor anyway.'

Craig slipped out of the room.

'I feel sick.' Ned suddenly stood up and turned around, clutching at his chest. Dave shot out of his seat, yelling to Craig to get an ambulance. Ned hit the floor before Dave could reach him, his sightless eyes staring at the legs of the wooden table.

Chapter 29

'Hello?' Gemma answered the phone.

'Hi, Gem, how goes it?' asked Pat with an unusual strain in his voice.

'What's wrong, Pat?' asked Gemma, picking up on his tone straightaway.

'It's Kate. I have to go back to Queensland as soon as I can. She had a fall from a horse – broke her leg and busted a couple of ribs.'

'Oh no! Go, go as soon as you can. Do you want me to book a flight for you?'

'I'm just about to do that. Will you be all right to manage the workload on Hayelle?'

'We'll be right. Leave the list of things that Dad wanted done on the kitchen table and we'll try to get to it,' Gemma paused. 'Pat, thanks. Thanks for everything. I don't think I would have got through this without you.'

''Course ya would've. I'm gonna go and see the olds tonight and tell them what's happened with Kate. Better tell 'em we're gonna get married, eh?'

Gemma smiled into the phone. 'Not a bad idea. Don't want the old man falling off the perch before you've told him that. Be careful you don't shock him too much though.'

'Hopefully it'll shock 'im into getting off his arse and back to the farm!'

As Gemma hung up Bulla appeared at the door, Ben close behind him. They both had grim looks on their faces and Gemma realised they had bad news for her – but she couldn't think what on earth it could be now.

Long after Bulla had left and the shock about Ned had begun to sink in, Ben was still at Gemma's side. Jess was helping Bulla in the yards, although Gemma knew she wouldn't be of great assistance.

'Why would he do that?' Gemma asked, not for the first time.

'I don't know, Gem.' Ben took her hand.

'Poor Rose. Her husband in a coma, only hanging on with the help of a machine, just days before her dream holiday,' Gemma said sadly.

Gemma jumped up from the couch. 'C'mon, I want to show you something.' She stalked out the door and jumped in the ute, Ben following.

'I'm so bloody angry,' said Gemma as she revved the engine and headed out towards her favourite spot on the farm. 'I can't believe this is happening. Do you think Dave and Craig will get into trouble since Ned collapsed while they were questioning him?'

Ben shook his head. 'My guess is there will be an internal investigation, making sure all the proper procedures were followed, but Rose told them he'd been diagnosed with a heart problem about three months ago. That's when they decided to take this holiday and put me on the road. He was a ticking time bomb apparently. I don't think you can blame Dave and Craig. The questioning and circumstance, possibly, but Ned was the one who put himself in the situation. I guess he never thought about the outcome. Anyway, I still reckon he's gonna be fine. Ned's a tough old bloke.'

'Would you want to live if you knew what trouble you were coming back to?' Gemma asked and then answered her own question by shaking her head. She turned the music up loud and let the cool breeze of the late afternoon caress her face. It was going to be a beautiful sunset and, if she tried hard enough, she might just be able to forget the events of the day for a couple of minutes.

Pulling up beside the creek where she and Jess had camped not so long ago, Gemma threw open the door and got out.

'This is my favourite place on the whole property,' she said, throwing open her arms. 'Adam and I used to camp here.' Gemma walked over to an outcrop of rock that was as high as her waist. 'This is the little table we used to use to put nibblies on and over here . . .' She indicated a flat spot next to the bank of the creek. 'This is where we'd roll out our swags. Look at the stars, talk, make love.' Gemma's voice was soft, remembering, but when she swung around to face Ben her expression was hard. 'It was all a lie. My marriage was a lie. My whole life as I knew it was a fabrication.'

Gemma leaned against an outcrop of rock and Ben moved towards her. He put his hands on her shoulders and looked into her eyes. 'Yes, it might have been a lie, but it doesn't have to stay that way. Once all this is sorted, you can start again. Learn to trust and learn to love again. Gemma, you are too strong to be eaten up with anger and bitterness. You have so many people who love you. Jess, Pat, me.' Ben stared at the beautiful face that looked back at him in wonder.

'Did you say love?' Gemma asked quietly, searching his face.

Ben looked slightly uncomfortable. 'Well, love might be a bit strong at this time, but I definitely want to spend a lot more time with you.'

Gemma put her arms around Ben and leaned into his chest. He tipped up her head and kissed her. Gently at first, but more passionately as the kiss continued. Around them, magpies warbled their evening song and galahs screeched noisily. Then they sat in silence and watched the sun set over the purple hills.

* * *

Jess was waiting in the kitchen for them when they got back, the excitement plain on her face. Waving her mobile phone, she yelled, 'The bastard has slipped up! He's sent a text message to me that must have been meant for Jack. We've got the mongrel!'

Gemma laughed. 'What are you talking about, you crazy woman?'

Jess held up her mobile again. 'Brad has stuffed up. He's losing the plot. He's sent me a text message saying he wants to start shifting the next lot of stock on Friday at 11 pm. Let me read it to you. Come on! Get inside! Hurry! Ben, make yourself useful, there's a love, and get us all some drinks.' Jess was too busy organising to see the look of amusement pass between Gemma and Ben. 'Here we are, okay you ready? *J stock shift 11pm Fri. Roch Rd. 40 cows + calves. Hold padd bjn.*' Jess looked up excitedly. 'What do you think?'

'Okay, he wants to get forty cows and calves on a truck from Roch Road at 11 pm on Friday. Hold padd would be holding paddock and bjn ... I don't know what that means,' Ben said.

'Hang on,' Gemma said slowly. 'BJN, wasn't that the abattoir mentioned in the newspaper article? Isn't that the abattoir that Brad has a half share in? I bet the B stands for Brad, the J for Jack. I wonder what the N stands for?' A look of horror crossed her face and she said quietly: 'You don't think it could be Ned, do you?'

There was a brief silence while the friends took it all in.

Jess said after some thought, 'But where's Roch Road? It wouldn't stand for Rochden Road, would it? That's the road that Hayelle's on!'

But Gemma had already gone into the office to ring Dave.

Craig headed to Adelaide on Wednesday morning. He had a street directory with him to help him around the unfamiliar streets, but the local officers had told him he wouldn't have any problems. Wide road, easy parking and well-signposted streets would make it easy to get around. Craig decided they were wrong. He'd made a wrong turn and ended up on some side streets that he couldn't find in the street directory. After driving around the same block twice, he pulled into the car park of a small motel – the side streets certainly weren't wide enough to park in – so he could study the street directory more closely.

When he'd memorised the easiest route into the centre of the city, he put his car into gear and turned around in the small car park. Two brindle dogs tied to a ute caught his attention. Stopping again, he grabbed at the street directory to make it look like he was lost, while his eyes scanned the car park. White ute, two dogs, Victorian number plates, naked woman sticker, out-of-the-way motel. Jack Marshall was here somewhere.

Easing out his mobile phone, Craig lined up the ute and took a few photos. He was trying to zoom in on the dogs when he saw Jack emerge from his room. Craig swung the phone around, took two photos of Jack, put the car into gear and left. What a piece of luck!

A few blocks down the street he pulled over and rang Dave, leaving a message on his voicemail when he didn't answer. Then he resumed his course to Dr Tom Dyason's psychiatric practice.

A mousy-looking secretary showed Craig into the office of Dr Dyason and told him to have a seat. The doctor would be with him shortly.

Sure enough, Dr Dyason bustled into the room within minutes. 'Good morning, good morning,' Dr Dyason said, walking quickly towards Craig. He held out his hand and Craig went to shake it. 'No, no, warrant please.' Craig obediently handed over the warrant.

'Very good. Now, how can I help?'

Craig opened his briefcase and took out a photo of Brad Manstead. 'We are interested in this man. Can you tell me anything about him?'

'Yes I can. Bradley Charles Manstead. Had a difficult childhood and quite a pronounced problem with alcohol. Father deserted at a crucial time in Bradley's development and took up with another family, leading to feelings of abandonment. His mother was poor and his father didn't help out in any way financially. Consequently, his hunger for money is quite unhealthy. Quite willing to take risks to achieve what he wants. Anything else?'

Craig pulled out a photo of the second POI. 'Do you know this person? We are trying to work out how Brad and this individual met.'

Dr Dyason took the photo and stared at it for a long time. 'This person is very disturbed. She was my employee for about four months while I was helping Bradley. They began a relationship. They were both banished from my practice of course. Completely unacceptable behaviour. I'd been having some problems with her already. A compulsive liar, manipulative and has trouble distinguishing fact from fiction. Should have been my patient, not my employee. This individual' – Dr Dyason tapped the photo – 'is dangerous.'

Chapter 30

On Friday night Dave had two officers following Brad, two observing from the bush at the end of Rochden Road and two following Jack out of Adelaide. Craig and Dave were in Hayelle's machinery shed with binoculars and a video camera. Everyone had night-vision goggles and radios.

The crackle of the radio broke into Dave's thoughts. 'Truck approaching Rochden Road.'

'Roger that, unit four,' he responded and nudged Craig. 'We're on, get that camera rolling. Have you got the infrared thingy all set up?'

'You're so technically minded, Dave. I don't know how you'd do your job without me,' Craig said from behind the camera.

Dave clipped him over the ear. 'Respect authority, thanks!' They fell silent as they heard the rumble of the truck.

'Attention all units, truck entering property now. Keep observing. Remember, no interception. We want to follow this truck to its destination. Understood?' Dave clicked off and waited for the quiet replies.

'Roger that.'

'Unit four to unit one. Ute, Holden with Victorian plates, turned down Rochden Road. Think it's suspect Jack Marshall driving. Copy?'

'Copy that, unit four, sit tight,' Dave responded. The team of police waited as the truck backed into Hayelle's loading ramp. The night was bright from the full moon and, other than the clicking of the truck's engine, there wasn't a sound.

Jack's ute, with his lights switched to park, drove slowly past the shed and out into the paddock closest to the yards. The men watched as Jack let out a piercing whistle and his dogs jumped from the back of the ute and headed out around the camped cattle. Working quietly they rounded up the mob of cows and calves, while Jack drove slowly behind, park lights on. Taken unawares, the cattle were agitated. The calves bellowed loudly, frightened by the unexpected activity, but within fifteen minutes, the cattle had been herded into the yards and the gate clanged shut. Jack and the driver swung the gates to allow the cattle to flow up into the truck and ten minutes later, the cattle were loaded and the driver had leapt into the cab, ready to leave.

'All units, truck and ute leaving the scene,' Dave

whispered into his mouthpiece. To Craig he said, 'How much of that did you get?'

'The stuff out in the paddock won't come out – too far away – but I caught them running into the yards really clearly. Did you get the plate number of the truck?'

'Yeah, I just got word from the station that it's registered to the BJN Abattoir. These guys might not be as smart as we thought. How stupid is it to use a truck that can be traced so easily? Things must be falling apart for them.' Dave started packing up his gear and indicated for Craig to do the same.

'C'mon, let's follow this truck.'

'Unit four to unit one?'

'Unit one,' Dave answered.

'Suspect Jack Marshall has dumped his ute in the bush and jagged a ride with the truck, over.'

'Has he now,' murmured Dave. 'Unit four, immobilise the ute, over.'

'Roger.'

Dave and Craig followed the truck at a safe distance.

'Unit two, can you pull suspect truck over in about thirty kilometres and check his paperwork?' Dave said into his radio. 'Let's get a couple of cars in his view and keep him company for a bit. Then we'll disappear out of his life until he starts unloading, okay?'

'Roger that,' came the replies.

* * *

Unit two waited until they had travelled the full thirty kilometres and flicked on the lights of the police car without the siren. They pulled up alongside the truck as it stopped, then two uniforms got out of the car and gestured for the truck's driver to get out of the vehicle.

'G'day,' the policeman said amiably, flashing his credentials at the man. 'Late night, huh?'

'Somethin' like that,' the driver replied.

'Where ya off to?'

'Wakefield,' he said, naming a town on the outskirts of Adelaide.

'Oh yeah? Well we're just doing a routine check of paperwork, mate. Can we take a look?'

The man climbed up the steps and got a folder out. He handed it to the policeman, who opened it and checked through the weigh bill. 'Got anyone travelling with you?'

'Ah . . .' The man looked back at the truck. 'Yeah, a mate.'

'Good thing.' The copper nodded. 'Helps you stay awake on these midnight shifts, hey?'

'Yeah.' The man scratched his head uncomfortably.

'No worries. Only thing I noticed wrong was the date. You need to put today's date on there; you've used yesterday's. But there's no other problems. Sorry about having to pull you over. Keep getting emails from the stock squad asking us to check a couple of trucks a week. Reckon those blokes haven't got anything better to do than make work for us lowly uniforms! Cheers, mate, catch you later.'

Looking relieved, the driver grabbed his paper-work, mumbled goodbye and was back in the truck as quick as a flash.

Jack looked over at the driver. 'All right?' he asked.

'Yeah,' the other man said harshly. 'Stuffed if I'm doing this again. Bloody cattle truck on the road at this time of night heading towards Adelaide. Bound to get picked up. It's too bloody obvious.'

'Hey,' said Jack, 'don't panic. It's the last shipment from around here. We're all disappearing after tonight.'

The two men watched as the cops drove past them. There was silence in the cab until another cop car raced by with lights flashing.

'Busy night,' commented Jack.

'Hope that's all it is,' said the driver sourly.

A few more kilometres along they passed another cop car sitting by the side of the road. As Jack looked down, he could see the illuminated face of a police-man talking on his mobile phone. 'Good to know the cops follow their own rules,' Jack said. 'Bloody stupid idiots. There's cops everywhere tonight and we're just sailing through with a truckload of stolen cattle. Wankers.' Jack stared into the darkness. It was definitely time to leave South Australia.

As they continued down the highway the occasional car passed them but the road was mainly deserted by the time the driver turned the truck onto a dirt road leading to the holding paddocks behind the BJN Abattoir. It wasn't the main entry; all the stock trucks that were carrying killable stock went through the front gate and unloaded in the main stockyards. This was the track that the truck followed when they had stock on board for keeping. Jack jumped out to help unload and the driver could see Brad standing at the loading ramp, ready to direct him. Throwing the truck into reverse, he backed it in slowly. Brad took out the pin that held the back door of the crate shut and slid the door open.

The startled Hayelle Stud cows with their calves needed some encouragement to leave the truck. Brad climbed onto the top of the crate while the driver moved inside it trying to encourage the cattle down the ramp and into the cattle yards.

Jack swore. 'C'mon, you bastards, we haven't got time for this.' He climbed up onto the crate as well.

'Let's go, go, go!' Dave yelled into his mouthpiece. Four cars flew around the corner with spotlights blazing.

'Police! Put your hands where we can see them,' Craig shouted through a loudspeaker. Suddenly there were men rushing everywhere. Police wearing bulletproof jackets, wielding handguns and yelling. The cattle started to bellow loudly as they smelled the fear of the three men in the truck.

One officer braved moving inside the crate to grab the cowering driver and quickly cuffed him.

Another two coppers were trying to control Jack. He was doing his best to fight back, throwing punches and yelling, 'I'm not goin' back inside, ya bastards.'

Dave couldn't find Brad.

'Shit,' he swore. 'He's not gonna get away.' Searching the inside of the crate with a torch, he finally found Brad hiding behind one of the big iron doors that kept the cattle in pens. Dave saw him and stopped. 'Gonna come with me, mate?'

'Get stuffed,' Brad replied, looking around desperately.

'Good thing these cattle are quiet. Get some of those friendly buggers from up north and ya wouldn't be hiding inside there. They'd all want to eat ya for breakfast.' Slowly he advanced closer to where Brad stood. 'You want to tell me why you've got it in for Gemma Sinclair?'

'Get stuffed,' Brad said again, edging away from Dave and towards the dead end of the crate.

'No worries. We'll ask you again when we get down to the station.' Dave had his handcuffs out, ready. He was sure that Brad was going to make a run for it through the cattle. Dave could tell he had no idea about stock and in fact he was frightened of these gentle beasts, so he knew that Brad wasn't going to get away. He could hear all the shouts from the ground and knew the two other blokes had been apprehended.

Suddenly, Brad let out a massive scream. 'You ol' bitch, get off me foot, ya fat bloody cow.' He crumpled in a heap on the floor as the cow tagged as Y38 chewed her cud and stood on Brad's foot. Dave laughed at the man who was covered in sloppy cow shit, writhing in agony on the floor.

'I'd stand up if I was you, buddy. You won't be coming in the bloody front of the cop car looking like that. We'll need to hose you down and even then you'll still bloody stink. C'mon, stand up, ya mug. You'll get kicked in the bloody head otherwise. Hey, Jonno, open the side loading gate, will ya? We'll get this bloody idiot through there so we don't have to get in with the cattle.' Dave waited until Jonno was near the gate and climbed down to haul out Brad. Two sets of strong hands grabbed at him and hauled him through another heap of fresh manure, smearing it over the front of his shirt and face. Dave cuffed him and said 'C'mon, let's get you over to the yards and hosed down. Jonno, he can travel in the back of the paddy wagon, stuff having him in the front. Cor, he bloody reeks.'

Jonno grabbed a sorry-looking Brad and said, 'C'mon, let's go.'

With all three men in cuffs and in separate cars, Craig and Dave headed back to the Port Pirie police station to charge them. Craig made a quick phone call to Jess.

'It's all done. We've got Brad, Jack and the cattle.'

'My hero,' Jess gushed. 'Now about that drink ...'

Craig laughed. 'I think I might be tied up for the next couple of days, but darlin', after that, you're on!'

Chapter 31

Jess packed her bags early Sunday lunchtime so as to give Gemma and Ben some time alone.

Ben had spent the weekend at Billbinya. Once Friday night was over and Brad and Jack were behind bars, Ben had seen a new side of Gemma. She was like a different person. She laughed, she sang – terribly, Ben had to admit – and the tension left her face. She radiated life and fun. When Ben had commented on it, she'd smiled at him and said, 'There's no one left to hurt me. It's all done.' He'd hugged her to him.

Ben and Gemma waved goodbye to Jess then shared one last cup of coffee and a kiss before Ben climbed into his car and headed back to Pirie. Ned's heart attack had left him a huge workload and it would start in earnest on Monday.

The phone was ringing as Gemma went back inside. Snatching it up, expecting it to be Ben even though he'd just left, she was surprised to hear Paige's voice.

'Hi, Gemma, it's Paige. How are you?'

Gemma settled back in her lounge chair, ready for a chat. 'I'm great, Paige, how are you?'

'Great. How's your arm?'

'Yeah, pretty good. Got most of the movement back in it now, and all the swelling from the bruising and stuff has gone down, so I'm almost back to normal.'

'Excellent, how did shearing end up?'

'Really well. The second week just confirmed my thoughts about the first. Good quality wool, and lots of it, equals profitability!'

'That's really good to hear, Gemma. I'm pleased things are working out for you. Hey, I have tomorrow off, and I thought that since you don't come to town much, how about I come out for the day?'

'That would be great, Paige,' Gemma said sincerely. 'We can have a proper catch-up.'

'Okay, I'll be out in the morning then. Can I bring anything?'

'Just yourself. It'll be good to see you. Bye.' Gemma hung up the phone. Smiling, she hugged herself. Between Friday night's events and Ben's warm kisses, Gemma felt the happiest and most relaxed she'd been in ages. Roll on life!

Gemma was helping Garry tidy up the shed and change the oil in the neglected utes when Paige arrived. She got out of her tiny vehicle and gingerly stepped over the dusty ground to the shed. Gemma came out to meet her, wiping her oily hands on a piece of rag.

'Paige, hi! Sorry, I'm a bit of a mess – just helping Garry. But look at you. You look great!'

Paige was wearing pale blue three-quarter pants and a white linen top. A red silk sash was tied around her waist.

'Thanks – you look better than when I saw you last!' Paige joked.

'Absolutely. Life is brilliant. Come on, I'll make some coffee.'

The girls went into the house talking nineteen to the dozen. Old times, recent times, life since school. Gemma was surprised at how much there was to talk about with Paige. She really must convince Jess that they all needed to catch up for a meal.

'So tell me more about Ben,' Paige said as the afternoon drew to a close. 'He sounds too good to be true.'

'He's the right medicine for me at the moment! He's so gentle, loving. Really considerate. Just an all-round good guy. And he can talk cattle and farming, which is really important to me. I've found it hard since Adam died not having anyone to discuss things with. Especially things I'm passionate about. I love farming, I love cattle. It's just fun!' Gemma watched as Paige got up to look at all the photos that Gemma had around her walls.

'Do you miss Adam?' she asked.

'Yeah. Not as much as I did, and I've found out some really terrible things about him since he died, but it's never diminished my love for him.'

Paige turned around to face Gemma. 'Tell me how you felt when Tim died,' she said.

Gemma raised her eyebrows at the change of subject and crinkled her forehead in thought. 'Yeah, that was nasty, wasn't it? I dunno. It was only my second brush with death, I guess. Claire dying was the first time I'd lost anyone really close and I think her death affected me more than Tim's. I mean Tim was in our group and everything, but he was just a guy, you know what I mean? I was with Adam; Tim was just … just … I don't know – *there* I guess. But the whole thing was crap.'

'Did you hate me?' Paige asked quietly.

'No! Well, maybe a little. But only for a while. I guess the whole thing was such a shock and none of us knew that you were involved with Tim. You guys did a really good job of keeping that quiet. Did you really think Tim was going to leave Claire for you? Was that seriously what was going to happen?' Gemma smiled to soften her words.

Paige flopped onto the couch and looked at her hands sadly. 'Yeah, I thought it was. As time's gone on though, I've always wondered. Tim had made quite a few decisions before that dinner and I'm not sure I was involved in them. That's why I threw the photo on the table in front of Claire, think I got pissed off at that and wanted to hurt him.' Paige picked at her fingernails.

'Had he broken up with you?' Gemma asked quietly.

Paige picked at her nails a bit more and then looked up, her eyes glistening with tears. 'Yeah. The morning of the party.'

'Oh, Paige. The whole situation was dreadful, but as Ben said to me the other day, you need to put it behind you to be able to get on with life. Forgiveness is the only way to be able to live in peace. You need to be able to forgive yourself for what happened.'

Paige looked at Gemma quizzically. 'Why do I have to forgive myself?' she asked. 'I didn't do anything wrong.'

Gemma was momentarily taken aback. 'Oh, but I thought . . .' Her voice trailed off.

Paige stood up and walked across to look at Gemma and Adam's wedding photo on the wall. She traced Adam's face gently and turned to look at Gemma. Her eyes glittered and, for the first time, Gemma felt slightly unnerved.

'I knew Adam quite well, actually – just in recent times,' Paige said conversationally. She looked at Gemma brightly and a cold feeling settled at the base of Gemma's stomach.

'Did you? Adam didn't say he'd run into you again,' Gemma answered lightly.

'Mmm. I'm not surprised that Adam didn't tell you. Meeting me, he would have wanted to keep a secret.' Paige walked over and stood before Gemma, towering over her. 'Met him again through Brad, in fact. They were pretty good mates.' Gemma couldn't hide her surprise as Paige continued on. 'Brad's a bit of a honey too. Bet you didn't know we're married?'

'Can't say I did,' Gemma answered as calmly as she could. Inside she was quaking. Could she shout loud enough for Bulla and Garry to hear?

'And you,' Paige spat at her. 'You've lived a charmed life. Unlike me. You and your friends have taken away every man I have ever loved. Like Tim. I had to fight Claire all the time for Tim's attention and he finally gave it to me. For six months it was bliss. He was kind and wonderful. Even though he was still with her, he kept telling me he just needed time to work out how he was going to break it off with her. Then on the morning of the dinner he decides he doesn't want me anymore. Cast aside like an old shoe. "My future really does lie with Claire. Sorry, Paige," he said. Like he thought I was going to take that lying down. No way, buddy. I proved that, didn't I? And then you, Gemma, you. You drove me out of town by spreading terrible lies about me ...'

'I did not,' Gemma interrupted, bewildered by the attack. She'd never done anything like that!

'Oh, but you did, Gemma.'

Gemma stared at her in surprise. 'Paige, I did no such thing. You must be mistaking me for someone else. The only thing I ever did was yell at you and if you remember, I rang the day after to apologise. I was wrong and I knew that. I was still smarting from Claire's death.'

'And then there was Adam,' Paige continued in a shrill voice. 'I wasn't really in love with him, he still always went back to you. Just like Tim, he always went to another woman. Now you've managed to get Brad taken away from me – but you know what? Even that's not the worst thing you did. You took my father's love!'

'Paige, you always said you didn't know who your father was. How could I take his love away?' Gemma asked.

'When I was eighteen I managed to find the records I needed – and I found out who my dad was. And you know what, Gemma? When I approached him, he shunned me completely. I was the "repercussion of a few nights when he lost his mind", he told me. Once again, cast aside. But I saw my father coming here a lot. I saw the way he looked out for you, encouraged you. Treated you with respect. Especially after Adam died, he did everything he could to support you and nothing to support me.' Paige's face was etched with bitterness. 'Brad was already involved in stock stealing so I convinced him to help me target you. Put the stolen stock here, make everything point to you.'

Gemma's mind screamed with horror. Paige was obviously crazy. What if she intended to hurt her? Scared and desperate to run, Gemma didn't want to upset Paige by moving too suddenly.

Paige continued. 'Want to know who my dad is, Gemma? My dad is Ned Jones.'

Gemma gasped. 'I never knew, Paige, I'm so sorry . . .'

Paige turned and walked back over to the photos. 'See, Gemma? See the pattern? Any man I ever loved, or I wanted to love me, you took. That's why you need to be punished.' She took out a needle and syringe from her pocket. 'I have access to all these wonderful drugs – some of which don't even show up in autopsies.' She advanced towards Gemma as a shadow passed across the kitchen window. Puzzled, Paige looked carefully around and moved towards the kitchen. Then, changing her mind, she came back to Gemma.

Gemma knew if she could distract Paige, she could make it to the bathroom and lock the door – but how to distract her? Her eyes fell on the coffee table book next to her hand and her fingers inched towards it slowly.

'Stock stealing, Paige. Why? There was no evidence of you in there at all. Jess and I tracked Brad and Jack, but you didn't come into it. How did you manage not to get a mention?' Gemma's fingers closed on the book.

Paige's eyes swung back to Gemma, after convincing herself the shadow must have been the sun going behind a cloud.

'BJN, Gemma. Guess what it stands for?'

'Brad and Jack, we worked that bit out, but

please don't tell me the N is for Ned. Ned wasn't bad, misguided maybe, but not bad.' Gemma's eyes pleaded with Paige.

'Ned? Stupid man. Wouldn't know a good idea if it hit him in the face. No, not your precious Ned, Gemma. Nicholls. Paige Nicholls. I'm a silent partner in the abattoirs.'

With a sudden movement, Gemma picked up the book and threw it towards Paige, simultaneously jumping up from the couch. At that moment the kitchen door flew open and Craig tore in, with Dave close behind. Craig disarmed Paige with a swift movement and forced her to the ground, cuffing her hands behind her back.

Dave went to Gemma. 'Are you okay?' he asked, his hand on her shoulder.

Gemma nodded mutely as Craig began cautioning Paige.

'How did you . . . ?' Gemma tried to get the words out. 'Paige . . . She organised it all.' Gemma covered her face with her hands as Paige let out a bone-chilling howl.

'We've had her under twenty-four-hour surveillance since we read Adam's letter. We thought she'd be at the pick-up on Friday night but she wasn't, so we stayed on her tail through the weekend and followed her out here this morning. Pleased we did. We got most of her confession on tape. It's all over now, Gemma.'

Gemma started to cry.

Epilogue

Gemma looked at Craig as she walked towards him down the aisle. He smiled at her but Gemma saw his eyes slide past her to Jess, who walked behind in a simple wedding gown made of satin. Taking her place at the side of the altar Gemma glanced over at Ben, who stood uncomfortably in his suit holding the wedding ring for Craig to place on Jess's finger.

After making the decision to sell Billbinya, everything had seemed to fall into place. Her dad had decided he didn't want to farm anymore. In fact, that had been the discussion he'd wanted to have with her in the hospital the day of his heart attack. 'I'm too old. I want to travel and enjoy my life,' he'd said. 'Take on Hayelle. You'll do well and your life won't be as stressful!' She had taken him up on his offer.

Gemma looked at Craig and Jess and thought about how their relationship had graduated from a friendship to a full-blown love affair. Gemma had never seen Jess bowled off her feet the way she'd been with Craig. Craig had returned to Perth and for a while the two had commuted back and forth, but at Ben and Gemma's wedding a year and a half before, Craig and Ben had sprung a surprise on both the girls.

Ben was leaving the stock agency to live on Hayelle with Gemma. He'd sold his farm in the south, knowing he'd never go back there again. He belonged with Gemma. So there had been an opening in the agency. Ben lent the money from the farm sale to Craig, who had become a great mate, and Craig had bought into Hawkins and Jones. It now was Hawkins and Buchanan. Gemma could still recall the excitement on the men's faces when they had told the two girls.

Before she left Billbinya Gemma had two final things to do. Needing to settle the question in her mind, she had plucked up the courage to ring Mike Martin from the Australian Transport Safety Bureau. Mike had told her Adam's accident was just that. An accident. There wasn't any evidence to suggest foul play. Gemma had smiled to herself when she hung up the phone.

She had then collected the box that held all of Adam's secrets and climbed the rungs to the cavity in the shed, where the box had been found. Gemma had pushed the box as far back as she could and climbed down again. It wouldn't hurt her again and she could now banish Adam to the back of her mind, where he belonged.

Bulla and Garry had waved her goodbye after she had secured their jobs with the new owner, but often called in to see her and Ben on Hayelle.

Out of the whole horrible saga, Rose was the one she felt for. Ned had never regained consciousness before he died, but hung on to life for another three weeks after the raid. Rose had packed up the house and moved to Adelaide to be near her brother's family.

Looking around at the other wedding guests, she could see Pat and Kate, holding hands. They had finally tied the knot after Kate had recovered from her fall. Gemma's mum and dad had made the pilgrimage from Adelaide back to Pirie for today's wedding. Leisha and her family were still in Canberra and Gemma's three nieces were excited about the thought of baby cousins to play with!

She had found her soul mate, still had her cattle, and her life would become richer by having a baby.

Hearing the laughing and clapping, Gemma watched Jess and Craig kiss. Ben winked at her over their heads as Gemma quietly thanked God for everything she had.

Gemma felt the baby move and her hand automatically went to her swollen stomach. Ben, noticing the movement, looked at her lovingly.

Gemma sighed with contentment. The bad dream of three years ago was nearly buried in her mind.

Postscript

Stock 'rustling' or 'duffing' is entrenched in the fabric of Australia's history. From the convicts to the bushrangers to the modern-day criminals, such as Adam, Brad and Jack, stealing other farmers' stock has been an easy way to make money. It's also very hard to prove who is responsible for the theft.

With the rising costs of diesel and fertiliser, it isn't only stock that is now targeted. It's anything from machinery to fuel to wool. Rural crime costs Australia $70 million per year and the frightening thing about this statistic is that only 60 per cent is reported.

Acknowledgements

Firstly, to my husband Anthony, thank you for loving me, supporting and encouraging me, for being my friend and providing a life that is full, rich, and so much fun with you beside me.

To my gorgeous kids, Rochelle and Hayden, thanks for making me laugh (and growl occasionally) and showing me that life isn't as serious as I thought!

Carolyn, thank you for being there from the start. The strategic-planning meetings over coffees, the phone calls (complete with kid interruptions from both sides!) and lunches were vital to the plotting of the book. Also, thank you for being my dearest girlfriend.

Jeff Toghill, my tutor and mentor, thank you for your support, encouragement, and belief in me and my work when I didn't even believe in myself.

To Dave and Bob from the Rural Crime Division in Perth, thank you for willingly talking to me about rural crime and reading sections of the book for their authenticity. Your help has been tremendous and you have made this book bona fide.

To Mum and Dad, my brother Nicholas and his wife Ellie, my sister Susan and her husband Nathan, thank you for everything. For loving me, encouraging me and understanding me – especially on my 'blonde' days! Susan, thanks also for reading the first draft and for your insistence that I finish it so you knew what happened!

Thanks to all the 'in-laws', Mrs McDonald, Sharon and Ron, for their support, love, encouragement and interest. I'm grateful for our friendship.

To my walking, talking thesaurus and dictionary, friend and spiritual director Mrs Mackay – all the big words in this book are because of you!

To my wonderful friend Sandy, who helped baby-sit, clean, pray, talk and who drank wine with me whether it was needed or not – thank you.

Thanks also to my mates Amanda, Marie, Tiff and Gill for reading the first few chapters and the feedback, for the phone calls and keeping me in touch with things. To Bee who also read the first draft and encouraged me forward. Also to Robyn who is always on the end of the phone.

To my unofficial editor, Shelley; Louise, Ali and Siobhán didn't have as much work to do on grammar because of your input.

Gratitude to my cousin, Tanya, who helped me the whole way, while busily writing her own book.

To Ali Lavau for the edit – wow! What an experience and learning curve, but I loved every second.

Louise Thurtell from A&U, thanks for this amazing opportunity and your visit. I feel very privileged. Thank you for your encouragement and making my entry into the publishing world so enjoyable.

Siobhán Cantrill from A&U, thank you for answering my endless phone calls, questions, and queries and for never once making me feel like I was interrupting your work or was a pain in the neck! I've really enjoyed our conversations and laughs together and I'm so grateful for your reassurance and steadying hand.

Last but not least, I thank God for this opportunity and I know it is because of Him and only Him that this has happened.

Extract from Fleur McDonald's upcoming novel, *Blue Skies*, available in April 2010

Chapter 1

2000 – November

Brian took his eyes off the road for only a moment. But that was all it took. The steering wheel tilted towards the edge of the road, the gravel grabbed at the front tyres, and next thing he'd completely lost control.

His wife's screams and his moan of terror stopped abruptly as the airborne car hit the ground and skidded. The sound of crunching metal and shattering glass echoed through the countryside, then everything was still, the only movement the spinning of a wheel and a broken aerial swinging from side to side. The occupants of the car were silent while above them a crow cawed.

Amanda gazed down from a second storey classroom at the people milling around the graduation hall, trying to spot her parents in the crowd. She could see her accounting professor and the dean of the university talking to her biology lecturer, amid beaming parents chatting to one another. She couldn't believe this day had come at last. After all the arguments trying to convince her father she needed to get an agribusiness degree, after three years of hard work and part-time jobs, all the while enduring the separation from her mum – not to mention the family farm, Kyleena. And now she had finally done it.

The dean had let it slip before the ceremony that she'd topped her class. Would that make her father proud? she wondered.

She smiled as she spotted Katie and Jo talking to their parents with the seriousness of newly graduated adults, looking nothing like the drunken, loud yobbos they could be when they weren't studying.

Her eyes fell on Jonno with a familiar stab of longing. He looked so handsome in his suit and tie. She'd only ever seen him dressed so formally once before – at Cory McLeod's funeral. She felt a pang of sadness thinking of Cory who hadn't made it to graduation; he'd been killed in a car accident in the first year of their ag course. His death had been devastating to all of his friends and she had taken a long time to come to terms with it.

Suddenly, the door to the room flew open, startling Amanda, who looked around to see Hannah coming into the room. Her friend looked so unlike her usual wild, straggly self as she rushed into the room, dressed in a black graduation robe and blue sash, her fly-away blonde hair swept up under her mortar board.

'Why're you hiding?' she demanded, her eyes bright with excitement.

'I'm not. I'm just watching everyone,' said Amanda, turning back to the window.

Sensing Amanda's sombre mood, Hannah moved over to the window and put her arm around her friend's shoulder. 'Are your parents here?' she asked.

'Of course! You don't think Mum would miss it, do you? I haven't seen them yet but they're always late – they probably snuck in after the ceremony started and have run into one of Dad's old mates,' said Amanda smiling to mask her concern.

'Well come on then. You can look for them later, Miss Dux! Right now I've been ordered to bring you back for the class photos and drinks.'

'And here I was thinking you cared,' said Amanda with a smile, following Hannah out of the room, switching the light off behind her.

Arranging themselves in front of the camera, the class of 2000 smiled and called out 'Bundy!', while their families looked on proudly. Between shots, Amanda searched for her parents.

Forcing a smile, she was hardly aware of the camera clicking and whirring as more photos were taken of the whole class, then a series of the dux of agribusiness with the recipients of the three agricultural awards and their teachers. As the final shot was taken of her with the high achievers from the university's other courses, Amanda caught sight of two policemen speaking with the dean. The look of shock on his face as his eyes searched the crowd and stopped on her, told Amanda the story and, without thinking, her feet carried her to them.

Seeing her friend's expression Hannah followed, motioning for Jonno to come with her. So it was that they were by Amanda's side to hear the news and gather their weeping friend to them, the graduation celebrations forgotten.

Amanda sat next to her father in the church, her mother's coffin resting on a gurney in front of them, while her uncle spoke from the pulpit. The cheerful flowers on her mother's coffin matched her mother's vibrant personality and Amanda had to close her eyes against the pain she felt looking at them atop the coffin. She could hear her mother's laughter, see her flashing eyes and feel her arms around her.

It wasn't until she felt a touch on her arm that she realised the pallbearers were making their way out of the church to carry her mother's coffin to the cemetery. She walked by herself to the hearse, tears clouding her vision.

Over the past few days, her father's rigid posture and continuing silence had been unnerving. Struggling with his grief and guilt, he had locked himself away, leaving Amanda to cope with the funeral arrangements. She felt like she'd aged dramatically in the two weeks since the accident.

She would never forget seeing her mother in the coffin, cold and unresponsive, her scars from the accident cleverly hidden. The lady at the funeral home had helped do her mother's hair and makeup, but it was Amanda who had chosen her outfit and fastened the silver bracelet that had been a gift for her fortieth birthday on her mother's lifeless wrist.

It was hard to believe that only two weeks before she'd been so full of hope and optimism for the future.

Choking back a sob, she ran to her car and sped away.

Chapter 2

March 2001

Amanda swung the pick, which bounced off the manure packed solid under the shearing shed. Despite the cold wind, a thin film of sweat covered her brow. Arms shaking she pulled up the hem of her shirt to wipe it off. Taking a breather she looked at what had to be at least about fifteen years' worth of compressed sheep dung – and she'd scored the wonderful job of digging it out. There was barely enough room to stand under the shed, let alone swing the pick.

She crawled out on her knees and tried to stand up, gasping in pain as her muscles screamed in protest. With blistered hands she hauled the full barrow out into the open, not seeing a big lump of manure before the barrow hit it and tipped on its side, its contents emptying onto the ground.

'Bugger!' Amanda shouted, unable to stop angry tears spilling down her cheeks as she swept all the manure back into the barrow with her hands. Wiping at the tears, all she managed to do was smear dung over her cheeks. Gathering herself she pushed the laden barrow over to the front-end loader's bucket, full now from her hours of work. Jumping into the driver's seat and turning the key, Amanda backed carefully out of the sheep yards and headed towards the huge pile of manure that sat on the fenceline bordering the laneway. Hitting the levers that controlled the bucket, she emptied the load onto the mound, then slumped forward, resting her head on the steering wheel.

Surely there was more to her life than shovelling shit.

It was now four months since she'd come back to Kyleena to help her dad. The death of her mum hadn't changed her plans – she'd always wanted, yearned, to come back to the farm – but her homecoming hadn't been anything like she'd imagined it would be. Her father had totally withdrawn into himself, not talking except to issue instructions. And far from being interested in the innovative ideas she had for Kyleena, he'd been stubborn and resistant. Last night had been a prime example.

After convincing her dad to let her into the office, Amanda had discovered that the computer lacked a security program. So when Brian had walked in with a cup of tea for her and wanted to know how she was getting on, Amanda had explained how important it was to have virus protection; it was one of the first things they'd learned at uni, she'd told him. His face had darkened in response and he'd slammed the mug down, sloshing hot liquid onto the desk, and stormed out of the room.

Later, Amanda realised that she should have been much more diplomatic. He'd probably thought she was questioning his office ability, implying that he was old and out of touch, though she hadn't meant that at all.

She'd been distracted all morning thinking about how she could fix what she'd broken. She was sure her dad wouldn't let her near the office again, and he'd be even less enthusiastic about her contributing to any of the managerial decisions. It was frustrating the hell out of her that instead of utilising her knowledge of budgets and farm improvements, she was fixing rundown fences, drenching sheep and, today's glorious job, shovelling sheep shit.

Although Amanda loved her father, they'd started to clash when she was about fifteen, after which her mum had often had to act as mediator between them. Being alike in many ways, there had been occasions when they'd locked horns, the worst being when Amanda decided she wanted to go to ag college. Her father had strongly disagreed that it was worth doing, much to her surprise, since he'd attended the same college she was applying to. But when she'd called him on it, he'd maintained that ag college was no place for a woman; the social culture was too rough for *his* daughter.

She sighed. He was so out of touch. Some of the

women at ag college had been way rougher than the blokes. And on the flipside, women had dominated the merit lists in different subjects.

The two-way suddenly crackled to life, jolting her out of her reverie.

'On channel, Mandy?' came her dad's gruff voice.

Sighing but not shifting her head, Amanda felt for the two-way receiver and responded.

'I'm in number one paddock and I've just checked the dam,' he said. 'It's getting a bit low and there's two dead sheep stuck in the mud on the edge. You'll need to come and pull them out.'

'Why don't you do it, since you're on the spot?' she found herself snapping, resentment sweeping away her good intentions.

The answering silence stretched into minutes, till finally Amanda swung herself up and drove the front-end loader into the shed, collected a rope and climbed onto her four-wheel motor bike, still fuming as she sped away.

Riding through the open gate into number one paddock, Amanda saw her father sitting on the edge of the dam staring at the dead sheep. She could tell that his thoughts were elsewhere. Her gaze shifted to the dead ewes. As far as she could see, he hadn't even tried to pull either of them out of the mud himself.

As she approached, he stood up and came towards the bike, an angry frown on his face. 'Don't ever question my instructions on the two-way again!' he shouted. 'The rest of the district doesn't need to know what's going on at our place. You do as I say and no backchat, understand?'

Amanda folded her arms, her face set. 'Dad, it would have been quicker for you to pull them out than for me to leave what I was doing and come out here. Time efficiency is important on a farm. What I've just done isn't efficient. Time costs money. It's not that hard a job. Not pleasant, granted, but not hard.'

Brian completely ignored her. 'Understand?' he repeated.

'Yes, Dad,' she answered doing nothing to hide her fury.

As she uncoiled the rope and tied it onto the back carrier, she heard her father walking towards his ute, the gravel crunching underfoot. As he closed the driver's door, she lifted her head to look at him, and felt a wave of pity wash over her. He looked so thin and grey and unhappy.

'Sorry about last night, Dad.'

There was a brief pause as he processed what she had said but then, without speaking, he turned the key in the ignition and drove away.

Staring at the sheep carcasses, tears threatening once again, Amanda suddenly understood that his silence and these sheep were punishment for the night before. More than that, she saw the blame in his eyes every time he looked at her – he thought she'd caused her mother's death! As if she didn't already feel enough guilt without him heaping it on her. Oh, she understood how deeply he was grieving – she was too. But to survive, they had to move on. She realised now that when she'd lectured her stony-faced father, he'd seen her as cold and heartless. If only he could understand her, see her own overwhelming sadness, then perhaps he would understand that her way of trying to cope was to focus on Kyleena, on their future. But her father was so immersed in his own grief and guilt he didn't have any understanding of how much she and other people close to her mother were grieving.

Ah well, she thought, coming back to the immediate demands on her. She needed to get the animals out of the dam before they contaminated the water any further. Fixing the rope around one of the sheep's legs, she rode slowly away, dragging the animal behind the bike. She steered carefully towards a cluster of trees which would become the ewe's final resting place. Breathing through her mouth to avoid the stench, she unhooked the rope and rode back to the dam to remove the other dead animal.

As the sun sank lower in the sky, Amanda made her way back to the house. She felt so lonely and sad knowing her mum wouldn't be bustling around the house when she got home. Instead her father would be in his office, listening to the radio and drinking beer. Avoiding her.

As a child, the house had been bright and cheerful, full of laughter and fun. Her mother, Helena, had been a wonderful cook and gardener, as well as working alongside her father and keeping up with her original profession, journalism, by writing an occasional article for the rural papers. Since her mum's death, the garden had grown wild and the house had lost its cosiness. It was as if it knew the life and soul of the family was dead and the remaining occupants were slowly self-destructing.

Pushing open the door of her mother's study, Amanda smiled at the fresh clean aroma. Finally the room smelled like someone loved it again. When Amanda had first summonsed the courage to come into the room, not long after the accident, it had still smelled like her mum. The moisturiser she used, her shampoo and soap. The book her mum had been reading was still on the coffee table and the latest editorial she'd been working on sat unfinished on her desk.

Her mother's fragrance had faded over the months until the room had started to smell musty and rank Amanda knew she had to do something. Deciding she couldn't bear to leave her mother's favourite room to become unloved, two weeks ago she had moved her computer onto the desk and claimed the room for her own. After giving it a thorough vacuum and cleaning down all the surfaces, Amanda had flung open the curtains, and set a vase of her Mum's favourite lavender on the table. Her father had been aghast when he saw that she'd moved in, arguing that it was Helena's space and should have been left the way it was.

Once again Amanda realised she should have been more sensitive to her father's feelings before making a decision. She hadn't used the room for a while but then after an argument with her father she'd found solace sitting in the study and after that, she'd kept using it. Tonight she opened the window and sat on the soft couch her mother used to curl up in and read on rainy days. She smiled at the memory of her mother chortling over some book, her feet tucked up under her, her long, dark, wavy hair tumbling over the couch's arm.

There was a photo on the desk of Helena, Brian and a young Amanda in the garden. Amanda could *just* recall the day it was taken. Drought-breaking rains had arrived from nowhere that day and a fierce storm had swept through, cooling the sweltering day. But it hadn't fazed her mum, who'd been wearing a thin cotton dress. She'd danced in the rain, her arms outstretched and face turned towards the heavens as she laughed with joy, with hope. Amanda remembered how her dad had run from the shed and taken Helena in his arms and together they'd delighted in the downpour, while their only child watched from the verandah in wonder.

Fifty-three was too young to die, thought Amanda, tears springing to her eyes. And twenty-two was too young to lose your mum. She buried her head in the soft cushion, hoping to catch a hint of the fading essence of her mother.

Later that night, Amanda woke from a restless sleep, thirsty. Stumbling out to the kitchen to get a drink of water she was alarmed by odd noises coming from her dad's room. She made for the door, but was stopped in her tracks by the sound of gut-wrenching sobs and muttered words. Carefully pushing the door open a crack, she peered in. Standing at the foot of the bed with his back to her was her dad, his shoulders heaving with sobs.

'Why, Helena, why? How could this happen after everything we've been through? After all we did to stay together? How could you leave me now?' he cried, clutching a photograph of Helena, its silver frame reflecting in the moonlight filtering through the open curtain.